THE CROOKED FINGER

The Crooked Finger

MAX RANKENBURG

Ravenous dogs, never satisfied,

such are the shepherds

who understand nothing.

They'll go their own way,

each to the last man

after his own interest.

Isaiah 56.11

Part One

Good Guests

~ 1 ~

U nit seventy-one was like all the rest: an eight by eight by twelve steel box. Storage by George was the name of the place.

Row by row by row, down to the bay. The symmetry of the place, rows and columns, polished steel lines and orange trim, impressed him. One could forget things in such order.

It was cold out, one of the coldest Decembers on record, they said in the news.

He stopped at the unit, drove on, stopped at the end of the row, turned the truck off. He left the heater on, drying his sneakers.

On the radio, Christmas carols across the dial. He shut it off, lit a cigarette.

Who was this George, he wondered, to care so much about self-storage, such a simple idea. He probably had other lots in other places. Maybe he ran other, completely different businesses as well. Gas stations, pest control.

He closed his eyes, a woman named Sandra materializing in his thoughts, the last time he'd seen her. It was a Friday morning, weeks ago. She was riding him. He made the mistake of glancing at his watch on the floor. She jumped off, took the watch and shoved it in her snatch, deep inside. He was stunned. Never seen anything like that before. He thought she was joking. She wasn't. She dressed, called him some unpleasant things, and left like that, his watch ticking inside her.

He must have dozed off. When he looked again, there was a man in the mirror, small figure at the end of the row, hands in the pockets of his long square coat. He wore a cap and dark glasses.

That would be Drago Momcilovic. He was late.

The man walked with a slight limp. He stopped at unit seventy-one. The driver, watching him in the mirror, waited, enjoying the warmth of the car, his cigarette.

Just past nine. The sky darkened with the approach of another storm. He'd been up since five. Dark, light, dark again. Call it a day.

He finished the cigarette and got out.

Momcilovic was flipping through keys. His jeans sagged in the seat. He carried some weight in his gut. Thick and callused fingers, fat hands. He fingered one key after another. "Blue dot he said." With a groan he bent down and tried one on the padlock. He tried another. "That a blue dot?" He held up a key. The third key opened the lock and the door went up with a roar.

What they wanted, what they had been told would be inside, was up against the wall. They'd come for a crate.

Too large for one man to pick up on his own, two could manage.

Momcilovic removed his glasses, tipped his cap up, leaned forward.

They'd met once before. You don't forget a face like that. Flat chin, wide mouth. A compact creature, balding but for some buzzed hair over his curled ears, on the roll of fat back of his head, Momcilovic resembled a toad. His face collapsed on one side. His bulbous left eye drifted, looked everywhere but straight. Maybe he'd had a stroke. It was unsettling to sit in front of the man for too long, as he had once, a year back, in conversation. He spoke gently enough but his ugliness made his presence difficult to bear.

The man took a small flashlight from his pocket, turned it on, swung it around, stepped in. The first impression, however, was not of darkness, of the pale blue spot of light flitting about. It was the stink. Musty, damp, rotten. Piercing, a lance through the nose, something spoiled.

Momcilovic walked right in. Snorting, clearing his throat, thumb to his nose, he turned away, blew out a string of snot. He held his light on the crate. Black stenciled letters, words in Spanish, a city in Central America.

Charly's attention was elsewhere. In the opposite corner a blue tarp, new by the looks of its sharp creases, covered what might have been a rowboat.

Momcilovic said something, hands on the crate.

Charly ignored him. He dropped to a knee, lowered his head, wanting to see what was under the tarp. The cement floor was wet. Something was dripping under the tarp.

Momcilovic was behind him in an instant, hand on his shoulder, pulling gently.

They stepped outside into a cold breeze. Charly returned to the truck and backed it up.

The row was desolate, nutty smell of rain on the air.

Both men pulled on gloves. In the darkness they crouched and lifted the crate, one man on each end. It was heavier than it looked. They tried again, counting to three, rising slowly, shuffling out. They slid it onto the truck bed. Momcilovic closed and locked the unit. Then he got into the truck and Charly left Storage by George the way he had come.

Momcilovic turned the radio on, flipped around the dial, settled on something light and bright.

Charly turned it off.

Half past, rush-hour behind them. In a minute they were on Interstate 80, heading south. They didn't go far before Charly pulled off at a pier. He parked beside a white van, Roto-Rooter decals on the sides: jolly fellow with a plunger skipping off to work.

They moved the crate from the Isuzu to the back of the van. There was fishing gear in the van. Momcilovic took it out. Charly returned to the truck, leaned inside the cab, looked over the interior. It was completely empty. He inserted the key in the ignition and closed the door.

Momcilovic, in sunglasses again, fishing poles, tackle box, bucket and net in hand, waited for Charly. The younger man locked the van and glanced over the parking lot. It was nearly full, which surprised him, given the weather. Then again, maybe it makes sense, fishing between storms this cold Monday morning.

The regulars were out. Momcilovic knew some of them by name. Men mostly, there were a few women among the strange company, bundles of coats and sweaters, scarves and hats. Dirty kids scurried about laughing.

They set up at the end of the pier. Momcilovic baited his hook with nightcrawlers. Four minutes later he brought up a small bass. He tossed it back, carefully baited the hook again, cast into the wind with a big smile. A minute later he had another, larger. This one he dropped into his bucket.

The bay was rough, frothy white and dark green. The wind was picking up, mist blowing off the waves. Black clouds filled the sky over the Pacific.

Charly wanted to go.

Momcilovic leaned into the railing, his head dropped so low he could have been sleeping. He smoked, said nothing.

Charly tapped his watch. Long drive ahead. When he closed his eyes he saw the blue tarp in the unit, heard it dripping in the darkness.

Momcilovic folded his line, pinched between forefinger and thumb. Slowly he pulled, released, pulled. He looked at Charly, his bad eye drooping and drifting, watching waves. "I know what time it is."

The other fishermen were packing their things. Charly did the same. Momcilovic brought in the line. Then he stopped, talking to himself, something rattling in his throat. His rod bending, the line went out some and stopped. Patiently he brought it in. But again, a strike. The fish ran. Momcilovic pulled, the reel squealing, the rod arcing over his shoulder. Some of the men who had been leaving turned and watched. Momcilovic tucked the end of the rod under his gut; he reached up with his free hand, finished his cigarette, tossed it away. He reeled in. Mechanically the rod rose and fell. The carp emerged, spinning white, black and pink under the surface of the water, thrashing in the cold air. The rod was bent to its limit, wrapped over the black railing of the pier. The line would break.

Charly reached out with the net and caught the creature in its throes. He pulled it up.

Carp on the pier, Momcilovic stepped on its tail and knelt, slipped two fingers into the creature's huge mouth. With his free hand he withdrew a knife from under his coat and cut the line. The carp watched its captor in curiosity and horror, big eye rolling. Momcilovic sliced open its belly. Guts and eggs spilled out on the pier. The fish flexed and then lay still.

They gathered their things and started back.

A Chinese boy nearby had watched the process intently. Now he watched Momcilovic. Without a second thought, the man held out the fish, longer than his forearm, two fingers up its bright red gills. Blood ran down his wrist.

"You want?"

The boy looked over his shoulder at his father, a brown defeated man, his tackle wrapped neatly in hand.

Momcilovic put the fish into the bucket with the bass, the body folded. He gave the bucket to the boy, who took it with two hands, face clenched in the wind.

Sudden cold downpour. Everyone on the pier hurried back to the parking lot.

Charly let the motor idle, the heater blasting. He took off his wet jacket, tossed it over his shoulder into the back. He blew on his cupped hands. The windows steamed up. Everything in the parking lot dissolved into colorful abstraction in the windshield.

He turned on the radio. There was only one classical station in the area. It was early in the *Tallis Fantasia* by Vaughan Williams. He thought of Sandra, of sleeping in with her on a Saturday morning, of the white of her skin, the brown freckles on her back, the feel of her long brown hair on his face. He could smell her, feel the sun on his arms, on his face, hear a windchime in the breeze on the deck. He was painting, having a cold beer, listening to Vaughn Williams in the hot afternoon light. That was last summer, the summer before.

Momcilovic put his seat back and lit a cigarette. "Know how to get there?"

The older man cracked the window. The rain was coming down hard.

Exit plan and cars: they called Charly for a specific purpose. Of course he knew how to get there. He said nothing.

At quarter of eleven they were back on the interstate, heading south toward the bridge.

~ 2 ~

It rained hard all the way into the city. Momcilovic fell asleep. Even when Charly stopped at a station off Van Ness, the old man slept. He came back with two cups of coffee, a muffin, two ready-wrapped ham and cheese sandwiches, a pack of Marlboros and a six-pack of beer, Anchor Steam.

Crossing the Golden Gate, strong wind off the Pacific slowed everything to a crawl. The van listed, rocking with each gust.

Christmas – in how many days?

Momcilovic woke without a sound. He righted his seat and reached out for the coffee. He sucked at it through the plastic lid. He set the cup back in its place. He lit a cigarette.

"What's your plan?"

The man's voice was loud and flat. There was something to his *a*. He looked away as he spoke, watching a fog shrouded hill in the bay to the east, where a solitary red light flashed on and off. San Quentin. He had acquaintances back there, some alive, others long dead.

"Plan?" said Charly.

"You don't have to have one." Momcilovic took the paper bag from the floor. "Leave me anything?"

Charly had picked at the muffin. There were the sandwiches.

Momcilovic ate the muffin in a couple bites, shoving it in. "Doing anything for the holiday?" Spitting crumbs. Sleep had opened him up.

The hiss of tires on the wet highway filled the air.

"Nothing special. You?"

"Off to LA. See my kid. I fly out tomorrow."

"You have kids?"

" ... He's in Hollywood. An *executive's* assistant," Momcilovic said with pride and disgust.

San Rafael exits. One, two, three. Charly pulled off. In two minutes they were on a narrow road in the countryside. The hills were lush and green. The barbed wire fences along the roadside sagged with age and disrepair.

"What's nothing special?" Momcilovic said.

Glance at the other man. "I'll stick around."

"Got a girl, a wife somewhere?"

What's with the questions?

"There's a girl."

" ... A girl. And?"

Momcilovic made a face, smiling. You could hear it in his voice.

"And what? She's easy to get along with."

"She pretty?"

"She is."

"Good lay?"

Charly looked at the other man.

"What's this girl's name?"

Occasionally the road sank into a gully and water rushed across the lowest part. Charly eased off the accelerator as the van hydroplaned.

He was concentrating on the road. He didn't care to talk with the man beside him, and would much rather have him asleep.

Momcilovic let the question go.

Ninety minutes later, along an inlet and approaching the Pacific, they entered a small village. Lights were on in the grocery. Everything else looked shut.

There was a garage and station on the edge of town. The garage was closed but a few cars – a BMW, two shoebox Volvos – were parked in front. There was a kid in the office. Charly pulled in. The rain had softened. He got out and filled the van. He watched the cashier in the office. One fluorescent bulb hung from a wire behind the desk, a stick of green light. The kid was looking down. Sleeping, reading a book.

The whole village was hard and cold, sinking like a dead tree back into the earth.

Charly went in to pay. It was freezing in the office. The kid was playing some kind of video game, buttons clicking. He had acne and big blue eyes under a hoodie. Without a word he raised a hand and took the money.

Charly crossed the yard, stepped into a phone booth. He called Sandra. No answer.

Ten minutes down the road, following a sharp left at a fork, he turned the van up a single lane. This skirted a hill, entered a forest, pine, redwood and eucalyptus. Now and then, a hidden turn-off, private drives.

It was the middle of the afternoon but already quite dark. Mist and fog drifted over the road, curling white in the headlights. He'd been on a similar road before, some years before, with a girl, when, coming around a bend maybe a little too fast, they'd nearly hit a black cow standing in the center of the road. The girl screamed. The creature stood directly in front of their little car. Slowly it turned its head to look them over, its big white eyes in its black face gleaming. Hearts in their mouths, there was something satanic about the scene. After a while the cow went on its way, but the incident stuck in his mind for the remainder of that trip and days to come.

What was her name? Georgia? Georgina?

At the end of the road they came to a gate. Momcilovic got out and opened it. Charly drove through, over a cattle guard. Momcilovic closed the gate and got back into the van.

On the Mexican coast of the Sea of Cortez, south of a place called Cajón del Diablo, there is a farm and bungalow, orange and lemon groves, avocado and mango trees, and, down a narrow path, a clean little beach in a cove. A girl there, Felicia, she runs a cantina, just a shack really. She does everything. Cook, clean, set you up.

Charly had a plan. He didn't like to talk about it. He was superstitious in that way. Giving words to the idea.

A house, white and square, appeared in the darkness, flickering first in the trees and then, a final turn, rising before them. The two-story structure stood alone on the crest of the hill, behind it a jagged stand of trees, the round dark sky over the Pacific.

They pulled into the gravel yard. A tall thin man with large ears emerged from the front of the house. He tipped his head and raised a hand to shield his eyes from the glare of the headlights. Then he stood very still, fists balled in the pockets of his jacket.

Charly shut off the van. Both men got out.

The tall man smiled. Momcilovic stretched and approached him. "How are you, Frank."

"Good to see you, Drago. Hello, Charly."

Frank stepped toward the van. His windbreaker, clinging to his frame, hung on bones.

His voice was cool and smooth, like the pale blue of his eyes. The smarmy Englishness about the man, his unflappable poise always cut Charly the wrong way. Frank was a man who couldn't be quiet, and in his effort at charm, palaver, he always seemed to be hiding something, holding something back.

They were all hiding things. Everyone Charly knew was hiding something. But at least some could be forthright in their privacy and stop talking when there was nothing to say.

"Traffic wasn't a problem, I assume. Let me take something. Here –"

Frank Conway was from Somerville, Massachusetts. Not England.

Charly opened the back of the van. He caught himself counting hours and minutes in his head. At this time tomorrow...

It took him a moment to remember that Frank and Drago knew each other. It was an element he should have considered earlier, should have planned for.

Simple oversight: that's how we get into trouble.

Momcilovic came around the back of the van. The air was cold and damp. Their breath clouded before them. There was some light luggage, things Charly had picked up a week ago. Frank took these bags into the house. The other two removed the crate and carried it inside. They set it down before a large wooden table. A fire blazed, crackling and snapping in a large stone fireplace.

Charly returned outside. He closed the van. He climbed into the driver's seat and looked over the interior. Except for the two coffee cups and paper bag of groceries, the front of the car was clean and empty. He took a beer from the bag and opened it, drank it quickly. He ate a ham sandwich. The other sandwich, remaining beer, and empty cups went into the bag. He got out of the van, lit a cigarette, looked over the yard. Through the murk there was not much to see. The van was the only vehicle in the yard. Not far behind the house, he knew, there was a barn, inside of which were three other cars, one a Jeep Cherokee, one a small Toyota pickup. He'd brought these over himself last week. The other would be Frank's.

He listened to the ocean, not far off, enormous waves rising and falling against the shore. A bird cried in the forest behind the house. Lonesome sound, he followed it blindly, wanting to hear more, wanting to see its source.

It was supposed to rain all week. Rivers in the area were rising. There was a flashflood warning for the Sacramento River, and the rivers in the north counties, here, the Russian and Napa rivers. The system was coming down from the Gulf of Alaska, two thousand miles up the coast. There was no thunder with this storm, no lightning. Just strong cold wind and a lot of rain.

Momcilovic was going on loudly about something, drink spilling over his hand, Frank laughing, mouth wide open. Miles Davis's *Sketches of Spain* played in the kitchen. The kitchen was spacious and remodeled. Charly poured himself a glass of Chivas. He drank it, poured himself another.

On a cutting board lay three bloody steaks. In the sink, heads of lettuce, makings of a salad. Something in a pot boiled on the stove: potatoes. Two bottles of wine were open, one, a Cotes du Rhone from Laudun he recognized, the other, a syrah from South Africa, was new to him. The label depicted the silhouette of a horned savannah creature. He never bought wine with animals on the label.

Frank said, beaming, "We're waiting for you, Charly. Pour yourself a drink. Dinner can wait!"

On the table were tools, a crowbar, hammer and power screwdriver.

Frank stood, whisky in hand, at one end of the crate. Drago went to work with the crowbar. He had it open in no time.

The crate was filled with straw and, beneath this, wrapped in heavy brown paper, pottery, bowls and plates and other dishes, some decorated with flowers, some with fish. Beneath these, under a piece of plywood in the center of the crate, was what they expected, and that was money, bound stacks of hundred dollar bills. Each in his own way, the men studied the smooth green surface deep in the crate.

Frank would do the math. Retrieving a small duffel bag from an adjoining room, he set this on the table and withdrew from it a yellow tablet and box of pencils, light cotton gloves, a ruler, a jeweler's loupe, and a rather large calculator. He pulled on the gloves, took out the first stack of hundreds, and carefully began counting. His thumb worked the corners like a machine.

Momcilovic poured himself another drink. He sat near the fire and smoked, drowsiness overcoming his fleshy face. In a minute his wet feet began to steam.

Charly went into the kitchen and started *Sketches of Spain* from the beginning. He took the potatoes from the pot and mashed them in a large bowl. He added butter and a dash of sour cream, a sliver of shallot, salt and a pinch of red pepper. He tried a little of the Cotes du Rhone. He looked around and found a case in the pantry. He poured himself some more and drank deeply. He made a salad.

Through a narrow door next to the pantry, an old, steep staircase led down to the cellar. Cold musty air crept up the stairs from the darkness.

He took his glass of wine and stood in the entry to the kitchen, watching Frank. The man was building a rectangular stack of money at one end of the table. He'd tap the calculator, slam the *equal* key, add a figure to his page. Start again.

Idly Charly poked the three steaks with a fork. "Sandra." He wished she could be here with him. She had such a great appetite. But some things are impossible to share. Impossible not by choice, but by their nature. An aspect of the individual's life that is his alone, painful and dark, ecstatic and bright, whatever it is.

We dream like we die, he thought, stabbing the steak, remembering something he'd heard. Alone.

He seared the steaks, one minute on one side, two minutes on the other, thirty seconds again on the first side. He brought these to the table on a platter.

The other two men were chatting quietly. Frank's tabulation was still a secret. That could wait.

They ate the steaks, potatoes and salad quickly, like men who had to get back to work. They drank two bottles of wine. Except for the clatter of their utensils, the mashing of teeth, the complex inner sounds of the body feeding, these hungry men leaned into their plates in silence.

The fire, burning for hours now, crackled in the wall.

Momcilovic got up and opened another bottle of wine. He filled his glass to the brim and dropped back into his seat. He pushed a piece of gristle around his plate. "I could go for another of those."

"There're more in the fridge." Frank, chewing, pointed at the kitchen with his fork. "We're set for days... Who knows what the storm'll do." Then, eyes on Charly: "But you'll be off early."

Charly returned to the kitchen, fixed three more steaks.

The house was quiet. Frank called from the other room, "What about you, Charly? What's your plan?"

"No plan," he said for the second time that day, watching blood sizzle in the skillet. "I'll go down to the city tomorrow."

A gust of wind rattled the old windows, rain skittered over the glass.

"And Sandra?" Frank said.

Charly brought the steaks to the table.

They all worked for a man named Percy Hamling. Charly'd known him for years, done various jobs for the man. He'd found out about Sandra. That Frank should know about Sandra, however, somewhat surprised Charly. Somewhat.

"She's busy."

"Sandra?" Momcilovic said. He sliced open his steak.

Charly stared at his plate of steaming meat.

"Sandra *Bizarro*," Frank said. He leaned back in his seat and stuck a finger in his mouth, chewed on the nail.

"Bizarro. What kinda name's that? She in the circus?"

"No," Charly said. "She's a pianist."

"A what?"

"It's Portuguese. A *pianist*. She plays the piano."

"A piano player. How nice."

They finished the steaks and another bottle of wine.

Momcilovic pushed his chair back, hands on his stomach. He belched quietly, cheeks puffing. Eyebrows up and down, he coughed, wiped his mouth, turned to Frank. "Well?"

Frank said there was one point one million in the crate.

Though Charly had done similar jobs before, he had never seen so much cash in one place. So that's what a million dollars looks like.

Still, he had been told there would be two million in the crate. One point one was not two, not nearly two, and he didn't need a big calculator to tell him that.

"That's all of it? You counted all of it?"

"I counted what was there." Frank took a breath, picked meat from between his teeth with a nail. He had hideous teeth, gaps you could run a piece of rope through. "Want me to count it again? Wanna count it yourself?"

Charly kept his cool. *Two million. One point one.* He got up, brought his plate to the sink. Water running, pop of the fire. When he came back he went over to the empty crate and looked inside.

Later he would wonder why he did this, why he questioned Frank, feeling cheated, why he made his way, inebriated, over to the crate to look inside. "What did you hope to find?" Of course it would be empty! Of course Frank had done his job, impeccable as ever.

There had been a misunderstanding, that was all. A miscalculation somewhere up the line.

But the crate was not empty. There was something in the corner, on the dusty bottom of the box. He leaned over, reached down.

Old newspapers, pressed smooth – he peeled these back, revealing a square piece of cardboard – and then, was it tissue? Packaging? At his back, Momcilovic quipped, chuckling softly, glug of wine, scrape of fork and knife on his plate... A purse, a bag, a piece of black... wrapped around... He stood and poured the contents into the palm of his hand – diamonds, and –

What...

It was folded in a piece of thin yellow paper, like a dry leaf. It was no bigger than a dime. Without a second thought, with hardly a glance, like a magnet sucking up a paperclip the strange yellow thing slipped from his palm to his pocket, and as he tipped his hand, dropping the rocks back onto their velvet bed, the difference was imperceptible. Nobody knew any better.

He put the diamonds on the table.

Frank had an eye on him but Momcilovic appeared distracted. He was telling a joke: a priest, an idiot, and a donkey.

There was also, scraping the bottom of the crate, wrapped in a greasy rag, a gun.

"What's this?"

The pistol was small, curved beneath the trigger guard. He'd held a pistol before. It had been nothing like this.

"I'm no *ordinary* donkey," Momcilovic was saying. He stopped. Frank lowered his chin, eyes down as if embarrassed. "What do we have here?" Momcilovic leaned forward, reached out. Dragging the pouch, he slid the diamonds to the center of the table, touched them gently, counting. He looked at Frank. He turned to Charly, smiling, his bad eye pendulating. "And that? May I?"

Charly handed him the gun.

Momcilovic turned the pistol over, around. "It's German," he said. "A Walther PPK. It's an antique." He popped the clip out, set it on the table, opened the chamber. A bullet slipped out, dropped into his palm. "Twenty-two caliber, semiautomatic. A very good gun. Doesn't make too much noise. It's a purse gun."

"A what?" Frank asked.

"A purse gun. For a lady. Deadly at close range. A neighbor of mine had one. He had all sorts..."

The man faded, thinking to himself, recalling something he couldn't say.

He set the gun down before his empty plate.

Charly looked at the gun, at the black wad of velvet, its sparkling eyes. He was tired. He felt slow and heavy.

Momcilovic was thumbing bullets from the clip and standing them on the table.

"The deal was cash," Charly said.

Frank tipped his seat back. Eyes on the ceiling. He wiped his hands together. He leaned forward, forearm on the table, and touched the diamonds one at a time, tipping them, turning them. He lifted the pistol and balanced it in his palm. He had a big hand, long fingers. "Look, Charly," he said. "What do you want? Siddown. You're making me nervous standing there. Relax."

Charly remained standing.

The money stacked at the end of the table formed a neat rectangular structure. A smaller structure, like a porch, rose before the larger. Frank's work, architectural grace. The wad of velvet was a different matter. It looked like a barbed rodent asleep on the table. If you touched it it would bare its teeth and run.

"Look," Frank said. "Obviously you are dissatisfied with how things have turned out." He waited for Charly to respond. He went on: "Why don't you... You want the diamonds?"

At this word Momcilovic moved in his seat, shifted his weight. He licked his lips, raised an eyebrow. Does he want to say something?

Frank placed the gun back on the table. "I'm willing to..." The man blinked. Just ten minutes ago they'd felt so good. Open the box and look inside! "Take the diamonds, Charly. I'm... I know we were expecting a bit more. And I... Maybe I feel a little responsible."

Keep talking, asshole.

"I'll run this by Sullivan tomorrow. I can call him right now. Meanwhile, Drago, unless you have something to add, Charly, you take the diamonds. Hold them. Put them somewhere safe. If things come together, Gary has some explanation, we can work something out later." The man raised his big hands in the air, palms out. "If things don't, well, then... You're a crafty guy, Charly. You'll figure something out."

The lights dimmed and flickered. Five eyeballs rolled up to the ceiling.

Charly waited for Momcilovic to say something. But the other man was silent, studying with his good eye the bullets he'd lined up in a row on the table.

Frank rose and went to the kitchen. He came back with the bottle of Chivas and three glasses. He poured three full glasses, pushed two of them along the table.

Then the power went out. The red light of the fire flickered on one side of everything in the room. The wind howled outside.

~ 4 ~

Charly's cut was two hundred and fifty grand. Proportionally, Frank reminded him, that amount was what he had agreed to. Frank was trying to be fair. Charly said nothing.

He went upstairs with a candle. He returned with a small black satchel.

Frank stood at the fire. Momcilovic wasn't in the room.

Charly put his pile of money into the satchel. He left the black purse of diamonds on the table. The pistol was still on the table, its bullets lined up as Momcilovic had left them.

Upstairs he took from the satchel a handful of stacked hundreds, five thousand dollars, and put these in the inside pockets of his coat.

From his jeans, he took out the yellow item. He was thinking about the diamonds on the table downstairs, about Frank's offer, about how Drago had hardly noticed them, his attention drawn to the gun, "A Walther PPK..." He unfolded the paper.

The room was dim, candle light fluttering on the walls. The diamond was a masterpiece, a big goddamn hypnotic crystal burning a hole in the palm of his hand.

They smoked cigars, finished the bottle of Chivas, opened another, pulled chairs up to the fire. When Charly opened the door to get more wood, he staggered into the howling dark, roaring fall of rain, the monstrous face of the storm wanting in.

Well past midnight he rose and went to bed, where he slept like a dead man.

He woke a few hours later. His head was clear. He'd have a cup of coffee and go. He could be in the city before noon.

The rain had stopped. He watched the Pacific through the bedroom window, beyond the woods out back. Above the ocean the sky was dark gray, rolling around like a dog in the grass. The reprieve from the storm would be short.

The place was cold. Water dripped in the chimney. The fireplace was streaked, dark and wet.

Momcilovic, rattling and wheezing, lay asleep in an armchair. His grotesque body, collapsed in the chair, his round white gut hanging over his open pants, looked like something washed ashore from the ocean deep.

The table was as they had left it the night before. The pile of money was gone. The gun, bullets, diamonds – untouched.

The kitchen was empty. Frank must be upstairs, in the other room.

A transistor radio hung from a string over the sink. He turned it on. On the classical station, a Bach cantata, but which one? A viol da gamba, he thought. *In deine hände...*

He moved dirty dishes around the sink, began stacking things according to size and function...

The coffee was excellent. Strength returned to every part of his body.

Momcilovic staggered into the kitchen, slurping, sucking saliva from the corner of his mouth. Charly poured a mug of coffee and placed it in the man's hand.

He stepped outside. Pack of cigarettes in his coat pocket. He took one out, shook the box, counting how many remained. He walked out to the barn. The ground was saturated. When he opened the barn door, an orange cat ran out, scurrying quickly down the edge of the building.

There was the Jeep and Toyota. Frank came in a black Audi S6. That didn't surprise Charly.

He got in the Jeep, turned it on and let it idle. He took from the glove box a map of California, the Golden State. He found Mt Shasta, at Chico, and the winding route that went up into the mountains through Quincy. There was a cabin there, outside of Portola. He would go there before returning to the city. He needed to make some calls. He could be in the mountains before dark.

Cry of kittens somewhere in the barn. He looked around. He found the nest in the back corner, under an old work bench. He waved a finger over the small blind creatures. They shook their heads, crying. When he looked up, the orange cat sat above him, upright on a shelf, watching, motionless. As he turned to go, it jumped down without making a sound.

He turned the car off. He wanted something to eat. He was not so pressed for time.

It was raining lightly when he left the barn. He stood in the entrance and smoked.

Inside, he made bacon and eggs, cornbread, sausage, toast, a fruit salad, and more coffee. Momcilovic served himself while the food sizzled in the pan. He bolted everything down standing at the counter.

Charly was impressed. He was coming around to the man.

Momcilovic said, his mouth full, "I'm thinking of going up to Conklin Creek before heading back. Join me?"

Charly had no idea where Conklin Creek was. "Can't. I'm expected. It's a long trip. I need to –"

"I hearya."

"I need to bring the van down the hill. Would you follow me?"

"It's done."

The two men finished their coffee.

Momcilovic belched and said, "I hate Los Angeles... How about when I get back –"

Frank came into the kitchen, very clean and well dressed, his slacks neatly creased. He smiled brightly and said good morning. He made himself a cup of tea. He stirred milk and honey into it. He leaned his tall narrow frame against the counter as he sipped his tea.

Charly prepared the house for their departure. He cleaned the kitchen and dining room. He cleaned the ashes from the fireplace. He knew the owner. Before the New Year he would need to settle up.

Momcilovic was in the shower, singing. Charly went for a walk in the woods behind the house. There was a path down to the shore. In silence he passed through the trees, pine duff soft underfoot, the roar of the ocean growing. The trees opened up and the path entered a small meadow and then went along the cliff over the rocky shore. The waves were high. The water looked dangerous.

He stood on the cliff edge watching the ocean, watching the sky come in, the day disappear. Wind rumbled in his ears. On a green peninsula half a mile up the shore was another farmhouse. A white fence, a barn. Cars in the yard. Lights in the house glared bright in the windows. Family and guests over for the holiday. Part of him envied those people; part of him was disgusted by the sort.

He watched the distant house for a minute. Then he turned and followed the path back into the woods. There was a pleasant peacefulness about the woods. It wasn't silence, not just silence. The woods weren't silent. It was something else.

Then, just as he was nearing the end of the path, a gust of wind came up behind him, chilling the back of his head. He ducked lower into his coat. Something snapped. Crack in the air, like a branch breaking. Not thunder. Something behind him? He looked back. The woods were dark and still. He looked down – had he stepped on something?

There it was again. A gunshot. Not loud, not exactly soft. Sharp. Muffled. *The last thing...* The last thing he expected to hear, wanted to hear on a day like this, in a place like this. It meant only one thing.

Pop!

Another. And another.

When he was a child – he recalled, standing at the edge of the woods, the house just beyond the barn – his parents brought him to a place like this on a weekend trip. He had taken his dog out. They went exploring, walking for miles in the long warm afternoon. In a field, he had run ahead, and the dog, a large and healthy German Shepherd, disappeared, went running off. He called it but it didn't return. He wasn't that bothered, actually. He was old enough to know that the dog would come back. But the dog didn't. In the evening, he and his father went out looking. At a nearby farm, they found the dog. It was dead. It was hanging from a scaffold by its back feet, its long body perfectly straight. Blood pooled on the ground beneath its snout. Next to it hung a sheep, in much the same position.

The farmer had shot the dog. It had killed the sheep. The farmer apologized. That was that. They put the body of the dog into the back of the car and brought it home.

Charly waited. The house was quiet. Go see what happened.

No.

As if with momentum he continued forward, toward the barn, keeping it between him and the house. He entered the barn by a back door. The cars, the Jeep and Toyota, Frank's Audi, were as he had left them ninety minutes ago. Stepping carefully, he noticed that the Toyota had luggage in the passenger seat, and papers, a map, an airline ticket. The hood was warm. Momcilovic was ready to go.

The cat and the kittens were gone.

A screen door slammed shut. "Charly!" *Frank.* "Charly! We could use a hand here."

The statement fell flat on the cold empty yard. Frank called his name again.

He heard the man go back inside the house. Rain pattered on the steel roof overhead. He climbed up to the loft and found a crack in the wall that gave him a view of the house. He could see nothing of importance. The house was still and quiet, the windows dark. Then he saw Frank in the kitchen window, the tall man glancing out on the yard.

Charly waited. There was no sign of Momcilovic.

He would have to go inside for his things.

Stupid, he thought, not to have left earlier, to have gone for a walk. Stupid!

But it was done. There's no going back.

What happened in there? Perhaps nothing. He'd heard what he thought was a gunshot. It could have been any-thing.

No. He'd heard what he heard. Which meant... Which meant Frank had killed Drago and now he was waiting for Charly to return. He'd kill him too.

Charly closed his eyes, tried to clear his head. Was there another possibility? No. He knew Drago better than he knew Frank. Which wasn't saying much. But he knew Frank just enough to know that...

But why? Frank was not a killer. They'd worked to-gether before. He knew killers. He stayed clear of them. Frank was not like that – he didn't have the habit, that soullessness. He was a thief, like Drago, like himself. Noth-ing more.

So what happened?

It didn't matter. If the scenario was as he imagined it, he had few options. He could get in the car, and leave everything behind, and take the chance of facing Frank on the road in some kind of chase and fight. Or he could stay – wait and see what happens.

If he left, would Frank follow him? He wouldn't need to. They worked for the same man. Frank had seniority.

It would be Frank's word against his. The story would get out before he could do anything.

Which meant stay. Wait. Keep Frank close, not too close. There's plenty of space here, and I know the area better than he does. Let him make the next move.

The barn was a trap. Charly left the way he had come, in the same steps, returning quickly to the woods. Once in the cold darkness of the pines, he turned off the path and pushed his way deep into the trees and bramble. After some ways, he cut back toward the house. When the house was in sight, he kneeled, brushed out a bed in the pine needles, and lay on his belly, his chin on his hands. It was cold. The cold, it seemed impossible, rose up from the earth, soaking into his pants and jacket. But he had little choice, few good options.

His position gave him a view of the front and south side of the house. There was the van. There, the barn.

It was noon. Already it was getting dark.

It started to rain. The wood filled with the breezy sound of falling water.

His hands were getting stiff. His jaw tightened, his teeth chattered.

The house grew increasingly dark. He began to wonder if Frank was even there. Perhaps he had fallen asleep and the man had already left. No, impossible. It was too cold for that. He was quite awake, though his eyes were tired.

Lights went on in the house. He saw as Frank quickly passed from one room to another. Then the man left the house, luggage in hand. He went to the barn. Charly heard him put things in the Audi. Then he returned to the house. Hardly a look around. A moment letter he came out the front door, went to the van and took a knife from his pocket. He unfolded the knife, knelt and sliced the valves from the tires. The vehicle sank to the ground.

He was moving quickly. He'd be gone soon.

That's what happened. The second time Frank left the house, he stopped in the doorway, tucked a bag beneath his arm, turned and locked the door. He looked like a man rushing to catch a commuter train.

Charly wanted to stop him, to sprint from his hiding place and surprise the man from behind.

He couldn't. He knew what would happen. There was too much space between the woods, the barn and house.

Frank was the larger man. And Frank was the killer, the one not only with the gun but the poison, the drive to defend himself.

The Audi started. Frank was taking too long. What was he waiting for?

The tall man appeared in the barn door. He smoked a cigarette and looked at the house, at the yard, the woods. He even looked, it seemed from the distance, directly at Charly. Then he turned and disappeared inside the barn.

The black car pulled slowly, quietly from the barn, followed the driveway around the edge of the house, and vanished from view. In a minute, a natural silence came over the yard, the house. Rain fell gently in the trees. A clamorous argument of crows rose in the distance.

Charly counted to a hundred. Then he stood, gasping with cold and stiffness, and ran to the house.

He broke the window in the back door. "Drago!" With the lights off, he walked through the bottom rooms. Everything in the house was neat and put away, as they had found it. Good guests. He ran upstairs and checked the two bedrooms, the bathroom. Nothing. Dead silence. Rain on the roof.

In the bedroom he'd used, his things were on the bed as he'd left them. There was the case in which, last night, he'd put his money. He opened it, feeling sick.

The first thing he saw was the note. Beneath this, the gun.

Bono suerte Charly

He held the piece of paper, neatly creased down its middle. Even the handwriting made him sick.

What the hell kind of joke...

He picked up the gun. He could smell it.

Everything was gone.

Bono suerte...

Gun in hand, he gently squeezed the trigger and listened as the mechanism caught and went to work, picturing in his mind catching up with Frank, overtaking him on the road, dragging him from his car and shooting him in the ditch.

But that – that would only make things worse.

Downstairs, he stripped and started a fire. The blaze took a few minutes to warm up. Patiently he added kindling and wood. Soon the fire was roaring, snapping and popping, and he, nearly in the flames, began to feel warmth in his hands, feet, the tip of his nose.

He knelt on the warm hearth, hands up to the fire. He wanted to think. He didn't have time to think.

"Drago, Drago, Drago…"

The rain began to fall harder. The world grew dark.

He put on dry clothes. He turned on all the lights in the house. He tried the phone.

In the living room, the wooden floor looked naked. A rug was missing: a dirty, red Turkish thing.

Then, brain warming up, something else. On the empty table, near the corner, splinters, a scratch. He bent over, looking closely, running his finger along the slightest of grooves. He'd seen this kind of thing before. As if looking through the sight of a rifle, his eye followed the direction of the groove and focused on a point on the wall near the front door.

Between doorframe and window, a tiny black spot.

He bent over, hands on his knees, and looked closely at a little hole in the wood. There, not far in, was the smashed backside of a bullet.

He'd missed.

Charly looked back, tried to visualize the scene, the struggle.

For whatever reason, the bullet in the wall reminded him of the diamond in his pants. From his wet jeans, in a pile on the floor, he withdrew the yellow paper. He unfolded it.

So, there was this. And the money in his coat. And the gun.

Did Frank know, one might ask, about the diamond he'd left behind?

In the kitchen he made a pot of coffee. He sliced some bread and made a cheese and liverwurst sandwich. He wanted to think. He knew he had to leave – his plans going to shit – but he couldn't. Not yet.

It was Drago. He needed to know what had happened to the man.

The obvious place to look, it suddenly dawned on Charly, noticing the door by the pantry, was in the cellar.

He opened the cellar door. An ice cold draft rushed up the stairs from the darkness.

"Drago! You down there?"

Just around the edge of the open door was an old-fashioned light switch, round and porcelain. Up and down, its loud glassy click echoed in the cold stairwell. Nothing.

He did not want to go down into the cellar. Nobody would want to go down into that cellar.

Flashlight in hand, Charly descended the stairs into the cellar. The plank steps creaked under his weight.

The descent took a long time. But then, naturally, in little time at all, Charly found himself on the hard earth floor under the house.

The walls were brick and mortar. Wooden beams, in a haze of dusty cobwebs, crossed overhead.

There was a small doorway into another room. Shining his light through the passage, he saw nothing.

Crouching, he stepped into the doorway. It was not a large room. At his left hand, an iron door – sharp and speckled with rust, crooked, falling from its rotten hinges – leaned against the wall. Directly before him – he nearly stepped into it before he saw it – was a pile of coal, a pyramid of coal from floor to ceiling. On the floor at its base was the body of Drago Momcilovic.

Its bad eye was covered in blood and black grime. It looked like that side of its head had been smashed in. There was another hole in its side. The shirt was black with blood. The rug beneath the deflated body – Drago seemed smaller to Charly now, like a popped balloon – was soaked with blood.

He took a step back, raised a foot and shined the light. He'd stepped in a pool of blood.

He went back upstairs. Staring at the clean counter in the kitchen, he felt like he'd just stepped from a movie theater, come to the end of some tedious and tearful drama. His eyes burned. He was suddenly, strangely, very hungry.

~ 5 ~

On the radio, something by one of the Strausses. At the best of times he couldn't stand Strauss, any of them. He turned the dial.

News: Kenneth Star. They were going on again about Clinton. So the president lied. Charly couldn't care less, though he did feel something for the girl, Lewinsky, her five minutes of fame.

He turned the radio off.

The house was quiet. He sliced two potatoes into strips, the knife clapping sharply on the cutting board.

He fried the potatoes in olive oil, adding salt, rosemary, a piece of garlic. In the same pan he fried another steak. There were three more steaks on a plate in the fridge. There was also a package of pork chops and a chicken. In a separate drawer were vegetables: lettuce, chard, tomatoes, zucchini, cucumbers, mushrooms, carrots. Two dozen eggs on the top shelf, various local cheeses, milk, cream, butter, beer, yogurt, three bottles of champagne, and white wine. Vanilla ice cream in the freezer. "My cup runneth over."

He opened another bottle of the Cotes du Rhone and poured himself a large glass. He sat and ate, slicing the steak with care, watching the fire.

"We're set for days."

The silence was then too much. He turned the radio back on. Ah, Stravinsky's *Pulcinella* – he never tired of listening to it.

It was getting dark. He poured himself another glass of wine and saw that he'd almost finished the bottle.

He was still hungry.

He lit a cigarette and studied the ceiling, listening to the music, the prancing patter of trumpet and flute.

There was something wrong, something he couldn't place.

Without a second thought he rose from the table and ran out to the barn, to his car. All of the tires were slashed. The Toyota, the same. Momcilovic's things were gone.

He knew he should do something, take action of some sort. He was in a bad situation. Something was coming, he felt, and he couldn't do anything to stop it. At the same time he didn't really care. He'd find a way out. He always did. He'd cook a little more, eat a little more.

The house was actually quite comfortable. It was warm and, apart from the backdoor window, secure, and it felt like his, like he could stay there for days, weeks, thinking, reading, eating, listening to music, waiting for whatever came next.

There was the body in the basement to deal with. He'd take care of that tomorrow.

He put water on for pasta. He chopped up some tomatoes and simmered these in a pan with olive oil, salt and garlic. He cut an eggplant up into small cubes. These too he simmered in oil. He turned on the broiler. He slid the pan under the fire, browning the eggplant. He opened another bottle of wine, a heavy cabernet from the Napa Valley, purpleblack in the glass. He sipped some. *Hmm...* He poured the bottle out into a decanter.

"Let that sit awhile."

He watched the tomatoes simmer, melt down to a fleshy juice. Then he mixed in the eggplant. He added capers. On the radio, what sounded like Bruch's *Scottish Fantasy* came on. It was hard to tell. It's a protean piece.

He drained the spaghetti when it was undercooked and dropped it in the pan of eggplant and tomato. He stirred everything together. He added shredded parmesan. What a marvelous heap of spaghetti! Far more, he knew, than he could actually eat.

He was dozing off in a chair in the living room, hard rain falling outside. The house creaked in the wind, shifting on its foundation, still settling after all these years. The fire had burned down to embers. He would need to get more wood.

He made a pot of coffee, Sandra on his mind. What was she doing? Practicing, probably. She was always practicing. Or performing. Every day of her life was given to the study of music and the perfection of her craft. He admired her commitment to the art. You didn't meet many people anymore, he felt, committed to the craft of making something beautiful.

In his drowsy, vague thoughts, he then watched her step from a steaming shower, holding a towel around her top – she didn't see him – pulling water from her hair, her head tilted, her round heavy ass rising as she leans over the sink toward the mirror, looking closely into each of her large dark eyes.

What was that?

A sound, a bump, something in the house moved and Charly was awake in an instant.

Black windows before him, whistle of the wind...

The house was silent. He'd heard something, he was sure. Not the wind, not the rain, not the radio, saccharine Christmas medley in the kitchen. A tree against an upstairs window, against the roof? There were no trees near the house. An animal, the cat wanting to come in?

Boldly, carelessly Charly threw open the front door. The yard was pitch black, curtains of rain blowing in the wind.

Then something occurred to him. He closed the door, locked it, went directly to the cellar door, opened it, stuck his head into the cold wet darkness, listening. Nothing. He took the flashlight and once again descended into the cellar, old planks creaking with every step. He thought he'd fall through. He rushed down, slipping, skipping steps, staggering at the bottom, catching himself on the brick wall and laughing, realizing he was drunk.

The air in the cellar was gritty, greasier than he remembered it being. It had a peculiar, particular stink now too, bloody, earthy, homeless. He went straight for the little door.

He should have been more frightened than he actually was. He was puzzled, rather. No. He was inebriated and careless. He had the flittering obsessive drive and curiosity of a drunkard, of a man desperate to focus his vision on a concrete detail, a utensil, a thumbtack, a button on her blouse.

He nearly fell into the pile of coal, tripping on the edge of the red rug.

The body was gone.

Head spinning, he blinked hard and looked again, furiously trying to steady his hand, the beam of light. No. Where just a few hours ago there had been the body of Drago Momcilovic there was now a dark impression, a gaping mouth.

He was going to throw up. Something too rich, the eggplant and capers, that horrid cabernet, everything mixing inside of him into a toxic and violent potion.

He kneeled and put a hand on the rug. Cold and wet, he turned the light on the palm of his hand. Blood. On his knees as well. What a sticky, awful goddamn mess. He wanted to stand and run, to get out of the cellar, out of the house and away as fast as possible. But such a crushing immobility came over him, an enormous hand dropping from the sky and pressing him down. His legs, knees shaking, could barely hold him.

Voice in the dark:

"Is that *eggplant?*"

Charly whipped around, spot of light slicing across the darkness and swinging back, wobbling, scribbling, a blazing streak in his vision. There was a body –

"Son of a *bitch!*"

The light caught a large, pale and clear eye. On the ground, two steps from where Charly stood, Momcilovic sat against the brick wall. When he moved, turning to better see Charly, the other side of his face came into the light, his head caked in blood.

Momcilovic's voice, however, was clear and steady. He could have been talking with his son on the phone.

"You think you know someone, eh Charly?... It looks worse than it actually is. The stomach shot is in the side. It went through. It's just blood. It can be replaced."

Charly, a quiet man normally, had no words, his tongue wadded up in the back of his throat.

Replaced?

"The head, you're thinking," Momcilovic said. "Okay. Technically speaking..." The man stopped. He sighed, adjusted himself, dragged a hand over the dusty floor.

"When... I was," he began. He stopped. He tipped his chin, reached up and pressed a finger to his head wound. He examined his finger.

Charly stepped forward and gently took the man by the arm and shoulder.

"Get your hands off me," Momcilovic said, pulling away. "I'll manage."

The man groaned, lifted his legs, knees up, rolled to his side, slowly climbed to his feet. He held his knees for a moment. He gasped and raised his shoulders, stood straight. Mouth agape, he looked like a surprised corpse. Charly watched, waiting to do something, catch the man. But Momcilovic didn't fall. He cleared his throat and spat and raised a hand to his forehead, man with a headache, and his face fell into a more appropriate expression. He was thinking, behind all that. He stepped through the little door.

"I could eat a horse. Save me anything?"

~ 6 ~

Momcilovic took a long time climbing the cellar stairs. When he finally emerged – Charly was frying another steak, with cipollini onions and brown mushrooms – he shuffled through the kitchen, went straight to the table and dropped into a chair. "One minute," Charly said. Momcilovic said something he didn't catch but then came into the kitchen, aiming for the sink, where he vigorously washed his hands. He followed Charly back to the table.

His face was a filthy mess but his hands were clean. Momcilovic ate like there was no tomorrow, shoveling it in.

"Wine?"

Charly opened another bottle of the cabernet and poured the man a glass. He drank it in two goes.

"Excellent!"

He put the glass back and gestured. He looked down at his side, poking at the wound.

"Missed the important stuff."

Charly poured the man another glass. He poured himself a glass as well. "So?" he said.

"So?"

Charly tapped a finger against his skull.

The look Momcilovic gave him was that of a man who didn't have the foggiest notion what was going on. He chewed, staring. Then his good eye opened wide. He waved his fork in the air. He scratched at the wound in his head, what was clearly a hole in his head. "When I was nineteen," he said, "this crazy fuckin Albanian went at me with a hatchet. He got in two good whacks before they pulled him off. But two was enough. I'd had it. There was blood, blood everywhere. It was in my eyes, in my nose, in my mouth, in my ears, in my throat. I was choking on my own blood before I hit the ground."

"Why?"

"*Why* he says."

It was a dumb question.

"WHY! Why are there Albanians in this world to begin with!? I don't know *why*, Charly. He was crazy. He'd go around town with a rifle, shooting cats... It was a little dispute. About a game, a bid. A watch or a shirt... I don't know what, I don't remember. He thought I owed him. I thought otherwise."

"So he tried to kill you?"

Momcilovic cut a bite of steak, stuck it in his mouth and chewed. "Well," he said, chewing. "Have you ever been hit in the head with a hatchet?"

"How'd you... Where was this?"

"Questions, questions! So I lived! My mother always said I was a blockhead. They took me to a doctor. They stuffed everything back inside and patched it up. I had to go – not then, later – to a hospital in Prague, where... Where they nailed this *plate* inside my head, on my skull. You wouldn't have known – had I not just told you, had I not gotten up... What? You thought I was born this way?"

The man pointed a stubby finger at the bad side of his face. He licked his lips. He slid his empty glass forward and Charly filled it.

They drank in silence for a minute.

"He left the gun," Charly said.

Momcilovic worked his jaw, his good eye staring at a point over Charly's shoulder. "He took everything else?"

"Practically."

Charly didn't mention the object in his pocket. Nor did he mention the note Frank had left.

"What's *practically* mean?"

Momcilovic was eating what remained of the steak slowly now.

"I have five grand in my jacket."

"Imagine that. Smart man." Momcilovic emptied his plate, pushed it away. He drew the wine glass to the edge of the table. Something was coming together in his head, his good eye.

Charly put wood on the fire. "I'm leaving," he said. "But I'd like to–"

"Here's what I need you to do, Charly. Get on the line–"

"Phone's dead."

"So go down to the village and use that payphone. I'll give you the number. You tell him where I am and how to get here. He's a doctor. You say nothing else to him. Tell him to bring blood. Then you do what you want."

"What about Hamling, what do I tell him?"

"What about him? Tell him what happened. Tell him nothing. That's between you and him. But I don't think it'll really matter, what with..."

"And Frank?"

"I'll take care of Frank."

" ... He left this morning. Twelve hours ago."

"I tell you what. You hear from him, tell him you came back from your walk, saw what happened... You don't need to know. Let him talk. He'll talk, you know he will. Go with it, whatever he says. You want your money, of course. But don't deal with him. Talk to Hamling. Let him sort it out. Frank... Frank got a little extra. Maybe he'll run. Maybe he won't."

"Why wouldn't he?"

"Simple. He likes what he does. He's good at it. And Hamling likes him. And – he left you behind."

"Meaning?"

"Meaning! Charly! I'm sorry but sometimes..."

"You think he'll come after me?"

"He'll certainly come after you. I bet he's already doing it. He's already talked to Hamling..."

"So what's my move? What's our move?"

"*Our* move? No. Let's make this very clear. I'm a dead man. That's *our* advantage, right? And to keep that advantage we need... This conversation remains between us."

"I'll tell Hamling –"

"Tell him what happened. You found me dead. Frank's gone. He took everything."

"Frank will tell him I –"

"No doubt he will. But I trust Hamling. He has a good head. You have a good head, Charly. And Percy knows that. So play it cool. Be up front with him."

"And you?"

"I need a doctor. Then, if I'm still alive Friday, we see what happens."

Momcilovic sipped his wine. He was slowing down.

"So you'll find him," Charly said. "You don't want me to–"

"You're not a bad cook, Charly. You ever wanna make an honest living, I bet you could find something at a restaurant, someone to take you on. I could even..." Momcilovic pushed himself up from the table, held on to the table as he made his way around toward the fire, the empty armchair. "You," he said, "can cook and drive. I know how to find people. We all have our little talents."

Charly smiled. He was as amused by the thing shuffling about the room as he was frightened. He'd never been this close to the mystery of death before. There was dead and there was alive, but the thing seated at the fire seemed neither.

It looked as if a ventriloquist were speaking through the wrecked body of Momcilovic, as if the body at the table speaking to Charly were but a mannequin or a puppet and Momcilovic was elsewhere. It looked barely human. Even the voice was slightly off, out of synch with the words, the movement of the mouth.

Momcilovic told Charly the number. Charly wrote it down. He put on his coat, took the flashlight and left.

The walk down to the village took twenty minutes. He went to the payphone in the garage lot. He was soaking wet. He called the number, spoke briefly with a quiet old man, gave him directions, hung up. He phoned Sandra, who didn't pick up. Her machine was off.

He tried to remember her schedule. He was sure he had told her that he'd be in the city this week.

Then he called another number.

"Daniel. It's Charly."

Daniel Ortiz was an art dealer. He helped Charly out time to time. "I've been calling you," Ortiz said. "You get my message?"

"Have lunch with me Saturday. I have a surprise for you."

Saturday morning would work.

"By the way, Charly..." His stomach turned. Ortiz's by-the-ways never led to anything good. The man got around. He was very observant. "I saw Sandra the other night, at a party. The mayor was there. *Gorgeous* woman! But..."

Here it comes.

"You oughta stick around more," Ortiz said. "Don't disappear so much. Where are you, by the way? Girls, they want attention. They want you there, Charly. They're social creatures. You leave her alone too long and she's gonna find other company. There's no stopping it."

"This coming from you!"

"Yes, coming from me! I know these things, Charly. I watch people! I talk with people! I'm not an animal."

On the road through the village a car slowly approached and passed. Charly could barely make out the driver, glare of light inside the booth. Dark form, a man, glasses. What time is it? It looked as if the car was slowing to a stop, then it went on.

"I know," he said. "I know. I'll try and be around more often."

"Try. Only bulls try, Charly."

"What?"

"Doesn't matter. There'll be others."

Charly wanted to ask what he meant, about what he'd seen, but Daniel said quickly, at a distance, already hanging up, "See you Saturday."

He approached the three cars parked in the lot, the BMW and Volvos. Back-up plan. He crouched, reached under the front bumper of one the Volvos, a brown, well-worn vehicle, withdrew a Lucky Line Key Hider. He got in the car, sat behind the wheel and relished the scent and tranquility that only a Volvo can offer. It started right up, as he knew it would. He turned the heat on, the radio on. He opened the glove box and took out two cassettes he'd left there, Palestrina masses and a Nigel Kennedy recording of the Mendelssohn and Barber violin concertos. The Mendelssohn did nothing for him. He pushed the cassette into the player and skipped ahead to the Barber.

The opening of the Barber violin concerto is like a ray of sunshine at dawn, coming through your window and warming the bed with its purity, its openness.

He sat in the darkness, singing along.

He drove back to the house. The lights were out. Through windows in the front, he saw the orange glow of the fire.

"Still alive?"

Momcilovic was sitting low in the chair by the fire. He turned his bad eye toward the door.

"Make the call?"

That clear, automated voice.

"Good. You're on your way then. I'll be fine. My man'll be here soon. I'll be fine, Charly. Just bring in some wood, will you."

Quite suddenly Charly wanted to go, to put the entire situation behind him, to forget everything that had happened in the last twelve hours.

How far can a man get in twelve hours?

Charly brought his things downstairs. He put the gun on the table. He counted out twenty hundreds, two thousand dollars.

"I don't want the gun," Charly said.

"You might need it."

"I won't. The money's for the doctor."

Quietly Momcilovic said: "That's yours."

"You'll need something to get yourself back."

"Charly. The money is yours. You did the right thing, putting some aside. Frank has mine. I'll deal with that."

He wanted to ask about Frank. He wanted to take the gun, to take back the money he was offering. But he couldn't, he couldn't say the words.

Momcilovic, not a large man to begin with, reduced by his injuries, had slid so low in the chair as to be almost out of sight. It was hardly a voice talking in the dark.

"Take the money, Charly. I have what I need."

He knew the man in the chair was alive, but the sense, deep in his brain, that the man was somehow more than alive, or somehow both alive and dead, made making such a simple decision very difficult. Just speaking with Momcilovic, now, felt illogical. "So give it to your son," he said.

That stirred the figure. He'd missed his flight, long ago.

It occurred to Charly that there might not be an executive's assistant waiting for this man in LA, that the ticket he'd seen on the car seat could have been to anywhere.

With that, he left. He drove down the hill, watching in the mirror the white house retreat into a foggy mist. There was the smallest flicker of red in the window, indication that something remained inside, that it contained some kind of life. And then it was gone. The forest came up around the narrow road. In a minute, he was back on the street.

He stopped at the payphone. He called a man named Ethan Burton and left a message on his machine, saying that he'd be coming up the next day.

He called Sandra. No answer.

He considered calling Percy Hamling. He felt he had to say something but he didn't know what. He also felt that the wrong word might muck up Momcilovic's plan.

He dropped in a quarter and made the call. The call was redirected and a man named Tom Brown picked up. "Hi, Charly."

"There's a problem."

"Go on."

"Frank's gone."

"Yes, and?"

Charly told him what happened.

Silence. He had the impression that what he'd said was news to Brown.

Our advantage...

"When was this?"

"This morning."

"And you're only calling now?"

"Yes. I was... I wanted to collect my thoughts."

"Collect your thoughts. And Drago?"

"The body's in the basement. There's a coal room."

"Okay. And the gun?"

"I left it."

"Good."

"So you'll…"

"You did the right thing, Charly."

The man was writing something down. He could hear the scratch of a pen.

"It's tragic," Brown said. "Really is. He was a good man. When can we expect you?"

"A few days. I'll call."

"Good. We'll, um…"

"I'd like what's mine, Tom."

"Of course."

"Then I'll be away."

"Of course. Some R-and-R. You've earned it."

"I'll call in a few days."

"Okay."

Charly hung up. Tendrils of water on the foggy glass, light rain falling.

Someday all of this will be gone, he thought. The oceans will rise, the mountains fall.

He tried Sandra again. This time, after the fourth ring, a man picked up.

"Sandra there?"

"Who is this?"

"Let me speak to Sandra."

"She's not here."

"Know when she'll be back?"

"No idea."

"She out of town still?"

"Is this Charly!?" The man's voice rose in excitement, kid on a schoolyard. "She doesn't want to talk to you, *Charly*."

"Just tell her I called."

"She won't talk to you! She says fuck off!"

"What's your name?"

"John."

"Thanks, John. Goodnight."

What happened? What always happens. Things go bad.

He drove east. The land was quiet and dark. He was not driving fast when, around a bend, a deer appeared at the edge of the road. He slowed to a stop. The animal stood absolutely still, its head back. Its ears fluttered once, twice. Then it bound up the hill and, as if stepping through a door that only it knew about, vanished into the forest and night.

Part Two

The Crooked Finger

He drove into the small hours of the morning. He stayed off the highway, making his way east into the Sierra foothills by two-lane roads. When he could no longer keep his eyes open, he pulled off and slept.

The sound of birds woke him. The rain had stopped but the sky was flat and gray beyond the canopy overhead. The cacophony of sound, birds singing in the morning, enchanted him. He got out of the car and stretched.

He unfolded the map and found the road he was on but, turning the map around and around, could only guess at his approximate location. Twenty minutes later, outside of the town of Montague, he stopped at a roadside diner. He ordered pancakes, ham and eggs. The coffee was good.

Sitting at the counter, he noticed a dark spot on the knee of his jeans. He studied this for a moment without moving. He scratched at it. Blood, a big fat stain.

He looked at his hands and nails. Except for the finger he'd used to scratch his pants, they were clean.

He went to the bathroom and washed his hands, his face, behind his ears. His eyes were bloodshot.

A few doors down from the diner was a bookstore. He went inside and looked around. He purchased a Zane Grey western and a mineralogy book.

He went back to the diner and had another cup of coffee with a cinnamon roll. He opened the western. *The Mysterious Rider.* He liked the simplicity of the story, how straight forward everything seemed. There was a quiet order implicit in the prose, world of the story, the mountains of Colorado as imagined by Mr. Grey. He laughed at the idea of being a scoundrel for cheating at cards.

"Hungry today, aren't we," said the waitress, a slender teen with a nice smile and ponytail.

"I'm always hungry."

"Maybe you're hypoglycemic."

"Maybe I am." He smiled at the girl. "Does it have a cure?"

"You'd need to check with a doctor. I don't think it's a disease."

"That's good."

"It's a disorder."

"Hmm."

The girl walked away to help two men in flannel shirts at the other end of the counter. She was wearing jeans, pulled high on her hips. She had long beautiful legs. He wondered what happened to such girls, growing up in a two-dog town like this. Did they escape? Or did they stay, and transform?

Outside McCloud, in the shadow of Mt Shasta, he turned down a dirt road to a fishing hole he knew of. Two men stood in the full stream. He stayed in the car and smoked, watching the fishermen, lines glimmering in the air.

When the sun dropped behind the ridge, the world once again got cold and dark.

An hour further east, a light snow began to fall.

He reached the cabin at sunset. Smoke rose from the chimney.

Burton, a huge bearded man, met him at the door.

Charly told him he'd be around over the holiday. He'd make a trip down to the city, but after that would be here through the first week of the new year.

He paid the man a thousand dollars.

The cabin was small, two rooms. A stag's head hung on the wall. Beneath this was a rifle, a Winchester 30-30 that he'd shot before, a good gun. There was a kitchen, a table, a small couch and chair near the fire; in the other room, a dusty futon, a bookshelf, a closet. There was a toilet and small porcelain sink but no shower. That was outside.

There was no television but there was a small, Sony stereo with a turntable. From a collection of LPs at the base of the bookshelf he pulled out two recordings, one of Sibelius's 2nd and 5th symphonies, Leonard Bernstein conducting, and one of Brahms string quartets. He put on the Brahms, opus 67, a piece he first heard, live, only a few years ago. Though he hadn't thought much of Brahms at the time, after that concert he went out and found recordings of the quartets, which were easy to come by. He listened to them carefully in the weeks to come. Those and the four symphonies.

He found a plate of what looked like ground beef in the fridge. (It was elk.) He made hamburgers and rice. He made a small green salad with lettuce and tomatoes from Burton's greenhouse. He opened a Montepulciano d'Abruzzo, something Burton, who had an impressive cellar, had brought down with the greens and toiletries.

He fell asleep before ten and dreamt of a desert. There were horses, though he was on foot, a girl he was following but couldn't catch up with, and a canyon he couldn't cross.

Later the next day he took a truck over the mountain to Reno. He played Texas Holdem for three hours, breaking even. At Blackjack he made two hundred and thirty dollars. He wanted to keep playing but thought better of it. He went to a bar, ordered whisky and beer, watched the dancers. At the end of the bar a group of young men, frat boys, were getting drunk, raising their voices, staggering, holding each other up, pushing each other around. One of them kept holding up ten dollar bills to the girls and then dropping them on the floor as they reached out. They all got a kick out of this. The dancers did too, it seemed.

His look caught the attention of one of them. Fratty looked away. Then something came over him. He stood and ran a hand down the length of the bar. Flush, with crewcut red hair, he leaned in close, swaying. He stank of orange vodka and cigarettes.

"My friend bothering you?"

It didn't come out so clearly.

"What's that?"

"I said is my friend *bothering* you?"

Charly nodded. "Yes, he is."

" ... " Fratty opened and closed his mouth. He closed his eyes, drifting off.

"Why don't I buy you and your friends a drink, and then you all go home. How's that sound?"

Fratty blinked, licked his lips, smiled. He had small teeth and puffy red gums. "You're alright," he said quietly, his hand on Charly's back. "That'd be real swell."

Real swell.

He bought them a couple rounds and then left. Like hungry dogs, they followed him a ways. Then they fell back, either unable to go on, or discouraged, unwilling.

In the parking lot, almost back to the truck, he heard the boys at some distance. He looked back. They were in another part of the lot, staggering drunk, arguing incoherently. One of them, "My friend," shoved Fratty on his ass. Fratty leapt to his feet and threw a punch, catching his friend in the ear. Friend screamed, bending, clutching his ear. When he stood up he lowered his chin, clenched a fist, went at Fratty like he meant business and in the blink of an eye Fratty was on the ground, holding his gut, spitting blood.

Charly was half tempted to go over and ask them what it was all about. But then they were laughing and Fratty was back on his feet and peace restored.

Ascending the mountain, he reflected on how in the wastelands of Nevada, where nothing lives, where nothing is produced, people do nothing but steal from each other, exploit each other for their weaknesses. "There's the land," he said, the argument taking shape, "and what *it* contains." But that's not production. "Production is the key."

Snow was coming down fast and accumulating. Traffic inched along. Near the summit he pulled off, followed a winding road down into the forest.

The town had one street and a number of bars. The air was cold and fresh.

The bar had a long plywood counter and not much else. A large bearded man sat at one end, hunched over in his seat. Green and red Christmas tree lights twinkled overhead. A football game played on a small TV up in a corner behind the bar. The sound was down to a slight murmur.

He ordered a beer. He smoked and watched the figures in the TV.

He heard the door open and close behind him, the soft tread of a woman walking back and forth. He heard her put a quarter in the payphone and make a call. Nothing.

He heard her make her way back toward the door. Then she sat down next to him.

"In town for long? Buy me a drink?"

He caught the look on the bartender's face as he dried a glass, the tilt of his head.

She wasn't old but she wasn't young either. Such a simple body, a farmer's daughter's body. Not much to fixate on, not much to remember.

She did have some long legs, great in jeans.

Her name was Mia Marconi. He took her to the only motel in town.

"Take a shower, Mia. Make yourself comfortable."

He lay back on the bed, kicked off his shoes, read *The Mysterious Rider.* He thought he could hear Mia singing in the shower, which bothered him. He wanted peace and quiet. The company was nice. Quiet company would be even better.

When she finished and came out naked, tall and rail-thin, he stepped past her without a word and closed the bathroom door and took a shower.

She'd put the heater on full blast. The room was hot and steamy, stank of old carpet and wet bath towels.

She had a long flat body, strong legs. She was on the bed, back on her elbows.

"So you like reading," she said.

Her nipples were flat and pale. Her ribs showed. Down the side of her right leg, hip to knee, was a long white scar.

His scrutiny didn't bother her. She watched him round the bed in silence, his eyes going over her, up and down.

He turned off the heater and bedside lamp and opened the curtains. There was nobody outside. The night was empty and cold. The red lamp of the motel sign hummed in the icy air.

Tying her up crossed his mind. There was so much to her: long gangly limbs. What ended up happening was she tied him up. He didn't understand how it came to that, but in no time at all there he was, arms out crucifix style, wrists fastened securely to the headboard, one in a bra, the other in the telephone cord.

Head down, bony spine up in the air, Marconi ground her body against his, groaning like some prickly scavenger backed into a corner.

Minutes later, somewhat bored, and sensing her immersion in the act, he managed to slip his wrist from the bra and, partly free, wrapped his legs tightly around her waist, pulled her over, and quickly unfastened the other wrist. She was stunned for an instant, surprised by the quick change in position. He took her upper arms and twisted hard, rolling her on her front. Leaning into her with all his weight, teeth in the side of her neck, her ear, he pushed himself in from behind and felt her catch her breath. Arm under her stomach, he squeezed, his hot ear against her back, the boom of her heart inside.

He opened the window a crack before going to sleep. Piercing cold air blew into the room. In bed he pulled the whore tight against his body and the blanket tightly around them.

When he opened his eyes, the room was full of milky light, freezing cold. A car passed on the road outside. He got up. It was snowing. He closed the window and pulled the curtain, went to the bathroom to piss.

Mia Marconi hardly moved. Her long body curled shell-like on its side. He listened to her sleep. From his jacket he took out two hundred dollar bills. He put these on the table beneath a glass ashtray. He got back into bed.

When he woke again he was alone. He listened for a minute before moving.

She was gone.

The money he'd set out was gone. On a napkin she'd written a phone number. Her numbers were beautifully drawn, antiquated, like something from a postcard a hundred years ago.

He checked his jacket and pants, to see if she'd taken anything. Finding the diamond in its yellow paper surprised him. She hadn't seen it. She hadn't looked.

Or maybe she had.

It surprised him, as well, to think about how dumb he'd been, first, to take the diamond with him to Reno, and second, to leave it where it was, almost in plain sight.

He didn't care, he realized. Somewhere in his mind he wanted the diamond to disappear, wanted what remained of his money, money he'd stolen, to be stolen itself. Somewhere in his mind he wanted to be left with nothing.

He went back to the cabin. He made hamburgers and fried potatoes and onions. He had a bottle of the Montepulciano. He put on the Sibelius symphonies, loud. The fifth impressed him very much. He thought he could hear the end in the beginning. He played the whole thing – it's a short symphony – over and over. He opened a bottle of Cutty Sark. In no time, he was on the floor, drunk to the marrow of his bones. He crawled to the door laughing like a madman. He staggered out into the forest and threw up. It felt good. The vomit steamed in the snow. His head cleared a little.

He could hear the 5th still playing in the cabin. *The swan song*, they called the last movement. He pictured – there, in the darkness of the forest, on his hands and knees in the snow, gasping for breath – pictured Jean Sibelius in his little shack on the shores of that lake very far in the north of Finland, all alone. Writing, drinking vodka, listening to the world without people.

There was a meadow not far from the cabin. He made his way to its center and collapsed. He turned on his back. The sky was opening for a change. Stars, spinning round and round, blazed in the heavens.

He felt like he was about to die. He was very cold, but it was superficial. Deep inside he was strangely comfortable. He was sinking into the snow, into the earth.

He could smell the woman, her long body, feel the coarseness of her armpit on his face. What was her name?

He heard something, edge of the meadow. He tried to raise his head and look.

"Mia?"

~ 8 ~

The rain started in the foothills. Cars were sliding off the road right and left. Red lights flaring all the way down.

He stopped at a station west of Sacramento. He called a man named Bernie Posner. "What's the word?"

"So there you are. Causing trouble?"

"Bernie."

"I know... You know what you need, Charly, is a good –"

Posner was an old man. He was doing well for himself in computers. He had a wife down south, your classic Tinseltown bombshell. Charly'd seen pictures. They'd traveled the world. That's Barcelona, Rio de Janeiro, Jerusalem. She liked the sun. She always looked the same. Some people never age.

Maybe the north didn't agree with her. It was cold. And it rained a lot. In any case, she was gone.

Posner was always telling Charly what he needed. Half of this was just impulse, the man's nature. Half of it was mentoring, Charly's eye in the sky.

"Things are quiet," Posner was saying. "You'd think nothing happened."

"You check the locker?"

"We had someone there. He said it was like you left it. Nobody'd even been there, he said."

"You check under the tarp?"

"What tarp?"

"In the locker."

"He didn't say anything about a tarp."

"It's not important."

"Where are you, Charly?"

"Nearby... Anything on Frank Conway?"

"Nada. The man is gone."

"He took my money."

"So he killed Drago –"

That was fast. Brown's moving.

"You could say that."

" ... Didn't take him for that kind of guy."

" ... He probably had his reasons."

Take the diamonds. Hold them. Put them somewhere safe. The man had his reasons. He had them all lined up. *You're a crafty guy, Charly. Figure it out.*

"My money, Bernie."

"What do you want me to say?"

"Get a word in with Hamling's boys and see what you hear."

"I can do that."

"I'll call Saturday. Let's meet. I'll come down to your place."

"I'm clearing my calendar. And then?"

"Then nothing. Then I'm on vacation."

"No, I meant... It can wait, Charly... Let's meet. Talk then."

The roar of the rain on the metal roof of the phone booth was deafening. The world on the other side of the glass disintegrated into a kaleidoscope of red and blue shards. A man, dragging a kid by the elbow behind him, ran from the Quickymart to his car. The boy had one of those of Nintendos in hand, a block of gray clay, thumbs pumping the buttons, enraptured by whatever was happening in the tiny screen. He didn't even see the rain. Kid didn't see anything except, in a glance, in the phone booth, uncanny familiarity, Charly.

It was just past midnight when he pulled up to Sandra's. The building was dark. The neighbor had lights on in the front room, an enormous Christmas tree taking up the entire window.

He climbed the steps in silence, knocked on her door. Nothing. He looked in through the front window. The shades were pulled. He tapped on the glass. He knocked on the door once more.

"Sandra."

He left. Went to his place down in the Lower Haight, a decrepit Victorian. A couple bums were asleep on the stoop outside. They were wrapped like mummies in filthy blankets, plastic bags, their few belongings, stacked in the corner. They hardly moved as he passed.

The mail was full of trash.

It's a long walk up to the fourth floor, old wooden steps winding round a center shaft, every step creaking beneath him as he climbed. No way to make a quiet entry.

The other flats in the building were abandoned, dark rotting holes, all locked up. If Charly moved out, the owner told him, the building would come down.

That his place should hold things up puzzled him. He didn't have much. And he wasn't there for half the year. He'd move into a newer place, if he wanted to. But the building had character, a certain ugly charm about it, like a giant tortoise.

On the landing outside his door he had two potted geraniums. They'd seen better days.

Rain fell on a skylight overhead. Pigeons murmured on the eaves. Down in the street, the hiss of a car quickly passing.

It was cold inside. The place was dark.

At the end of a long corridor was the kitchen. The fridge had beer and some jarred things – artichoke, olive paste. Mustard. No butter, no cheese. No bread in the cupboard.

He opened a small window over the sink. The sounds of the city on this dreary midnight came through – music, some kind of hiphop, playing nearby, a car down in the alley, a siren. The rain, its endless patter and swish.

No end to it.

There was a small black dish there, on the sill. He pulled it inside and rinsed it out. Before closing the window he called outside: "Cat!"

Nothing.

His hands were cold and stiff.

He ran water in the sink, waiting for hot to come. It took a minute. He held his hands under the steaming current. He held them up to his nose. He checked beneath his nails but it was too dark to see anything.

He took a long hot shower.

Midday through he stepped out – leaving the water running, filling the little room with steam – and got a beer from the fridge. He brought it into the shower and carried on with his thorough cleansing.

Afterward he took another beer to the bedroom. He threw a couple extra blankets on the bed and crawled in naked. He read a little more from *The Mysterious Rider*. He thought about becoming a cowboy. He'd need to learn how to ride a horse, throw a lasso, and shoot a pistol from the hip.

Reaching over to put out the light, he noticed, remembering, a leather bound book on the bedside table. *Tales of Terror and Suspense* by Edgar Allan Poe. It was Sandra's. There was a bookmark in the middle of a story called "The Tell-Tale Heart."

The book smelled like her. Lying back, he pressed it to his face and imagined her neck, her great legs and hips.

He finished the beer in the dark. Downpour outside, the sky crashing to earth. He could hear a shutter swinging and banging in the wind.

Bap! ... Bap! ... Bap!

But he couldn't fall asleep. Insomnia? He pictured himself sinking into the bed. Dissolving, melting like an ice cube.

He was more hungry than he was tired. His stomach felt turned inside out, so empty it was.

Then he fell asleep, suddenly, surprising himself.

He woke startled. He thought there was someone in the room. He reached out, as if to stop or catch something.

There was nobody there.

It was early. He could hear the guys downstairs on the stoop, laughing, drunk already.

He went to his pants and pulled from the pocket the yellow pod, unfolded its delicate leaves, the diamond.

"Look at you."

Would it have impressed Sandra? Not at first. At first, she would accuse him of doing awful things, of breaking the law and getting her tangled up in his world, with his awful, dangerous friends, and the bad consequences of everything they did.

Then she would take the diamond. Then she would hold the rock in the palm of her hand and shut her trap.

He pictured her trying to say something. The woman always had something to say. Always. Her lips parted slightly, the word caught somewhere back on her tongue.

That was the kind of rock it was.

~ 9 ~

Tom Brown was a slight man. He wore what looked like an expensive gray suit, a dark blue shirt. He did not wear a tie. He sat at his desk in his home on Telegraph Hill with the posture of man who wakes early every morning to run ten miles. Even relaxed Brown looked ready to strike, like he was already in motion.

Charly stopped by his place without an appointment. It was ten to nine, Friday morning.

"Let's back up," Charly said. He'd described, again, what had happened Monday. "The first question is the amount. I was told at least twice there'd be two million, about two million in the crate."

"That's correct."

"No," said Charly. "Well, incorrect. Because there was one million in the crate. One point one. Frank counted it. Frank himself said he expected two. That's what he'd been told. This has not happened before."

Tom Brown said nothing. A vein pulsed in his forehead.

"Explain it to me," Charly said.

"You're correct in saying that the estimated amount was two million. I was with Frank when the opportunity was first brought up. So I heard that as well. I'm not sure what happened to the rest of the money. I have my theories, which I'll keep to myself for now. We have people looking into the matter. What I want to understand is what happened between Frank and Drago."

"I told you what happened. I was outside. I heard the gun go off."

"Whose gun?"

"I told you. It was in the crate. Lincoln's gun. I don't know whose. It was there. Drago seemed to recognize it. That's the gun Frank used."

"But you didn't see this."

"No. *I was outside.* I heard the gun. I –"

"Why didn't you go –"

"Back to the house? You *hear* a gun go off. There's a million dollars on the table. Right? Would you walk into that house? Tom? No. I didn't go back to the house. I stayed where I was. When I saw Frank come outside, I knew what was what."

"You saw Frank come outside."

"Like I said. He came out, called my name."

"And you waited. You wanted to see what would happen."

"I wasn't sure what would happen. Wasn't sure if he'd come after me." Charly replayed the episode in his head, hiding in the woods, watching Frank Conway in the door of the house. He wanted a cigarette but didn't bother asking. "I don't think it was planned," he said. "He might've, but..."

"Interesting."

"... Interesting? *Quasars* are interesting!"

"I mean –"

"Interesting! *Fuck!* Tom!"

"Language, please."

"My money is gone. Drago is dead. There's nothing interesting about that."

Brown smiled. "You're right," he said, hands up – *Slow down.* – in a gesture Charly'd seen before. "What I meant to say –"

"He could have had others coming, guys to finish the job... But he didn't. He waited for me. Then he left. He took care of the cars. He took the money. He left the gun... Was it planned? I don't know. I don't think so."

"So what do you think happened?"

Charly waited. He'd said too much. He was telling the truth, but holding back.

That's our *advantage.*

He suspected Tom Brown knew he was holding back. "I think something was going on between them. And there was a last minute change of plans. A disagreement. I didn't like the look on his face to begin with. He was up to something. I see these things. I think I'm a good judge of character... You know – he brought enough food up there for a week. Did you know that? Was he going to stay? Was he expecting someone? Was he..."

"What about Drago? Tell me more."

Through the window behind Brown's head, the towers of the Golden Gate rose out of the fog, worn and abandoned, like ancient ruins.

"We did one job before. Maybe two. I think he was straight. I didn't have a problem with him."

"No. What *about* Drago, what was he like? He say anything, do anything?"

" ... We did the job. We went fishing."

"*Fishing?*"

"He likes to fish. He was flying to LA to see his kid. If he was up to something, he played it real cool." Charly stopped. Then he said, redirecting: "What about my money?"

Brown didn't blink. Tom Brown never blinked. Glasses like two postage stamps of ice balanced on his long thin nose. He fixed his blue eyes on the man across the desk, reading the smallest details in his posture, his face. Scum, he thought. I should never have let him in the house. I'll never do it again.

He smiled suddenly and began to rise.

"I need to make a phone call, Charly. Please excuse me."

Brown left the room and closed the door behind him.

Charly stood up and looked around the office. The furniture was spartan and toneless, beige, cream. On the desk there was a telephone and what looked like a calendar. Nothing else. If you caught its surface at the right angle, you'd see there was hardly a speck of dust on it. Like a window, like ice. What's it made of? Wood? Glass? Steel?

There was an abstract painting on the wall. Four hazy colors, blue, purple, orange and yellow, stacked in layers, like fog, like a color sandwich. He didn't care for it at all. He wondered if there was a safe behind the painting, like in the movies.

Brown returned after a few minutes. He was moving quickly, speaking clearly. He did not sit down.

"Here's how we're going to do this. First we need to locate Conway. No question about that. Then we want to recover your money. What's yours is yours, and if what happened happened as you say it happened, then we need to right this wrong."

Charly worked his tongue over a sore spot in the back of his mouth. He thought of Mia Marconi, the scar down her leg. He thought of Columbine, the young woman in the Zane Grey novel he was reading.

Brown went on. "Then we'll need to settle up. Accordingly, you owe Hamling, accounting for the adjusted take, ninety-nine thousand, nine hundred and ninety-nine dollars."

The man said this with a straight face. Charly wanted to laugh. It wasn't a joke. After a moment he said: "Hamling doesn't get anything from me so long as Frank is gone. Get Frank back. Then we'll talk."

"Sure. That's about right."

"That's the way it's going to be."

"Charly." Was that fluster? Impatience? "I'll get back to you on this. One final matter –"

Cup of coffee'd be nice. *Criminy!* this guy can talk. *Ninety-nine thousand nine hundred and –*

"What's that mean," Charly said, "you'll get back to me on this? The money's gone, Tom. Frank Conway has it. You'll get back *to me* on this?"

"Charly?" Again, that look. "I have kids in the house. Let's be civil. You're not listening. We like you. We can count on you. We've done right with you, these years. We'll find an equitable way to settle the matter, I'm sure."

The painting was really getting to him. That and the desk and this man, every word those tight lips produced.

"Can I offer you something?" said Tom. "Tea?"

Tea.

Charly wanted to go. He'd said enough. "What about Drago?" It was a move he had to make carefully. He wanted to know what Brown had discovered at the house. Still, if he thought he could get away with it, he wouldn't have said anything at all. But not saying anything might say too much.

"We've sent someone to take care of it."

They appeared finished. Charly looked out the window, at the homes of Tom Brown's neighbors. *Fat Cats. An equitable way to settle the matter.* "And the cars?"

Brown nodded. "Those too."

"... So I'll hear from you."

Brown said nothing. Then: "One more thing. Why did you wait an entire day before calling me?"

"For all I knew," – *careful, Charly* – "Frank was waiting for me at the end of the driveway. I was figuring things out. What would you have done?"

Brown smiled, cheeks stretching.

"What I would have done is not the issue. I am not you, Charly. What *we* will do is what we can about the house, but you've got to realize... The longer one stays around the scene of a crime, the more likely it is that one will leave a clue for the police. That is basic, Charly. You should not have stayed there, having dinner, drinking wine, making a darned fire in the fireplace! What you should have done was pack your things and left as quickly as possible. What you should have done was call me before even going into the house, minutes after you saw Frank leave. That's what you should have done. But you didn't. You made a mistake. You have made several, big mistakes, Charly, in the last seventy-two hours, and though I want to help you rectify what can be done about these mistakes, you know there is only so much I can do."

Brown stared at the young man by the window.

He continued. "So. For now, we need to end this conversation. I will get back to you. Is there a number you can be reached at? I recommend not going far."

He's lecturing me. I bet he eats sushi every night. Has his tea mailed directly here from a little farm in Japan.

I would like to watch this man eat sushi, how he uses chopsticks, how he opens his mouth and wraps his teeth around that tongue of fish.

Charly left a number.

~ 10 ~

He walked down to Vallejo Street, stepped into a cafe. He had a large cup of coffee, black, a bagel with lox, cream cheese, tomato and sprouts.

People get salmonella poisoning from sprouts. Charly ate spoiled meat once in Mexico. He was in bed for four days, what felt like dying. Then it cleared up.

Christmas carols chimed overhead.

It was cold out. Through the window he watched dark forms bent against the wind and rain. Rain blew sideways in the street. When others came into the cafe they gasped at its warmth, blowing into red hands, wiping water off their arms and legs.

They seemed cheerful, these locals. It was the last Friday before the holiday. In a few days, everyone would be gone. The streets would be empty.

He could feel the cold creeping in, on his feet, around his ankles. His socks were already wet. Everything was wet.

In the darkness of his coffee he saw a beach, white sand, sunlight gleaming on the waves, he could hear gulls in the breeze.

Where is Frank Conway?

Drago Momcilovic?

He flipped through a weekly and skimmed the calendar. There was a concert that evening at a nearby church. A string quartet. Maybe he'd stop by. Maybe he'd go back to the mountains. Maybe he'd hunt Sandra down.

On the steps outside his place, clustered tight together under the eave, all shoulders and lowered heads, heavy black jackets, the regular gang – these black men drinking, playing dice, smoking pot, all of them without work. One of them stood up at Charly's approach. He held a wet piece of cardboard over his head.

"People lookin for you, where you been?"

"Emmett. What's happening... In Reno a few days. Before that, Austin."

"You do get around, don't you. Here it's the same old."

Emmett stepped in close. He smelled like gin and cigarillos. He had a bruise beneath his eye, a burst blood vessel in the eye, filling the white with red.

"But these suits... come around asking for you these days."

"Like yesterday, the day before?"

"Like that."

The men on the stoop were there every day, from dawn to late in the night. They'd scatter in the afternoon to sleep and sober up a bit, maybe play with the kids after school, but then they'd be back, back to the cards and dice, malt liquor and pot.

In this neighborhood, they were good men to have on your side.

"Tell you what, Emmett."

Charly reached into his coat and took a card and pen from his shirt pocket.

"You see these men here today, call these numbers. You see them this weekend, next week too, you call me. I want to meet my guests."

"Will do."

"If I don't answer, that's okay. I'll come around. If it's something you think I should know right away, you find me. I won't be far. I'm at Sandra's, on the hill. Or ask Rita. She'll know how to find me."

He gave Emmett twenty dollars. He went inside.

He plugged in the stereo and put on Mahler's fifth symphony. Militant trumpets, soaring and sobbing string choir, sweet antidote to the Christmas music playing everywhere now. There was something approaching in the music, he felt, something terrible. It was composed in the first year of the twentieth century. He tried to think back to that time. Impossible.

He was in the army once. He didn't remember much of his life before then. Nothing important had happened. Too much had happened since.

He turned the music up loud.

He made a pot of coffee. He put on the heat.

A dark flash in the corner of his eye – a mouse scurried across the kitchen floor, one corner to the other. Down where the wall met the floor he found a hole that hadn't been there before. From the other room he brought in a lamp, plugged it in and brought it as close to the wall as he could. On his hands and knees, he peered inside the mouse hole. It was very dark in there. He started to stick a finger in and then pulled back and stood. A fan of black mold crept down the wall near the ceiling.

From a cupboard he took down a bag of cat food. He filled the dish he'd cleaned the night before. He opened the window over the sink, onto the grimy backside of the building. A soft rain blew in. He set the dish on the sill.

Clicking his tongue, he called the cat.

He closed the window. Coffee in hand, he went to the front room.

The men down below, laughing, playing, getting drunk. Busses coming and going, nearly on time. The occasional cab. A cop car crept around the corner, rolled down the street, pausing ever so slightly outside his place – a little exchange through the passenger side window between the cop and the guys outside. Nothing unusual about that.

What do you call it? Would that be a parasitic relationship?

A month ago a kid was shot dead on that corner.

Years ago this was a clean, safe, up and coming neighborhood.

So was the Tenderloin, not far off.

Everything changes. Everything turns to rot.

In the kitchen, a shadow in the window over the sink. He opened it and there it was, the black cat that had no name, eating its lunch.

"Hello fucker, what're you up to these days? Get in here and do some work."

Gently he lifted the cat from the ledge and brought it inside, set it on the floor. It looked around quickly, studying its environment. It did a few circles, found the hole in the wall, turned and walked away.

Best to be patient with some things. To give the impression of nonchalance.

Charly shaved and took a shower.

At a few minutes to noon, the phone rang. It was Posner. "You were right," he said. "The job was rigged."

"How's that?"

"This is speculation, but Donny Lincoln was this close to being brought to justice, and it would seem that a large sum of money has put that off for another day."

"By large sum we're talking –"

"A million, give or take."

"I see."

"And what's more, our friend Hamling, according to my source, had a stake in this exchange."

"I'm listening."

"The legalese is beyond my ken, Charly, but apparently Lincoln owed Hamling something – I don't know what or what for – and the circumstances, then, were propitious for both of them. Lincoln cuts down his debt and steers clear of the law, and Hamling gets his money back. And then some, I'd say."

"That means Frank knew how much was in the crate."

"We can't know for sure what Frank knew or didn't know. But that's not a bad guess."

"Which means we were set up, Drago and me. Which means –"

"Like I said, let's not jump to conclusions too quickly here. Hamling might –"

"Frank knew what was in the crate," Charly said. "I'm going with that. I'll make this assumption."

"Very well. What's that do for you?"

"If Frank and Hamling told me the job was for X, knowing that it was actually for Y, it was because they knew I wouldn't do it for less. But still they wanted me for the job. Then the question is how they deal with the blowback, once I discovered –"

"Good question. How *did* they deal with it?"

"You know part of the answer already," Charly said, his brain beginning to hurt. "But I don't think Frank wanted to kill Drago. I don't think that was his plan. Something happened in the house. Drago caught on..."

"And what's the other part?"

"That's the thing, Bernie. The crate... There was something else in the crate."

"Go on."

"There was the gun, first of all. Strange little thing. Drago recognized it. A *purse gun*, he called it. Frank offered it to me… I didn't touch it. Not then. And then – that's what he used…"

"And that's it?"

"There was jewelry. Diamonds."

"Diamonds?"

"Yes." *Mexico, Mexico, Felicia, Felicia*, he sang in his head. "I said… I said I didn't know what to do with diamonds, that… And that the job was for cash."

"And? That it?"

"And he offered them to me."

"*Offered* them?"

"Like a token of his appreciation for my help. As collateral for…"

"And you took them!?"

"No."

The day was quickly fading outside. Through the bay window in the front room, a lonesome ray of light, full of ash, flickered on and off.

It was raining hard. The Mahler was long finished. A chill was creeping back into the air. On the battered floor, the blue spackle of rain on the window.

There was a painting on the wall before him, something by George Bellows. A city street on a summer's day, trees flush with green, a woman in a red dress hails a cab, reaching out – her hand like so, her wrist so, her ankle and raised heel, like so…

Something was growing in his mind.

He lit a cigarette. He studied the woman in red.

The cat ran into the room and sat down suddenly, upright at his feet. It glared at him with narrow green eyes.

Posner: "What happened to them?"

"They were on the table. I couldn't... You know, it was *obviously –*"

"You did the right thing, Charly."

"They were gone the next day."

"So he took them. He killed Drago. He took the diamonds, he took the money."

"That sums it up."

"And so you're wondering why he offered them to you in the first place."

"Right."

Posner said nothing. He could hear the old man breathing, hear and feel the cat purring on the floor.

"Rather strange move," Posner said, "if you think about it. Especially if, as you say, he wasn't planning on murder. A double murder."

"That is what I'm sitting here thinking. Did he want me to walk away with those diamonds?"

"If I hear anything else, I'll call. You'll be there?"

"... Hamling wants his cut. I need a hundred grand... Here or there, Bernie."

"I'll see what I can do."

~ **11** ~

He could not play an instrument. He didn't understand them. He thought of himself as mechanically minded – he could fix most cars without any trouble – but the mechanics of a piano, for instance, baffled him. How such sound could be produced by such a simple device. It was almost like magic.

He didn't listen to much music before meeting Sandra. In his life before her, he never listened to classical music but would skip over it on the radio, preferring rock or heavy metal or, on occasion, jazz. Classical music was stuffy. It was something his father had listened to. He had memories of the old man sitting alone in his study, nearly in the dark, Tchaikovsky on the record player.

Then something happened. An accident, a series of accidents, actually.

Tommy Arminski was a clerk in a prestigious law firm downtown. Their chief was a bigshot for a while. She ran for DA a couple times, lost both times. Doesn't matter. When Tommy came home after pushing paper all day, he'd unwind with booze and coke and a harem of Asian girls. He was insatiable. He could fuck three girls in one night, pass out twice, and then get up for more. He had a real problem.

Charly'd seen this, seen him. He was like the walking dead. It's five in the morning, and *it hurts*, Arminski's practically crying as he follows his monster cock down the hall from one bed to another.

It was through Tommy that he got tangled up in some rotten business. Dangerous material, dangerous people. When he felt things had gone too far, he decided to walk away. Tommy said it wasn't an option. Then one evening he came by. He walked in in a panic, high, said to pack some things, they were going for a drive. They wouldn't be back soon.

They took Tommy's car, an MG Midget. Charly drove. Tommy was going on and on about how he'd tried to cut them loose, about how this hadn't gone down well. But then how they'd let him go too easily, no questions asked. He didn't like it. They were following him, he said. He'd seen them outside his office, outside his place. Charly said maybe he needed some time off, some fresh air and exercise. No more coke for a while.

"Exercise!" Tommy screamed.

Tommy was turned and looking the other way, out the rear window. They were just off the bridge, on 580, Oakland passing quickly on the right. Maybe they'd go down to Yosemite, hike Half Dome by the light of the moon.

"Is your seatbelt on?" Charly asked.

Tommy was all stare.

Suddenly the whiteness grew, first covering half the man's face, then filling the car.

The SUV was moving fast. The MG was like a puddle to it. It split and splashed, spinning all over the highway, rolling, it seemed to Charly, who was in a curious state of bliss, transcendent, forever.

When it stopped, Tommy wasn't there.

Charly crawled from the wreckage. White head lights sparkled at a distance, like bugs on a summer evening.

His head was spinning. It hurt to breathe. When he pulled his shirt up he saw that his left side was black, bruised. His ribs were broken. Not so bad, actually, all things considered.

Tommy wasn't so lucky. Mixed on the road with various pieces of glass and metal, parts of the MG, were various pieces of the insatiable Tommy Arminski. It looked as if, while flying from the spinning vehicle, something in the man had unzipped. As if, while spinning in the air, something sharp had pierced a hole in Arminski's side, and that was the end. Everything came undone.

"You okay man?"

Some guy approached Charly. Then he noticed a whole line of them, people standing clustered at the edge of the road, looking on, holding their faces. He heard sirens.

"I think my ribs are broken."

He looked at his hands. They were shaking. They were cut up.

The stranger put his hand on Charly's back.

"Sit down. Help is coming."

Charly walked away. The stranger told him to sit, again, tried to help him with this, but Charly brushed his hands away. The man watched stupefied as Charly staggered off toward an array of bright yellow garbage cans and then down the offramp.

He felt his way along in the dark.

The sirens got louder.

"I really think you should wait for help!" the stranger called behind him.

He walked to the nearest subway station. He took the next train back to the city. In the tunnel beneath the bay he noticed a ringing in his ear. "I have a concussion."

He made his way home.

He had some leftover pizza and potato gratin. He had a beer. He took six Advil. He took a shower.

Before midnight he'd pulled some things together. He took a taxi to the bus station downtown. He boarded the next bus for Seattle. He got off in Portland and crashed at a friend's. The next morning he boarded a bus for Denver, where he stayed for a few days.

There he went to the hospital. The skin from his right shoulder to his pelvis had turned black, blue and purple. He was having trouble breathing. He could barely move his arm.

The doctor told him he had four broken ribs and a fractured clavicle. He was lucky man. The important things were intact.

"So what happened?" the bald man said, smiling.

"I was in a car accident."

"You walked away from it?"

The doctor was writing on a clipboard, taking notes, looking at Charly in quick glances over the rim of his glasses.

"Didn't seem that bad at the time."

He took a bus back to the city. He couldn't go back to his apartment so he stayed with a friend. He wanted to do something new, something different. Without saying so much, he told his friend that he wanted to reinvent himself, to become a new man.

They started that evening, when the friend took him to a recital in a nearby church. It was in a small place. There weren't many people in the audience. Scarlatti, Chopin, Scriabin were on the program. The pianist, a pale young man with a great head of hair, came out and bowed. Then he sat down and got to work. The sound was marvelous. How could such a small instrument produce such sounds? Was it amplified? He looked around, studied the structure of the place.

He didn't understand any of it. But it was a pleasant kind of confusion. Better than pulling yourself from the wreckage of a car, than seeing your friend chopped into a dozen pieces on the roadway.

The next week he went to another concert, in a different church. Again, the play of sound around the interior of the place was incomprehensible and enchanting.

Why hadn't he noticed this before?

He began going to concerts on a regular basis, three, sometimes four nights a week. Then one day he realized his life was different. He was changing. The life he had known, a life he was happy to forget, was that of another man.

One evening he saw Sandra Bizarro play Dmitri Shostakovich's *24 Preludes and Fugues* and he left the hall much more than enchanted. The woman's figure, the woman's movement with, over the instrument, it was unlike anything he had ever seen.

It was not about beauty, nor passion. It was all mechanics. It was as if, in overcoming the machine of the instrument, in mastering it, the performer transformed herself into something else, into, not a musician, but something equally mechanical, not even human, but, mad with concentration, a greater machine.

The recital shook him up. He couldn't get the music out of his head. He couldn't get the image of that woman out of his head, her large body rising from the bench, her long arms spread out, hands pressed down, focused on a point before her, on something only she could see, as if by pressing just a little harder she could win, she could kill.

He wanted to touch those legs, the ankles, the muscular thighs, wanted to feel those hands on his body.

He went after Sandra Bizarro. She was not available, they said.

Didn't matter. He'd make her available.

So he did. He wedged himself into her life, and very slowly she made room for him.

Near dark, he walked over to the Castro. On the marquee of the theater at the bottom of the hill, *The Entity*. He liked that theater. He'd spent many hours there, forgetting himself.

On a small side street just up the hill, he stopped at a white iron gate and pressed an intercom button. He waited. He was about to press the button again.

"Who's that?"

"It's me. Charly. I'm early."

"Charly... I'll come down."

He heard him before he saw him. Like the flop of an unfurled sail, this huge red umbrella opened at the top of the stairs. Ortiz came down. He looked like hell. He'd lost weight. His eyes were bugging out, his hair was falling out. His baggy clothes clung to his frame. He had a ratty blanket pulled up around his neck and shoulders.

The man blinked at Charly through the gate.

"Weren't we –" he started to say.

"Let me in. I've a question for you."

"Everybody has a question," Ortiz said. "All these questions... Busy times, Charly. Shoot."

"Can't we go upstairs? You'll get sick out here, like that."

"Hee hee ha ha. Too late for that."

The man licked his lips, smacked his gums. Even his teeth were falling out. Heavy eyes, in the darkness it looked like he might fall asleep standing.

"I have something to show you."

Ortiz opened the gate. Slowly they climbed the steps to his place.

The flat was impossibly packed with odds and ends, old furniture, paintings – on the walls, stacked against the wall, on the floor – books, magazines, newspapers, posters, dishes, clothing, rugs, shoes, an aquarium, bird cages, a motor of some sort, computer monitors.

The place was stifling. It smelled like chorizo.

Ortiz shoved some things off a leather chair and told Charly to sit. He positioned himself behind a large green desk and turned on a fluorescent lamp. "Talk," he said.

"People die like this, you know. Buried under their own shit. Found days later."

Hunched over his desk on his elbows, Ortiz reminded Charly of Peter Lorre, of a very sick Peter Lorre.

Ortiz said, "Yes but those people are sick. They have no one."

"You're sick."

"Not sick like that sick, Charly. I'm cared for... So whadda you want? What is this you gotta show me? I'm going out."

"Going out? Like that?"

"Like what?"

"Danny…"

"A sick man can't go out and enjoy himself?"

Charly set the diamond on the desk.

"What's that?"

Ortiz carefully unfolded the yellow leaf.

He looked at the diamond without moving.

"Want a drink?" he said quietly. "Help yourself." He pointed with his chin at a Chippendale cabinet in the corner. Various bottles were gathered there on a dusty shelf. From the back Charly pulled out a twenty-year old Glenfiddich. He poured two glasses. He sipped one and then poured himself some more. He returned to his seat, placing both glasses on the desk.

Ortiz had brought out a lamp and magnifying glass. The bulb at the end of the curved neck was large and bright. "What you have here," he said. Then, looking under the bulb: "I can't drink that. You have it. Maybe you deserve it."

Charly enjoyed his scotch. It made him feel connected with everything. He settled into the chair. He thought Ortiz lived in despicable conditions, but he wouldn't mind staying in this chair, drinking this Glenfiddich all night, well into the next day.

Ortiz went on. "I can't help you with this. Not directly. What I can do is refer you to a man named Joseph Gideon Lasker. He knows diamonds. His office is in Manhattan but I know he's in LA from time to time. He could tell you what you have here."

"What's it worth?"

"You didn't hear what I just said."

Ortiz sat back in a shadow. He licked his lips. He raised his hands and did something funny with his fingertips, wiping them hard against his palms.

There was a sound somewhere in the murk of the apartment. Charly turned to look.

"That's Aldo. Don't worry about him. He's taking me out."

A tall stately man appeared in the doorframe. "Hello," he said. Then he turned and disappeared.

"You'll need to see Lasker to confirm anything. But I would guess – and I've only seen a few diamonds – like this one – I would guess somewhere between seven and *ten* million."

Charly drank his Glenfiddich, gears turning.

Ortiz said, "But it's not my business, Charly. I'm probably wrong about that. Let's be realistic and say five."

Charly was thinking about Frank Conway. The scotch was opening something up inside him, moving him far far away from Daniel Ortiz, across the desk.

Conway knew this diamond was in the crate, and knew, without a doubt, that Charly now had it.

"Where'd you get it?" Ortiz asked.

"Say I'm just a courier. Just moving it from point A to point B."

"And you want to know it's value. So..."

"So nothing. It'll be in the hands of its owner on Monday. Say I was just curious. So I know what to ask for diamond-sitting over the holiday weekend."

"And... Who knows you have it?"

"You. Old buddy."

"We're not buddies, Charly. As *a colleague*, may I suggest that you put this away somewhere safe. Tonight. That you put it away and forget about it until the phone rings and its owner tells you where to bring it and when. That's my suggestion."

Rain pelted a dark window behind him, gravel being thrown up against the glass.

The intercom chirped in the hallway. In the heat of the apartment this electric burp sounded thick and far away.

Charly heard Aldo say something. He had an accent. Such a gentle voice, Aldo's, for such a large man.

"He's not in. May I tell him who's calling?"

Charly finished his drink. Then he had Danny's. He rose, reached out. Ortiz folded the diamond into its paper, as he'd found it, and placed it in Charly's hand.

"Get rid of it, Charly. That's all you can do."

In the hallway, Charly said over his shoulder, "Call Lasker. Give him my number."

Ortiz sighed, fell back into his chair, further into shadow.

"You still think about Mexico? That chica. Como se llama? Nadia?"

"Lasker, Daniel."

After a moment: "Of course. I'll ring him tomorrow."

He had a burger and fries in a twenty-four hour joint down past the theater. The meat tasted good, just undercooked and bloody. The tomato was flavorful and crisp. They knew how to make burgers at that place.

He had a cup of coffee, flipped through the weeklies.

He'd go to the concert after all. They were playing Sibelius.

He drove over to Sandra's. Her light was on. He was running up the steps when the door opened and a man stepped out. "No, really!" he was saying.

Charly got right in his face.

"Sandra in?"

"Who?"

"You John?"

"John? Am I John? No. Who you..."

He pushed past the young man toward the door.

She was gone. Her things, her place, she wasn't there. There was another man inside, a thin guy in a white undershirt. Boxes everywhere. He was unpacking. It sounded like Elvis Costello singing, playing.

"Help you?"

"I'm looking for Sandra. She lived here."

Over his shoulder he heard the other man laugh. "She's gone."

The inside man opened his hands. "Don't know her. Sorry. I'm just –"

He backed up a step. Looked at the front of the place, at the number beside the door. It was her place all right. Had been her place.

The outside man said, as he passed him, leaving, "She moved out. Two days ago. You're too late."

Was he drunk?

Charly felt like smacking him, throwing him down the stairs.

It wasn't worth it.

What's done is done.

He went to the concert.

~ 12 ~

The first violin was a ferocious looking Japanese woman. She played to kill. She was in pain, she wanted to cry, it seemed to Charly. She looked – for an instant, he thought – directly at him, and what rapacity in those black eyes, what violence he saw in there coming for him.

Her black slacks crept up her legs. Her heels in black stockings rose in unison off the floor.

But the music was not painful, or violent, or demonic. So where did it come from, that anguish he saw in the body of the performer? Why should it hurt to make something so beautiful?

At the intermission, he went up to a man he recognized, a guy he always saw at these things, and asked about the violinist. Yoshiko Wada was her name. She played frequently around the city. Maybe he'd seen her before but hadn't noticed. She taught at the conservatory.

The guy mentioned a bar they sometimes repaired to afterward, he should stop by.

"Maybe I will."

The woman came in later. She was accompanied by a Japanese man. Short fellow with a small round gut, he dressed well, in black and white, no tie.

He found out that the guy was her brother, in town on business. He spent a minute listening in. The brother did something in restaurants, in design.

It wasn't hard to approach Wada. You just needed to be patient. Everyone had something to say to her, but she was remarkably quiet. Politely responding to questions, giving little else away. She looked tired, with a long face, dollops of flesh beneath her eyes.

For a moment she was alone at the bar, waiting for a glass of chardonnay.

"You played beautifully this evening."

"Thank you," she said, tight smile, eyes down.

"I don't know anything about Sibelius," Charly said. "I sometimes listen to the fifth symphony... I thought your performance was excellent."

Her wine arrived. She looked him in the eye.

"I didn't think so. We were lazy. It was too soft."

"What was too soft?"

"The entire thing needed to be sharper... It has *edges*, you see... What's – do I know you? – what's your name? You came in with Sally?"

There was a dark smudge beneath her cheekbone. A slender neck, strong chin, red tongue. Small breasts under the black blouse. Strong arms. There was something about her hand that caught his eye.

She spoke softly but with force, sort of like she played, Charly thought.

"Charly. I came in by myself."

Her eyes moved over his face for a second. She looked irritated.

He wanted to touch her hand, look more closely at what he had noticed.

Another woman interrupted, appearing out of nowhere, her long fingers falling over Yoshiko's shoulder. She was tall, with a small square face and brilliant blue eyes. As she said something to the violinist that he missed, these eyes followed him, wanting a reaction.

Yoshiko smiled and began to cover her mouth. She blushed, looking at the other woman, whispering behind her hand.

Then, pulling Yoshiko away, the intruder smiled at Charly, her large, white, square teeth too much for her small lips. Those eyes, again. They made him feel small, like a stranger. It was a challenge, that glance.

He was a stranger among these people, and he didn't have the slightest notion of what to say to save his chance.

Then Yoshiko smiled, the expression hollow, and said, "A pleasure, Charly. Excuse me."

She took her chardonnay and left the bar, joining a group of women.

He ordered a Cutty Sark.

Over his shoulder, he heard her laughter, warm, deep, wide.

After a minute he turned and looked back. She was facing him from behind two rather tall women. Her dark eyes met his for an instant.

When he left the bar he noticed the brother seated on a couch in the corner, talking loudly with two other Japanese men.

It was nearly two in the morning when he got back to the apartment. Cold dark night. The rain had stopped but everything was saturated, dripping.

Two bums, again, asleep on the stoop. He wondered if he'd ever even seen their faces, these two.

Keys in hand, brain catching up, he heard a car door close and the steady tap of a heavy man in leather shoes coming down the sidewalk. There's only one reason why such a man would be on the street at this hour.

He was big. He had a pony tail. Named Jaime something. Charly'd met him before. One of Brown's.

"Jaime. What brings you out on such a lovely night?"

"Invite me in for a drink? Or we do our business out here?"

The man's head was so big and hard, like a wooden stump, it looked to Charly like the mouth could barely get the words out, how something in the neck and cheeks pushed forward, cramping the lips.

What a week. The sun is shining in Cajón del Diablo, no doubt.

"Come in, Jaime. Watch your step."

They sat in the front room. Jaime sank low in the couch, his arm over the back. He crossed his legs. Pointed leather shoes.

"Wanna beer, booze?"

"I'll take a Calistoga water."

"Just ran out!"

"Then whatever you're having, Charly. Nice place."

Charly poured him a scotch, J&B.

Jaime sipped the drink and winced. He held up his glass. "Can I have it with ice?"

Charly opened a beer. He poured himself a scotch. He went to the window, studied the street far below. It was empty. Jaime's car, a black Cadillac, was parked a ways down at the edge of a pyramid of darkness, where a street-lamp was out. "It's late," he said. "I'm tired. What do you want?"

"Hamling gives you until Friday."

The man's voice was higher pitched than it should have been. For something that big.

"You came out on a night like this to tell me that."

"It wasn't so bad when I left. You've kept me waiting. How's Sandra?"

"Cut the crap. I wanna go to bed."

"Okay then. You know the policy. Nice and simple. Let's say by five, Friday. Don't be late. Thanks for the drink."

The big man stirred his scotch and ice with a finger. He took a long sip, flash of teeth, grimacing.

Charly lit a cigarette. "Before I agree –"

"*Must* you smoke?"

Jaime waved a hand in the air, disgust on his wooden face.

Charly stared at the man, speechless. He stepped closer to the couch, to a bookshelf. In a little plastic frame he had a polaroid of Sandra. Stinson Beach, last summer, the wind in her auburn hair. In a motel there they'd had sex for hours, all day long, sleeping like the dead in between.

He could taste her, hear her, feel her weight, her breasts, her heavy legs.

"Before I agree..." He pulled on the cigarette, enjoying its crackle and flair in the near dark of the room.

The big man smiled. He had a nice smile. But the pony tail had to go. "Agree?" he said. "There's no agreement. It's not an agreement, Charly. Friday. On Saturday, a week from now, if the payment is not made in full, I'll come back. Not to talk, Charly. Saturday we foreclose." The man looked at his drink, spun it around, ice tinkling.

"Sure enough," said Charly. "Now may I ask a question?"

"Ask away."

"Where's Frank Conway?"

"Frank Conway."

"Maybe you didn't hear. I spoke with Tom earlier."

Jaime started to say something and then paused, lips parted. You wouldn't take him for a thinker. He looked like a man acting like a man pausing in thought. Then he shook his head, realizing the futility of what he wanted to say. "I heard," he said.

"You heard. So?"

"It is irrelevant to your, *our*, situation. In other words, Charly, that's your problem. Frank Conway is your problem. My problem, and your other problem, is the fact that my man wants his cut. And so long as you are here, within the reach and reason of my hands and poor little brain, you are the one I will speak to. You are my concern, and you *will* get the money, Charly. Conway is not my concern. He is the concern of another man who, I have no doubt, is working very hard on that nut. So. The money, Charly, by Friday. Or else."

"Or else?"

Do people even say that anymore?

"Or else things get ugly. Want me to put it in writing for you?"

"Please do. And then, Jaime, try to understand my position –"

Jaime Dossantos laughed. "*Your* position!?"

"I would pay what I owe Hamling," Charly said, "I always have. But that money was taken from me. Conway has the money. Does this not compute? I understand that I might be a problem in Hamling's view of things, but how is *this problem* separate from the other problem, namely Frank Conway. He is one of us. And he took my money, which includes Percy Hamling's money. I don't know what else to tell you."

"Tell me about Momcilovic."

There was a twinkle in the big man's eye and it was not the prelude to a kiss.

"What about Momcilovic? You already know. He's dead. Frank shot'm. Wrapped the body in a rug and dragged it into the basement. Then he took the money. Then he drove away."

"Dead, is it?"

"Am I speaking Chinese here? Yes. Dead! As in food for worms. The big sleep! What about dead do you not understand?"

"In fact." Jaime raised a fist, cleared his throat. "The matter does not concern us. I should say, it doesn't concern me. What concerns me is getting a certain amount of money from you. I'm sorry if I sound like a broken record, Charly. Really! I just want to get my message across. I'm a simple man, after all. I don't want to argue. I don't want to fight with you. I'm just doing what I'm told to do."

The big man sipped his drink. It was going down easier now. "However," he said. "I will say this... It was a curious thing – yesterday morning – to hear that the house – that house of yours, that you secured – beautiful place – was empty. The house was empty."

"What's that?"

"EMPTY. Want me to write it down?"

"They checked the basement?"

"Basement, cellar, attic, pantry, the barn, the woods, they turned that place upside down. No body. No Momcilovic."

"That is a curious thing."

"Isn't it."

Charly felt sluggish, feebly trying to anticipate his next move, to see the situation from that other point of view. *Drago Momcilovic.* But he was so tired, the night so cold and wet. He was shutting down, a knot of fear and apathy tightening in his throat.

He left the room to pour himself another drink.

"Where you going?"

"To get myself a drink, Jaime. Be right back. Get you something?"

In the kitchen the black cat sat on the dining table, where he knew he shouldn't be, still as an Egyptian idol.

He returned. His guest was on his feet.

"I was just leaving," Jaime said. "But first, back from our interesting tale to the question at hand. Hamling's money. Okay. Now, when you say Frank Conway ran off with it, after killing Momcilovic dead, dead as in food for worms, do you not see how I might be a little dubious."

"Dubious?"

"Do you not see how the fact that the house was empty, that no *body*, no corpse of any kind, turned up, strongly suggests that what you are telling me is not true. Although, I will grant you, the semantics here do not exactly indicate to me that you are lying – but what is a lie, after all? – do you not see how this complicates matters? Or does it? Rather, Charly, maybe the empty house simplifies things very much. Simplifies things for me and for you very, very much."

"He was dead. How many times do I have to tell you? Ever looked in the eye of a dead man, James?"

"Tell me, tell me again, you've told us. We know the story. All I'm saying, Charly, is that... The house was empty. So the story doesn't hold up. What we conclude from this scenario, this new scenario, is that something happened up at the house, but not exactly as you've told it. Whether or not there is a body involved, a corpse waiting to be discovered, disinterred, whatever, is neither here nor there –"

Neither here nor there? Where on earth is this guy from?

"Our concern is only, simply, the money you owe us. I don't know what happened up there. I don't know where Frank Conway is. I don't know where Drago Momcilovic is. All I know is that you have a deadline for this payment. Without a body to substantiate your claim, Charly, what you are giving me is hokum. I don't want hokum. I don't want words of any sort. I want money. I want the money you owe Hamling. And if you don't pay my employer, *our* employer, what you owe him, Charly, then you are going to pay in other ways. But I don't need to tell you that. You know I'm a man of my word."

"Of course you are, Jaime. I'll have the money. It's not a problem."

Charly listened to the man descend the stairs, around and around, the diminuendo of his hard feet on the wood, and then on the wet cement outside. From the window, he watched the man get into the black Cadillac and drive away.

He poured himself another scotch.

He stripped and climbed into bed.

He lit a cigarette and studied his filthy ceiling.

Momcilovic got away. He's after Conway. Does Conway know? Do they know where Conway is? It's only a matter of time, now.

~ 13 ~

The image of that gun, the one they'd pushed around the table, a game of hot-potato, of Momcilovic standing those bullets up one by one – it played again in his mind, back of his closed eyes.

It was late. He had to get up.

Everything was heavy and cold. He heard his grave calling.

He wanted a gun. It wouldn't solve anything. It might get him an extra day or two, before nature took its course.

He fed the cat.

"Get that mouse?"

He could hear it, or others like it, a whole family of them, in the wall. They were eating. Scratching.

The cat was crouched over his dish. His tail swept the floor, back and forth.

"You still have work to do, cat. Nobody gets a free lunch here."

He took an umbrella and went for a long walk around the neighborhood. Rain fell steadily, straight down. Thin sheets of water ran in waves down the street. A bus passed, the windows steamed up, its motley colored occupants like souls being shipped off to the next world.

He made his way down the hill to a Safeway. "Little Drummer Boy" piped in overhead, playing endlessly, variation after variation as he ran up and down the aisles gathering things for breakfast. He bought eggs, sausage, portobello mushrooms, swiss cheese, ricotta, coffee, organic whole milk, oranges, apples, honeydew melon, pineapple, and a loaf of bread, artisan style. He also bought an *Examiner*.

On his way back up the hill, laden with groceries, he had an idea. Beginning of a plan.

He stopped by a garage. It was twelve-thirty, they were just closing for the day. He knew one of the mechanics there. He asked about a certain car, an old BMW they kept around for errands, if it was available for a few hours.

It was.

He'd be back.

At the apartment he put on Bach, partitas, Rosalyn Tureck at the keyboard. He cooked. He made omelettes with the mushrooms and cheese. He fried the sausages. He toasted bread, buttered it, made a pot of coffee and a fruit salad.

For two and a half hours he enjoyed himself, the large breakfast, the newspaper opened on the dining table, music filling the apartment. When he finished the first pot of coffee he made another. He smoked, drank his coffee, and read. He forgot about the rain outside, forgot about

Sandra, about the holiday, about people like Frank Conway and Jaime Dossantos, about the rodents in his wall, about the yellow wad in the pocket of his jeans and what it contained.

Then he had to clean up and everything started coming back.

It was nearing four when he descended the hill again, to the garage. He found the BMW where it was always parked. It was a CS 3200 with nearly eight-hundred thousand miles on it. Someone had loved this car very much. The interior was clean, polished. Faintly, the smell of a cigar. In the glove box was an envelope which contained a key and nothing else.

He went north, over the bridge. The 101 was empty. He drove fast.

He did what he knew he shouldn't do, and that was go back to that white house.

It was dark when he came to the village. Gentle rain falling. He pulled into the garage, stopped directly in front of the office, dark now.

He walked quickly up the hill. When the house first came into view, white and skeletal on the rise, he stopped. There was a vehicle in the yard. He wasn't alone. But then he saw that it was the van.

That wasn't supposed to be there. Brown said he'd take care of it, the van, the cars. Didn't he? And if they'd been up Friday...

EMPTY. Want me to write it down?

The place was quiet. Rain fell through the trees. He was soaked to the bone, that cold stiffness coming back.

In the barn the two cars he'd brought up were as he'd left them. The Jeep and Toyota, sunk on their slashed tires. He heard the kittens but couldn't find them. The cat had changed locations, picked up each kitten one by one and moved them to a safer place.

He stood in the barn door watching the house in the rain. Then he ran across the yard, went in the back door, unlocked. The power was out. Didn't matter. After a thirty seconds he knew the house was as he'd left it a few days ago. Minus Momcilovic. The chair before the fireplace was empty, streak of dried blood on the leather armrest, on the seat, what was obviously a bloody footprint on the brick hearth.

He went down to the cellar, God knows why. Five steps down, Zippo extended, his foot plunged through a rotten board and he screamed, juggling the lighter in one hand, flailing for the railing, imagining the possibilities, the odds. "They found his mouldering corpse at the bottom of the cellar stairs. Broken neck."

He made his way into the coal room, ducking through the small door. The rug lay where they'd left it. Black stain of blood in the dust.

In the back of his mind he felt he was missing something. The fact was bright as a spring morning and right before him but still he could not see it.

Brown's men had not come up to the house. Nothing had been touched.

But they knew about Momcilovic. Knew, that is, that his body was not here. *How?* Someone had either come to the house and found it empty, or...

Water dripped in the corner, in the darkness.

Plink. Plink.

He stepped toward it. Stopped.

Drip, not a drip. Something else.

Plink!

He turned suddenly and the lighter went out and the darkness, like a bucket of oil in his face, covered him, his frantic cry, spark of the Zippo wheel blasting, spitting, blasting and finally catching, the long blue flame revealing the stairs at his left hand. He took them two at a time without a glance back, thinking of nothing but getting away – "Watch that step!" – getting far away from all that had happened.

He slammed closed the cellar door. He did a once-through of the entire house. Nothing had changed. The gun was gone. The money he'd left Momcilovic was gone.

He ran down the hill, back to the garage. He sat in the car, blowing on his hands. He turned on the radio. A boys' choir. "O come all ye faithful..." He turned it off, went out to the payphone, isle of serenity on this dreary frightful night.

"Bernie. Charly."

"What's happening, where are you?"

"Heard anything?"

"Nothing."

"I was paid a visit by Jaime Dossantos last night. You know Jaime?"

"Never heard of him."

"He's a piece of work. One of Brown's guys."

"And?"

"And he told me..."

"You have to come up with that sum."

"I have until Friday. I'm betting Conway turns up and Hamling sees what's what... It's still a lot of money I don't have."

"I might be able to help."

"There's something else. Something Jaime said."

"... I'm listening."

"Jaime told me..."

"You're fading, Charly. Speak up! Where are you? I'll come for you."

He regarded his reflection in the glass of the booth. He looked old and tired. *What'd the guy say? To speak or not to speak - that is the question. That is the question.*

"Charly!?"

"Drago Momcilovic, dead when I left, is missing."

"Missing, what's that mean?"

"The body's gone. They checked the house, came to clean up, and found nothing. No Momcilovic."

"No Momcilovic," Posner said. "The dead Momcilovic?"

"Right."

"So someone took it."

"Or Drago rose from the dead and walked off himself."

Posner ignored the comment. "Why would someone take it?"

"I have no idea."

"Is it possible your friend Jaime's trying to mislead you?"

"Mislead me?"

"Goading a reaction."

"Sure. I considered that. So I, I went out to the house."

"Today you went?"

"I did. And sure enough. Empty."

"You know how stupid that is."

"I had to check. What's more... Something Jaime said. He was just reporting, telling me what he'd been told to say. And thick as he is – it's hard not to trust the guy."

"Really stupid, Charly. They're going to throw away the key, they catch you. Fish you outta the bay."

"He's a peon. He couldn't make up a story like this. He said they turned the place over. Looked everywhere. He's never been here, Bernie. He told me exactly what he was told to say. That's fine."

"Your point is?"

"They weren't here. That's the point. The house is empty, yes, but it's the same house I left on Tuesday. The car I came in is still in the yard. I don't think anyone's been here."

" ... Wait. Let me understand this. You called me when, Thursday was it? Told me Frank Conway had killed the other guy, this Momcilovic, and taken his and your money. He was on the run. You told me you were in a tight spot because you owed Hamling. You told me you thought the whole thing was rigged to begin with, which I have tried to confirm. That's that. *Now* what you're saying is –"

"He was dead."

"No. Let me understand this. You're saying the body you left behind is now gone. And without a body, Hamling doesn't seem interested in listening, in dealing with you. Right? That's clear enough. What's not clear, Charly, is how the body of a dead man disappears. Someone took it away. So. Who do we know who knew about the body and who might want to move it? Conway?"

"Could be. Could be he came back."

"But you don't think so. Someone else then? Hamling? Who'd you talk to before talking with me? Brown. Brown sent someone up."

"Sure. He said he would. But that doesn't explain things. Why would he then come at me with this empty house story?"

"Right."

"Why's he twisting my arm, Bernie?"

"So let's go with the possibility that Conway went back to the house."

"Conway went back to the house," Charly said. He could see it in his mind, Momcilovic seated before the fire, bleeding in the armchair.

That's our *advantage.*

Who's misleading now, eh Charly? You are building a house of cards over the only man who might help you. Why not tell him the truth?

"He went back to remove the body," Charly said, "with a million dollars in the car. With a twelve hour lead. I don't know Frank Conway that well but I don't think he came back. That'd be stupid. Not even stupid, it wouldn't make sense."

"Well then, tell me."

"I can't. I don't know what's going on. The body was there. Now it's gone. Brown knows this, but..."

"But?"

"Something's not right. He might know there's no body but not because he or his men found this out."

"I don't follow. You told him Momcilovic was dead. He said, he said what?"

"That he'd take care of it."

"Right. So? He sent up some guys and they stepped in and stepped out. All they needed was to see a body. Right? You told them where it was, it wasn't like they had to dig it up or anything, right?"

"That's right."

"So they took it. It's the simplest explanation, Charly."

"I don't think that's what happened. Brown would clean up. He's like that. He doesn't miss a beat. And the place is as I left it."

"Well then. Tell me. There must be an explanation. Maybe it's Conway, still. He's giving Brown a story in the other ear. About how you lost your shit about being gyped, about your suspicions of Conway and the other guy all along, about how you were going to take what you deserved after all these years, about all the shit you took from the likes of Conway and others. About how you were going to disappear for a long time. About how you forced them into the basement at gun point, disabled the other vehicles and made a smooth, foolish, getaway."

"And then walk into Brown's office empty handed? It wasn't like that. I talked to Brown Friday morning. If Frank did something like that..."

"So it's complicated! You plan these things step by step. But they never work. You know that. And that's why I believe you, Charly. You wouldn't do something like that. Turn against the likes of Conway, Hamling. All I'm saying is there's probably a simple explanation."

"Of course there is."

"It's the case, isn't it, that Conway is closer to Hamling than you are."

"That's right."

"So there you are."

The thing needed to be sharper, she said. Yoshiko Wada's lips flashed across his mind, in the bar, that other world.

He could see her in the dripping glass of the telephone booth, standing before him. Her long strong arms. That peculiar hand on the stem of her wineglass. "Don't ask me how I know it," he said, "but that's not how it is. Conway is running. He's long gone. Holing up who knows where. All Hamling wants is his money. He has people after Conway. At least that's what Jaime told me. In that sense, yes, things are simple. But this missing body is getting to me. I need to know how Brown knows that Drago's missing, and that I –"

It then occurred to Charly that he might be the butt of a joke. He was the guy caught with his pants down round his ankles, dick in the breeze. "I'm the only one left," he said, realizing this obvious fact for the first time. "With nothing... With –"

But there was something. Two things, in fact. *Momcilovic. He –*

"Charly? Slow down. What did Churchill say?"

"Who? You have nothing to fear?"

"No. You're a mystery inside an enigma. You are complicating things! Don't! Get some rest. I'll do what I can about that sum. Really, if that's all there is, if what you're telling me is all there is to it, then come Friday everything's settled and you're off to that pretty little island in... Where was it, Charly, that place you told me about?"

"Nowhere, Bernie."

"Go home and get some rest. I'll put things to work for you. I'll drop by in a couple days."

"I'll be there."

"I'm sure you will. Don't get killed in the meantime."

Forty-five minutes later he pulled off at a roadside motel. The rain was too much, falling like there was no tomorrow.

There was a light on in the office but nobody home. He rang the buzzer several times, then gave up.

He drove out to the coast, to a little beach he knew of. He stopped in the parking lot there. He turned off the car but let the heater run. On the radio, finally, something different for a change, through static, what sounded like George Antheil.

Curtains of water ran over the small windshield. Of the world at night there wasn't much to see. He could barely make out the Pacific, fifty meters off. You could hear it though, rumbling down there, the waves high, white, boiling, curling and crashing on the shore, one after the next. And beyond these, the darkness of the ocean on a moonless night.

You could hear that darkness, and feel it, so massive it was.

He put his seat back. He smoked and listened to what was maybe Antheil. He wanted a drink, something hard. He opened the glove box. He knew there was nothing there but he'd thought he'd check anyway.

He thought of Henry Miller, who wrote "That's my Georgia cunt," a line he always liked.

They couldn't find him out here. Nobody knew where he was. He didn't have to go back. He could stay here for a few days. Go back to that motel. Wait for the storm to end. It had to end.

No. He had to go back, had to pay what he owed, had to face what was coming.

He thought of *The Mysterious Rider*, which he'd left behind. That world seemed so simple. Everyone's intentions and desires seemed so obvious. One could see where everything was going.

And that's why it's fiction, he thought to himself, proudly.

It seemed like a good thing to know, the difference between what is real and what isn't.

Then again, he still didn't know who exactly the mysterious rider was.

He pulled the key, shutting off the heat and radio.

The car rocked in the wind. It felt like being in a casket, afloat somewhere in the middle of the ocean.

He thought about Yoshiko Wada. About her legs, her black stockings.

What was she doing?

Practicing.

At this hour?

The whole thing needed to be sharper.

Practicing for a perfect performance.

And that's where Charly's thoughts ended. He fell asleep, the possibility of Yoshiko Wada practicing her violin in the middle of the night, playing Bach all alone in her apartment, a shadow in the center of his brain. Slowly, precisely, the sound of the violin expanded, glowing red like a filament, its heat cutting open the night and pulling forth a kind of light from the other side.

He was stepping out when the phone rang. Joseph Gideon Lasker identified himself and gave him the address of a place in the Richmond District, off Lake Street. A man there would look at what he had.

Closing the door the phone rang again. He let it ring.

He walked up Haight under a soft rain. He stepped into a vegetarian restaurant. The girl behind the counter had thick blond dreadlocks. She wore overalls, bushes of brown hair sprouting from her armpits.

Charly tried not to stare. She was repulsive, but fascinating.

He thought of Mia Marconi, who had hard armpits, and of Sandra, who had wide ones.

He ordered a tofu sandwich with avocado and tomato. He had a couple cups of organic, "free trade" coffee.

At the Red Vic they were showing Rambo movies all afternoon. The first started in about an hour.

He walked around the Panhandle with his hood up, smoking. The grass in the park was intensely green, blinding with color. The park was empty except for a few intrepid runners.

He went back to the theater, bought a ticket for the 12:30 showing of *Rambo: First Blood Part II*, and went inside.

A punk couple sat in the front row, whispering intimately.

He lit a cigarette and slid down deep into the old seat. There's nothing like being almost alone in a movie theater on a wet day, bottom of the year, watching John Rambo kick some ass.

The lights had just gone down, the trailers starting, when a man sat down behind him. The click of his shoes gave him away.

"Jaime. Don't be a stranger. Come closer."

"I would but I can't stay. Things to do. Anyways, I hate Stallone."

"It's a great movie."

"So is *The Sound of Music*. Work comes first."

"What do you want?"

Charly turned to look the other man in the eye. He was bothered to be interrupted like this, just as the picture was about to start.

Jaime could barely fit in the seat. His knees were up to his shoulders. He spoke quietly, hardly moving his lips.

"Frank's paid his due."

"What's that supposed to mean?"

"That means he's clear. Money's in."

"I'm..."

What? You're what, Charly?

"I'm speechless. I have no words."

Jaime smiled. "I thought you'd like to know."

"How considerate of you. So you saw him – Frank?"

"I don't spend my days in the office, Charly. I do what I'm told and that means I'm out here, like you, getting exercise. I was told that Frank is clear. You're next."

"Drago?"

"Like I said, I do what I'm told." He raised his hands. "I know nothing about your dead friend."

They looked at each other for a moment. Then Jaime slapped his hands down on his big knees, got up and left. "Have fun." He shoved his way passed a couple who were just sitting down. "Scuse me."

The movie started.

So Frank's back. Can't be sure. If Jaime's right, and Frank is clear, then...

He's going to turn up. It's just a matter of time.

He tried to enjoy *Rambo* but his thoughts wandered.

Frank couldn't have paid up. He couldn't have just walked in the door.

And why not?

Because...

An M-16 would be nice right about now. That would do the trick. A couple full clips, a grenade launcher. Yesss.

He ended up staying for the next show.

It was dark when he left the theater. The streets were empty.

Down the block from his place, Emmett appeared and fell into step beside him.

The bruise under his eye was healing but the blood in the sclera hadn't gone anywhere. In a flash of light from the streetlamp overhead, that eye glowed red.

"Keep your head up, man. There's trouble looking for you."

"Who's that?"

"One smooth dude. Little guy with deep pockets. Maybe Asian, maybe Mexican, I can't tell. Some of them look all the same... Anyways, he's making friends quickly round here. And he wants to know all about you."

"Get a name?"

"Nah."

"A cop?"

"No way. But he'll be back... I tell you. You turn the other way you see this one coming. I've seen the kind before. He's cold, man. Got that psycho look about'm. Determined, *meeeean*, know what I'm sayin? Don't cross him."

"Thanks, Emmett."

"It's nothin. But I'd skedaddle. Go back to Reno or someplace, don't come round here for a while."

"That's the plan."

"What we'll do is this... This guy come around and get in –"

"Get in, how would he get in?"

"I don't know how he'd get in, but he will. They do that. So he gets in, and I know you're there, I'll whistle, like this –"

Emmett didn't whistle but he put his index fingers in his mouth.

"You hear me whistle three times fast, loud, then you go out the back door and don't look back."

Emmett took a flask from his coat pocket, undid the lid and tipped it up quickly, twice. He offered it. Charly took it and drank. Whatever it was was strong, like toilet bowl cleanser, burning his insides. It did the trick.

Charly took out his cigarettes and offered one to Emmett. They smoked in silence. They watched the empty street. Then Charly gave him a twenty and went inside.

He showered, shaved, had a ham and cheese sandwich and glass of prosecco. Then he took his book and went back to that bar. Maybe Yoshiko'd be there. You never know.

It was a quiet place, unlike most. Even the music was off, which took him a moment to realize. Imagine that – the sound of people in hushed conversation, of glasses rising and falling on the bar, these hard little tables, the hush of air settling around them.

He sat in a booth near the back, reading Zane Grey, drinking very slowly, watching with one eye couples come and go.

He was more or less sober at one-thirty, when they started to close. He ordered a night cap. Glenfiddich, neat.

Then she came in, alone. Since the place was nearly empty, she spotted him right away, came with her drink and sat opposite him.

Under a black wool coat she wore a dark maroon dress. Faded yellow flowers. Black stockings, like before.

"You don't see that anymore," she said. "A guy reading alone in a bar, at this hour."

"Did you used to?"

"No. I guess not. Actually I've never seen a single guy read alone in a bar, at any hour. The guys I know don't read."

"What brings you out so late?"

"What's wrong with you? Reading alone in a bar... I always come out late. It's my time."

"What's wrong with me." He smiled. He tried to tell her, tried to explain the situation. It was hopeless. After a moment he stopped midsentence. He looked the girl in the eye. She had a freckle on the tip of her ear.

She found his feebleness, his inability to explain anything, charming, which didn't please him. So he asked her about music. Which didn't please her.

"You practice a lot?"

Her face fell. That was precisely what she would not talk about.

He'd play it carefully.

"Last call!"

"I'll take you home," he said.

She stared into her drink.

There was a tap on the window a few tables away. On the other side of the glass, a woman, smiling, cheerfully waving beneath an umbrella in the rain.

Something about the woman's mouth – nobody smiles like that on a night like this, at this hour.

He recognized her from somewhere.

She was coming in.

He felt that the fragile balance he'd quickly established between him and Yoshiko was about to come undone. Everything would fall back to earth.

Yoshiko glanced over her shoulder and frowned.

He wanted to ask her again if she was ready to leave. But he couldn't push her.

It's like fishing, he thought. Let the hook set. Wait –

She looked up and said, "You're not dangerous, are you?"

He thought about it. "Do I look dangerous?"

"You a pervert?"

"Do I look like a pervert?"

"You look mysterious," she said.

The other woman had gone straight to the bar, ordered something, and was now approaching. "Yoshi!" He wanted to throw something at the intruder.

Yoshiko Wada said quietly, "Let's go," and they stood up together, taking their coats.

"Mary," she said, turning to face the other woman. "We were just leaving."

Charly noticed how Yoshiko quickly turned away from the woman, this Mary. She kept a shoulder between them as she put on her coat.

Then he remembered. He'd seen her here, at the bar, the other night. She was a tall, striking woman, in some kind of suit under a slick, dark blue raincoat. Black hair, cut short, Dutch Boy. Square face, broad shoulders, a long athletic body. In her small head, blue eyes that could cut glass, the barbed look she gave Charly.

"Mary Mullen," the woman said, pointing her hand at his gut. Her grip was firm, pulling at him, lips dipped in a tight smile.

She looked tired, beneath the forceful front. He could smell her, sweat wafting up the *v* of her coat at her neck, the smell of a long day, a woman in a hurry.

Yoshiko introduced him.

They were leaving, she said again.

"Another time then," said Mary.

It was her eyes, Charly realized, in a glance back, that made him so nervous. Not the blue, supernatural and captivating. It was the lower eye lids, tiny bumps rising over each eye, like styes, like rifle sights, so that it looked like she was squinting when she wasn't.

She watched them go. She sat at the bar, laughing with the bartender.

"Friend of yours?"

He waved down a taxi. A cold mist was blowing.

"We know each other." Climbing into the cab, she said: "That's trouble, Charly. Mary Mullen. She's crazy. Stay away from her."

He turned, looked back.

Sure enough. Mullen's gimlet eye was boring a hole in the back of his head.

~ 15 ~

He poured whiskies. She put on a Heifetz recording of the Bach violin partitas and sonatas. For almost ninety minutes they drank in silence, listening.

It was something he and Sandra would do.

At four in the morning he got up to leave.

"No way," Yoshi said. "It's too late to send you out. And it's raining. You stay there. Sleep there."

She disappeared for a minute, returning with sheets and blankets. He fixed a bed on the couch.

He listened to the woman move around other places in the apartment, rinsing something in the kitchen, showering, brushing her teeth.

The apartment was large and, for the exception of the study – with the piano, music stand, violin and music, music everywhere – clean. Polished steel, wood. It looked hardly lived in.

He lay back on the couch in the dark. What floor were they on? High up. He could hardly hear the city at all.

From the lit entryway to the other room, she stood for a moment, shadowed, in some kind of pajamas. She said goodnight. She disappeared.

He heard music on in her bedroom. Jazz, the particulars of which he didn't recognize. He heard her talking on the phone in Japanese.

He stood at the window to the balcony and looked out on the bay, on the bridge in the rain, lit up in red, green and white Christmas lights.

Without a sound he stepped outside. It was cold, a hard wind blowing. He smoked. He thought of Sandra. He'd never see her again, he was sure. He'd been too far away. Ortiz was right. They wanted attention, company all the time. She'd found someone else.

He thought of Drago Momcilovic, alone in that white house, bleeding in the chair before the fire. Had the doctor come in time? Or had he been the one to take the body away?

They wouldn't find him here, in this apartment.

Nobody knew where he was. Right?

But he couldn't stay. He wasn't even sure if he liked this Yoshiko Wada.

He'd never been with an Asian woman before.

He liked the way she played the violin. Maybe that was it, that was all.

When he woke, the room was full of light. She stood in the door with a steaming cup in hand.

"You awake finally?"

"I'm awake."

She threw a white towel across the room at him.

"Clean up. I'll fix lunch."

The shower was large, all white and chrome. Extravagant. Even the hot water smelled good. He took his time.

She made vegetable broth, rice, a green salad, fish. On the fish, some glaze, sweet, hot.

"I didn't ask you. You like fish?"

"I like everything."

"Of course you do," she said. She smiled.

Yoshiko Wada was suddenly very beautiful to him. Warm, caring. Innocent, he thought.

They ate slowly for several hours.

They traded stories about their lives. She told him where she studied and with whom, all of which meant nothing to him. She knew that. And he told her about his on-again off-again years in college in LA, about his stint in the army, in Panama, about drafting work he'd finally found with an advertising agency. All of which meant nothing to her.

He cleaned up. She had very sharp knives.

"I like your knives."

"My father gave them to me. Careful. Look at them the wrong way, you'll lose a finger."

"What's your father do?"

"He was a cook."

She made tea. She asked him into the study.

He sat down near the window. She took out her violin and began playing, first scales, an etude. For an hour she did this, scales and exercises. He'd never seen anything like it.

The ease with which she produced such powerful sound puzzled him.

Later, slowly at first, she played parts of Tartini's *Devil's Trill Sonata.*

Charly was enthralled.

How does she do that, play so many notes at once? How does such a small instrument produce such a large sound?

He closed his eyes, trying to discern all of the parts. He leaned forward. He stood up and stepped toward her.

She stood behind a wire music stand, beside a large black piano.

He stepped behind her. She didn't stop playing, didn't even pause.

He'd never seen a violin, activated, so closely before. It was much more mechanical, close up, than he expected it to be. All of its various, simple parts, quivered with energy. A small cloud – is it smoke? steam? – rose over the steel strings.

He thought he could hear sound behind the sound, a kind of deep hum inside the instrument itself.

Or was it her?

He could see, glancing without comprehension at the music on the page, muscles in her shoulder, arm, wrist and back shift, flex, relax.

There was something alive beneath her skin.

He began to reach out, like a kid putting his finger close to a candle flame.

Then she stopped. But she kept her position, the violin up on her shoulder. Only her eyes moved around, turning toward the man at her shoulder.

"What are you doing?"

"Please. I've never…"

"You've never…"

"Your arm. Your arm… It doesn't… And how do you know where to put your fingers?"

"I don't know. I practice. They remember what they're supposed to do."

"Would you…?"

She resumed playing. He was so close, then, that he could hear her breathing as she played. Not loudly, not humming, but in time with what she played.

Her body is a part of the music, he thought, as much a production of the music as the sound itself.

Very lightly he touched the tricep of her right arm, her bowing arm.

"Stop, Charly," she said suddenly, bringing down the violin, turning to face him.

"How do you *do* that?" he asked, ignoring, or not hearing, what was rising in her voice. "Do it again."

She set the instrument in its velvet case and unbuttoned the top of her blouse. She came at him quickly, wrapping her arms around him, beneath his.

"Stop. Enough gab. I want you to –" she began to say, pulling at his shirt.

He took her to dinner and then to a movie. *Ronin,* Frankenheimer's last film, was running at a small theater in the Embarcadero. She enjoyed it, to his surprise. Afterward, walking with her, he went on and on about the car chase scene, trying to imagine and recreate its production.

They went back to her place and had sex. She was very good at it. He hadn't expected that. She knew how to relax her body in such a way that he couldn't help but sort of relax himself, fall into her little trap. He was hypnotized. He could only follow her lead, which was unusual for him. And yet, she kept such a grip on him, deep inside, these countless muscles at work, as if all along he wasn't following but being pulled, his body being directed into a precise position, a precise feeling. Yoshi was in absolute control. Strength had nothing to do with it.

They woke late the next day. He watched her walk around the apartment naked, birdlike, hardly touching the floor, ripe with perspiration, with sex.

In the kitchen she was slicing a pear, an apple, eating these piece by piece. He had a green apple, whole.

She went into the study and closed the door. He listened to her do scales, slowly, faster, eventually at such a breath-taking speed he thought something might break. Then she stopped. There was a minute of silence.

He heard her on the phone, talking with someone in Japanese.

When she began to play the arabesque first movement of one of Bach's sonatas, he couldn't remember which, he quietly opened the study door and entered.

She was turned away. She had a small ass, but it looked heavy. Or her legs were too short for the rest of her.

Beautiful ass, he thought.

Then she heard him, acknowledging his presence only with a turn of her eyes.

He lay on the floor at her feet and listened. He watched her towering body, the muscles in her arms, her neck, her chest, even her stomach, contracting, relaxing.

Her toes curled up like caterpillars.

On his hands and knees, he crawled up to her and touched the dampness behind her knee, raised his head like a dog to put his nose between her labia.

Yoshi hardly reacted, such was her concentration.

She was like a machine. Every part, bone, muscle and tendon, moving in perfect, practiced harmony. The sound she produced was at once of the violin, a small, simple wooden instrument, but also of her, of a spirit in her that found an exit to the world only through the instrument's union with her body, through the precise recitation and punctuation of a code, a sequence of movements and sounds.

The next morning he awoke suddenly. His head was clear, he knew exactly what he had to do. Then he noticed something. The action he needed to take and what he noticed had nothing at all to do with each other, but for an instant he thought they did. He thought it was perfectly logical, his escape, on the one hand, and Yoshiko Wada, this violinist, on the other.

She was asleep, on her stomach. A milky beam of light was playing tricks with a fine dark fuzz in the small of her back. There was a tiny red freckle on her coccyx.

But it was her right hand. Part of it was beneath a pillow, pulling at the sheet. Part of it was not.

It was her index finger. It was long and crooked.

He blinked. He rubbed his eyes. He looked away and looked back. He was not mistaken. Yoshi had a crooked index finger. It curved inward, as if wanting to point at the middle finger.

When she woke up he asked her about it. Had she broken it?

"Didn't I show you that? It's my favorite part."

She held up her hand, her palm to him. A normal sized hand, quite slender fingers. But the index finger was clearly bent, crooked. It was no trick of the light.

"What happened?"

"It grew that way. I started playing when I was three years old. This finger is very important. It controls the pressure in the bow, which regulates volume and tone."

"The bone grew like that?"

"That's right."

Astonishing.

He was learning so much, so quickly.

He had never been so happy before, naked in bed with a beautiful naked woman, his hands and face smelling of her juices. Who knew you could learn what regulates volume and tone on a violin while sleeping in on a – whatever morning it was – with the body of a beautiful woman up against yours.

The violin is a part of her, he thought. Her body is made to play this instrument.   He didn't know what to say. He didn't entirely know what he was feeling. It was almost like a religious experience, an awakening.

Almost like, he realized – in a dim voice, far inside his brain, in his gut – like coming to life after being dead.

He pressed his face into her chest, between her breasts.

"I wish I were your violin," he mumbled into her skin.

To be a part of her body like that.

After a minute he pulled himself away. "Now let me show *you* something."

He went into the other room, looking for his pants, where he'd left them on the floor in the hall.

She had pulled open the curtain when he returned. The city was a field of steel flowers, the sky bulbous and dark. It was just starting to rain.

She looked at the world stone faced, her eyes half closed, out of balance.

"Put out your hand."

She did.

He dropped the folded yellow paper in her palm.

"What's this?"

"Open it."

He thought he saw the sparkle of the diamond flash in her dark eyes.

She blushed. She smiled in a strange way.

"Where's it from? Where'd you get it?"

"I'm delivering it to someone."

"Delivering it? But you're in advertising."

"It's a side job."

"Is it stolen?"

"What kind of question is that?"

Charly folded the diamond back into its yellow sheet and left the room. He was awake now. He could see where things were going. It had been a mistake to show her.

Her voice followed him down the length of the hall: "Where are you going?"

"To work. I'm late."

"Will you come back?"

He was dressing. She came after him, pulling on a red kimono.

What day was it?

"Of course I will."

"Of course, he said. Tonight?"

"Yes. By eight. You'll be here?"

"I will. There'll be company. My brother and a friend of his, for one."

"Company. Sounds good. Who's cooking? I won't be late."

She pulled him by his collar.

"Do you have to go?"

He didn't have to. He didn't exactly want to. But –

"Aren't you teaching later?"

"I can cancel. They're all on holiday anyway."

"There's a man I need to talk to in person this afternoon. We're closing a deal later this week."

"At Christmas."

"Before the end of the year."

"Is he a man like you? A draftsman," she said, pulling her body up against his. The kimono came open. He pressed a hand against her breast. Then he realized what was happening.

She'd reached into his pocket. He felt her crooked finger. She took out, pinched, the yellow wad and held it up.

"My guarantee of your return," she said.

He thought about it for a moment. It was simple enough.

There was nothing he could do. Nothing short of wrecking everything.

"You won't lose it," he said.

"I'll put it in a safe place."

"It would mean my head."

"I know. So one last thing..."

He was in the door. He kissed her on the lips. He felt he just might do anything for this woman.

"What's that?"

"I'm going to Tokyo on Saturday. For a concert."

"One of yours?"

"No. A friend. But I might record some things while there."

"How long will you be gone?"

"I don't know… Two weeks? I'd like you to come. You'd like it there. And when I'm finished we can go to the mountains for a few days."

What was there to think about?

"Let me check with some people at work. But yes. I think it should work. I'll come with you. I'll get the ticket as soon as I can."

She clapped her hands like a kid on Christmas morning.

"Wonderful." She kissed him. "Bye, Charly. See you tonight. Don't be late."

He walked quickly down the hall to the elevator, feeling her eyes on his back the entire way.

~ 16 ~

Outside the streets were dead. It was the twenty-third or fourth, he didn't know which. He'd lost a weekend and probably a Monday too.

Didn't matter. He had a way out. The solution was so simple. He laughed at himself for not having seen it sooner. *Give the diamond –*

"You let her get some rest?"

The voice was just behind him, in a recess in the building. Standing before a red iron door was a woman he immediately recognized.

"Wud'you say?"

"I was on my way up. She's there?"

"She was when I left."

"Great."

Taunting him, wanting a fight, tall Mary Mullen smiled and lowered her eyes. Her lips gleamed in the shadow of the recess.

It was raining properly then. What had been a patter turned hard, a dull rush in the air. Water in a sizzling sheet ran over the street.

He was tempted to step closer to the woman, get out of the rain. But she stepped forward, turned toward the building entrance, walked quickly away.

"Were you waiting for me?" he called after her, greasy rain in his eyes.

She didn't answer. At the door she glanced back, said something, smiled through the turning glass. A moment later she pushed open the door and yelled into the downpour, "Seeya later maybe!" Then the door closed again, she disappeared inside.

The long wet avenue before him was so desolate a god might have come down in the night, taken the city, tipped it and scraped its inhabitants right into the ocean and not done much better.

At the bus station he called Bernie Posner.

"The fuck you been!"

"Merry Christmas to you too. What happened?"

"I've been calling all weekend. Thought your line was out. Then I started thinking other things. You worry me, Charly. Stop it. Stay close. Things happen."

"I was out. Sorry."

"Sorry! Fuck. Daniel Ortiz is dead."

"What!?"

"I said your friend Ortiz. The collector? They found him last night."

"How'd it happen?"

"A big mirror fell on him. In the tub. Split him open and drowned him. It's homicide, for now. At least that's what I heard."

"And Aldo?"

"Who's that? *Oh.* The manservant. At large. He's on the list."

A Greyhound started with a roar, curl of blue smoke and dust, lonesome souls lining up and boarding, heading east.

"He's dead too," Charly said. "He'll turn up."

"Why do you say that?"

"He saw the killer. He let him in."

"How do you know that, Charly?"

"It's just a hunch. The man was taking care of Danny. He wouldn't have been far off."

"Whatever. Doesn't matter now. What matters is how you might be closer to the center of this shitstorm you've been telling me about than you think. When were you at Ortiz's? Friday night? There'll be a knock on your door. Count on it."

"Great. I'll make cookies."

"Don't get cute, Charly! Get moving. Let's get you on your way. I have something for you. Come over. Today, now, before I –"

"You read my mind. Listen. I need two hours. I wanna stop by my place. Feed the cat. Washup."

"Fine. Don't talk to strangers."

"I'll be there about noon."

"That's fine."

An hour later he found himself on his barren stoop. Everyone really had taken off for the holiday. That or some plague was going around.

He checked the street, up and down. Nary a soul. Everything looked tired and forlorn, gray and heavy with rain.

In the entry to his apartment, the dusty shadows of the place he called home, he thought suddenly of moving. Maybe he'd go south, to Palo Alto. It was always sunny in Palo Alto. Maybe he'd go further. San Luis Obispo. Get some roller skates, a VW Bug.

He'd take Yoshi. Would she need convincing?

She's a migrant at heart. Like a samurai, only with a violin.

They were all like samurai, he reflected, *ronin*, wanderers practicing their ancient craft in an era indifferent to tradition.

Don't get cute, Charly.

The cat was nowhere to be found. But he'd left a gift. The mouse looked asleep. Still wet with the cat's saliva.

He'd crushed its little bones without even puncturing the skin.

He put on Shostakovich, the eighth symphony, loud. It starts hard and only gets harder. Music for the apocalypse. He poured himself a scotch, fell on the couch and lit a cigarette, eyes on the wall. His painting: the woman in red, waiting for her cab...

Slowly the walls of the apartment began to collapse inward.

Shostakovich.

He fixed himself an omelette with a remaining portobello mushroom and asiago cheese. He brewed a pot of coffee. He ate and drank everything quickly. He took a shower.

He was about to step out when there was a knock on the door.

He hadn't heard anyone coming up the stairs. Then again, he hadn't been listening.

He stepped to the front window. The street remained as empty as before.

Again, the knock. Not too hard, *bapbap – bapbap*, but not the knock of a woman, either.

A knock on your door. Do you answer? One is under no obligation to answer the door every time someone knocks. The same goes for the telephone – but we don't seem to have a problem with letting that go, letting it ring or letting the machine pick up. With doors, it's another matter.

But what is logical out here, in the bright clarity of day, never makes sense in there, on the other side of that door.

So Charly opened the door.

It was him, the one Emmett had told him about. He knew it instantly. The face, the body, the look. He was small, hollow cheeked, narrow eyes that turned up at the corners. Charly probably had twenty pounds on him, but he knew in his gut it wouldn't matter. You can tell with some people, in the way they hold themselves, like Tom Brown – they attack with accuracy, not force. These are the types of men who exercise muscles in their hands.

But Charly got lucky. The killer, if that's indeed who the man was, only wanted to say something.

"You are Mr. Bingswanger."

"You asking me or telling me?"

"May I come in?"

"No. You are? I was just stepping out. One sec –"

Charly left the man in the doorframe. In the other room he turned off the stereo. The silence that came down over the place was sudden, ringing in his ears.

"You were saying."

The man in the door watched Charly come back from the front room. Then he looked at the floor. He said:

"My name is Chuchu, Mr. Bingswanger. The man I represent –"

"You mean –"

"– has sent me because –"

"Frank Conway."

The stranger spoke deliberately, too slowly for the context. English was not his first language. That or he had an odd speech impediment, the line between his brain and tongue clogged.

"You are in possession of an item –"

"An item."

" – that he would like returned immediately. No questions –"

"Tell Frank – Chuchu, was it? - that he can come for it himself. But he'd better hurry. I won't be holding it much longer."

"He won't ask a second time."

"He won't be able to. I won't have it. Did you hear what I said? Now –"

Charly began to close the door on the stranger, but the man raised his hand and gently pushed back, tilting his head ever so slightly forward, as if pushing the door open only to peek inside.

"Excuse me," Charly went on, "I'd offer you a cup of coffee but I'm late for a meeting. Your employer has my number. I'll deal with him directly. Tell him that. Let's arrange a meeting. And if I see your mug again, Chuchu... Nothing personal but I'll call the cops."

That made the stranger smile. Charly's heart skipped a beat. Despite everything else, the man's teeth were shit. Tiny, like kids' teeth, yellow and pointed, missing in places. Reminded Charly of Panama. "You see my mug again," the man said, "and I assure you, Mr. Bingswanger, it will be the last thing you see."

The man winked. He had long black eyelashes.

"Good day."

Descending the stair well, Chuchu hardly touched the steps. Maybe he knew exactly where to step, but his exit was in complete silence.

Charly watched from the window. Nobody left the building.

Was he waiting downstairs? Under the eave?

He called Emmett, who lived down the block. His wife answered. The man was supposedly at work, wouldn't be back until late.

"But you see that nigga!" she screamed. It was something about a leaky roof, and mops.

"I'll do that," Charly said, hanging up.

Charly went out the back door. There, off a small wooden porch, a narrow flight of stairs was tacked to the side of the building. At the bottom was a patch of earth, flush, green, hip high in weeds, a collection of garbage cans.

He made a circuitous exit of the neighborhood, eventually boarding a streetcar for the Sunset District, where Posner had a house at the beach.

It was getting dark when he arrived, a new storm and bank of clouds filling the sky. The wind was picking up.

Bernie Posner stood in a tinted deck window, three flights up. He raised a hand at Charly's approach.

The man was pushing eighty, but he acted half his age. He worked out and didn't look all that bad. But what can you do? His hair was falling out. He had chronic pain in his hips, when he sat down too long. He was developing a hump.

He was a very tan man, for December. He wore a white shirt, opened to his hairless sternum, hung out over linen pants, the sleeves all the way down to his palms.

"I tell you to come right over, Charly, you come over."

"I was delayed."

"I'll give you delayed, smartass. Picture your funeral. I'm the last one to arrive. Only there's nobody there! Some schmo lowering your box down into the hole. That's forever, Charly. Delayed my ass! I say come over, you come over. Like a German train. On time."

"Frank's back."

"Tell me something I don't already know! Know what your problem is –"

Long, bony finger.

"He sent someone," Charly said, "little guy who tried to talk me to death."

"You don't follow directions. You wanna live to see spring? *Do as I say*. Clear?"

Charly nodded.

"Sorry about Ortiz."

"He had it coming."

They went into the kitchen. There was a young woman there, a blond in a tight t-shirt with Chinese calligraphy on it and the words "Labor is glorious!" written beneath the red figure of a farmer, his fist raised in the air. She was in gray sweat pants. She was reading a magazine at the table. She had nothing on under the shirt.

Posner said, "Have some mussels." He pushed a plate of steaming mussels at Charly. He poured him a glass of wine. "Marie-Laure made them. She's French," he said. "And can she cook! Marie-Laure, Charly. Charly, Marie-Laure."

The woman didn't stand. She raised her hand, fingers down. Charly took it, he didn't kiss it. He felt, rather, like biting the woman, just to see what would happen.

Charly sat. The mussels were delicious. He made a pig of himself sucking them down. When he finished, Marie-Laure went to the fridge and pulled out a platter of cheese and sliced meat. A loaf of bread materialized. He poured himself another glass of wine.

If this is what I get when he's pissed…

"So what I have for you," Posner said, "is cash to settle up with Hamling. I want you to do this immediately. That means tomorrow morning. Call Tom Brown and arrange for a meeting. Take care of it. Tomorrow morning! Then I need you –"

"Where'd the money come from?"

"It's mine. I'm giving it to you."

Posner was standing. He lit a cigarette. He gave it to Marie-Laure and sat down across from Charly. Then he lit one for himself.

"It doesn't fucking matter where it came from," Posner said. "You'll give it to Brown and be done with it. And then you'll do something for me."

"I ask because," Charly said, "I'm wondering if –"

Posner leaned back, a hand to his mouth, smoking, cutting Charly into a thousand pieces with his eyes. But Charly, stuffing his face, didn't seem to notice.

"I'm wondering," he was saying, "since you know Percy Hamling, why didn't you –"

"I do not know Percy Hamling. He doesn't know me. Get your facts straight. And I'd write Tom Brown a check and send it with a Christmas card, Charly, but it's not my fucking problem. It's yours. Why on earth would I stick my handsome nose into your shitty business?"

"Which you are."

"Which I am. But carefully. My way. This way. I give you the cash, you give it to Brown. He ask you where it came from, you say you found it. You say whatever the fuck you want. But I find out you connect me with this money and *I'll cut your balls off* and Marie-Laure here will fix something tasty out of 'em."

"I'm fine with that."

"Goddamn right you're fine with that, Charly, because you have no other choice. This is not McDonald's. I serve balls, you eat 'em!"

"Alles klar Herr Kommissar."

"Very good. I'm glad we have an understanding."

Posner balanced his cigarette in the teeth of an ashtray and took a slice of bread and smeared a wedge of brie over it. He shoved it in his mouth and chewed. He poured himself a full glass of red wine, BV vineyards, Charly noticed, and drank.

A sheet of rain struck the window.

"When will the storm *pass*," Marie-Laure said, flipping a page of her magazine.

"There's a phone in the other room. Go call Brown."

Charly wiped his mouth and excused himself.

It was a small study. A long wooden desk, bookshelves built into two walls. A window looked onto a well-kept garden, bamboo swaying in the wind. There was a TV in the room, as well, and it was on, its volume low. A football game was in progress. The Dallas Cowboys and Pittsburgh Steelers. It was the fourth quarter. It was snowing. The Cowboys were down by five, with forty yards to go.

He turned it up. The crowd was screaming, going nuts.

He called Tom Brown. "I'd like to talk with you," he said. "Drop by in the morning."

"Where you been, Charly?"

"Out and about."

"So you want to stop by? You know what tomorrow is?"

"Wednesday."

"The celebration of the birth of our savior Christ. You Jewish, Charly?"

"I never really thought about it. Can we meet or not?"

"Okay. If it's early, and quick. But what for, if I may ask, on my one and only holiday morning of the year?"

"I want to show you something."

"I take it Jaime didn't tell you."

"Tell me what?"

"I can't imagine what you've gone through these past days."

"Can't you."

"You gotta get an answering machine, man. It would make things so much easier."

"I'm not much of a talker. I wouldn't use it."

"No kidding."

"So what is it?"

"You're clear, Charly."

"Clear?"

"You are *clear*. I was told –"

Exactly what Tom Brown then said Charly missed. But apparently Charly didn't owe Hamling a dime. The money was there.

His brain was doubling back, sprinting forward. *Think laterally* Charly thought, something a girl at a bar once told him.

"Which reminds me," Brown said. "There's that incident you spoke of."

"Yeah."

"It's still..."

In the distance, a cheering crowd, figures scrambling over the white turf. He didn't hear what Brown said, what *the incident still* was. "There's something else," Charly said, interrupting the man.

Brown was silent. Screaming fans. "Something else?" Brown said, shift in tone. But Charly, emptied out, seconds behind himself, something sizzling in the kitchen, said nothing. "Can it wait?"

"Yeah."

"Okay?"

"See you in the morning, Tom."

Charly hung up.

Clear. Paid up.

Marie-Laure, laughing in the kitchen, slammed the refrigerator door.

Posner appeared in the doorway. "So it's set."

"It's set. All set."

17

They asked him to stay for dinner. He said he had other plans. Marie-Laure pleaded, pouting.

"But it's raining. You *can't* go!"

Something funny about her *a*, high up in her little French nose.

"You call me tomorrow night," Posner said from the top of the stairs.

"I will."

"I'll expect your call."

The bag was a small carry-on. Rectangular, blue. It wasn't heavy. Inside were toiletries, a couple magazines. *Forbes*, *The Economist*. Beneath these, some socks and underwear. Beneath that, what looked like someone's mail. Like you'd been on vacation for six weeks and come home to this motley stack of envelopes. Only these envelopes contained hundred dollar bills, a thousand of them.

He took the streetcar downtown. At the Mission Street station he called a man, a travel agent.

"SFO to Tokyo, Friday morning. First class."

"I'll take care of it."

He went for a couple fish tacos. He had a beer. He smoked. A fat Mexican kid came out from behind the counter and told him he couldn't smoke there. He went outside, to a little white plastic chair and table under green and red Christmas lights. Or were they Mexico lights?

Does it even matter?

He finished his cigarette and beer. For the first time in a long time, he felt good. In a few days all of it would be behind him.

On the stoop, he saw from some distance, was the regular gang. They were high, drunk, laughing. Emmett was back.

He went around back, up the stairs.

Still no sign of the cat. Maybe he was on vacation, thinking he'd done his job.

Mice snickered in the wall.

He showered, shaved, dressed. He put on a tie.

He phoned for a taxi. They buzzed the door five minutes later. Ten minutes later, he was outside Yoshi's place.

The building was new. Tall, round, polished. Most of the windows were dark. High up, a couple lights on.

There were three elevators inside. Just as he was entering one, another opened and a man stepped out, immediately turning away, leaving quickly. Charly only had a glance at the figure. It was tall, slender, and on one side of its head, a white –

The elevator door closed.

Then it caught up with him, the tall man. His fingers scrambled over the numbers. 3, 4, 8, 10. The elevator stopped at 8. He pushed the lobby and down it went. He ran out.

The building was empty, the street was empty. Far down the way, a car pulled out, slowly moving away from him. It was too far off to tell.

It was probably nothing, his imagination racing ahead of him.

He went up to Yoshi's.

Immediately he knew he'd made a mistake. Maybe several.

First, Yoshi was drinking. Red-faced, all gums and tears, the poor thing couldn't find her feet, bouncing like a pinball from the wall to the counter, and counter to –

Second, Mary was there. She seemed to have put back a few as well, but this did nothing to her cement-wall charm. She knew what was what. If anything, she looked more dangerous drunk than sober.

Third, the diamond was out, on the dining table, blazing in the yellow petals of its paper bed.

He didn't know where to start.

Then the brother appeared at his side, the other Wada.

"My name is Haruki," the man said with a slight bow. He took Charly's hand and squeezed it, shook it once.

"Yoshi tells me you're in advertising. And the diamond delivery business."

"I draw," Charly said.

Another Japanese man appeared, this one taller than Haruki. Tall, thin, in John Lennon glasses, the man wore a black coat and stiff white shirt buttoned up to a gargantuan Adam's apple. He said something that Charly missed, smiling. Again, the little bow.

"Call him Joe," Haruki said. "He's here with me, on business. He speaks no English. He's an architect."

"Good to meet you!" the man called Joe said.

"Sure."

There was quite a spread in the kitchen. Broth, sashimi, zosui, rice, octopus, tamago-yaki.

Charly looked it over. He was hungry but not ready to eat just yet.

Yoshi was saying something nearby. Mary was laughing.

He took the diamond and its yellow wrapper from the table. He folded up the rock and dropped it in his pocket, where it pricked the edge of his leg.

"A man came by," Yoshi said suddenly, coming at him with a glass splashing in her hand.

"A man?"

"A gentleman," Mary said.

"He was *frightening*, Charly," Yoshi said.

"Like a wounded RAF officer," Mary said, drawing on a long and thin cigarette. "Lovely diamond, by the way."

"He had a bandage over his head," Yoshi said.

"And it looked like – he'd lost his *ear*," Mary said, cutting her hand across the side of her head.

"His ear. And what did this man want?"

"Well," Yoshi said, her words slurred together, "you, Charly. Obviously he came for you."

She was unsteady on her feet, reaching out.

"How did he know I was here? I would be here?"

"He said you were expecting him. You have something of his? You'd spoken on the phone."

"On the phone? About his ear?"

"No, dummy. *The diamond.*"

Charly poured himself glass of Cutty Sark and sat down. The cushion in the couch sank low to the floor. The room seemed to be getting smaller. Haunting shadows filled his periphery vision.

Mary was such a tall woman. She was in a tight black dress. Her bare shoulders looked even broader from this angle, like weapons, like she had wings folded up back there.

She brushed a strand of black hair from across her eye, over her ear. Those blue eyes, boring deep down into the poor man.

What did she know?

It was about a game, Momcilovic said, the man, the words suddenly floating in his vision. *For a watch, or a shirt. I don't know what.*

Mary put her hand on Yoshi's shoulder, pulled her in close, whispered something in her ear.

"Did he see it?" Charly said. "Did you show it to him?"

"No!" Yoshi said. "No way! We didn't like the man. We said you weren't here."

"So only after he left – just now…"

"That's right," Mary said. With her free hand she pinched her dress at the hip, pulled up a fraction of an inch. Something was slipping. She had such big hard hips. "After he left we were all so curious. What could this be about? And so Yoshi showed us your little gift, your item. What a –"

Charly's glass was empty. Haruki came around with the bottle, filled the glass and then poured himself one.

"You're not in trouble, are you?" Haruki said quietly. "Because…" And then: "My friend, please. Why don't we get some air."

It felt like the floor was falling out from under him.

He stepped out onto the balcony. It was windy, a hard drizzle blowing, slapping against the side of the building in waves.

The bridge flickered colorfully in the dark.

He lit a cigarette.

So Frank is back. And he knows about Yoshi. Which means –

Haruki joined him. He slid the glass door closed and came up close to Charly. He was not a big man. "What is with *that woman*?"

Charly laughed. It was the right thing to say, exactly what he wanted to hear. "What *is* with her? Someone will hafta do something. Throw her off a balcony, for starts."

"Lookit. I don't like her –"

"I didn't mean that, Haruki. That was being... I'd never –"

"I *understand*, Charly." Haruki fixed the younger man in his gaze. He said: "What I'm saying is I don't like what she's doing to my sister. The woman is seducing her, if you didn't notice, and infecting her with all sorts of bad ideas. Yoshi is a good woman."

They smoked together in silence. A mile south, down 101, toward the airport, flashing red and blue lights, the wail of a siren waxing and waning in the wind. Some kind of accident, an offense in progress.

"Our parents are dead. Yoshi is my care. She is the light of our family. She is a maker of beauty in a world full of filth and pain."

"Lovely, Haruki."

The man blinked. He lit another cigarette.

Charly said, "I like her. I like your sister, Haruki."

"So do something about it!"

In the corner of his eye he noticed the two women inside, and the other fellow, the architect, seated now, his tremendous legs crossed before him, a drink in hand. He was watching them. He reminded Charly of a picture he'd seen of Igor Stravinsky.

A Japanese Stravinsky.

"I need you, Charly," Haruki said. "I own restaurants. Yoshi tells me you know something about food."

"I don't know anything."

"She says you do. Says that you know how to cut vegetables. That's a start."

Charly laughed.

Haruki smiled. "So what do you say?"

"To what?"

"To my proposition."

"I didn't hear any proposition."

"Come to Tokyo and I'll get you into a world-class kitchen. Teach you things. I reward hard work and you're a hard worker, aren't you, Charly?"

"I have a job here. I like it here."

"Sure you do."

"I don't speak Japanese."

"I'll teach you everything you need to know."

"I've never worked in a restaurant before."

"You won't be on the floor."

"I can't cook."

"Don't lie to me, Charly. Anyways, think of it as a vacation. As a working holiday... To get away from your troubles."

Haruki was not a big man. He wore his pants pulled high, around a small pot belly, but there was a lot of muscle in that gut, in that frame. You could hear it in the way he spoke, see it in how he carried himself. His lower jaw would shoot out when he said things like "Don't lie to me" and "your troubles."

He was also very persistent. Charly felt that. "I'll think about it," he said.

"I'll book you a ticket tonight."

"I've already got a ticket."

"No kidding."

"I got it today. I guess I'm going to the mountains with Yoshi. After she does her music thing."

Haruki smiled ear to ear.

"And here I thought I'd have to force you. To beg. You were tricking me!"

Can't a man have some peace and quiet?

Charly could work for this man. He trusted him. And the change would do him good. To get out from under Hamling's thumb, even out from under Posner, who, in twelve hours or so, he'd owe a hundred grand to.

"So you'll take care of it?" Haruki said.

"What's that? Getting to Tokyo? Sure."

"No. The woman. *Mullen.* You'll look after her."

"She's not a problem, Haruki. In two days she won't know what hit her."

"Very *good*, Charly! I like the way you think, young man. I'm glad we had this conversation."

He pointed a finger at Charly's heart.

How many deals is that for one day?

18

His appetite was back. They ate for two hours. Gerry Mulligan and his band played on the radio, the sound warm and lush, fine tonic for the cold wet darkness outside.

Yoshi began to sober up but, as happens, then became increasingly morose. She and Mary started bickering. You could see Mary gradually freezing, getting cooler, harder, ice crystals spreading over her eyes, over her made face.

Nobody wanted to start cleaning up.

But then there was no avoiding it and everyone was up, clearing the table, sorting things in the kitchen. Haruki took a minute to inspect Yoshi's knives.

Mary was standing alone by the balcony window, studying something out in the night, her reflection in the glass.

Yoshi sidled up to Charly in the hallway.

"I'm sorry about this evening. What a wreck I've made!"

"Not at all. I enjoyed it. Your brother is an interesting man. He wants me to work for him!"

"No he doesn't. He says that to all my boyfriends. He wants you to save me from –"

"But do you want saving? That's the question."

After a moment Yoshi said, up close, in a whisper, "I can't take her anymore."

Mullen watched the two of them from the end of the hall. She'd pulled on a red raincoat. It gleamed in the light, looking covered in grease. "Yoshi," she said.

Haruki and Joe cornered him. Haruki was flush in the face, smiling stupidly. His words slurred together. "So I'll see you in Tokyo then!"

"I'll drop by. But I make no promises."

"Very good. I look forward to it. You'll love Tokyo, I'll take you everywhere, Charly."

Joe shook his hand as before, bowing.

The door was open. Where was Mary?

Charly stepped out.

Yoshi said, "See you tomorrow."

"Tomorrow evening. I'll bring champagne."

"For?"

"For the holiday. The completion of a long project. A trip overseas."

"Grand," she said. She pulled herself up to him and pressed her small dry lips to his.

Mary was at the elevator, sulking. Her golden reflection in the elevator door watched Charly come up. She turned. "That was fast."

"Thought I'd walk you out."

"So what is it you do, Charly?"

"I'm a draftsman."

"Really."

He looked at her reflection in the door. A couple at the bathroom sink, long late faces, dipped in gold.

"I arrange getaways," he said.

"Vacations?"

"The other kind. Robbery."

She smiled, raised her chin. She looked tired.

"What do you steal, Charly?"

The elevator arrived. They got on, Mary first, and then turned, facing the doors as they closed.

"Whatever pays the bills."

"And it pays?"

Charly looked her way, at her long, strong neck.

"Usually. When things work the way they're expected to."

Red numbers descending: *12, 11, 10, 9…*

She stared at his reflection in the doors. He looked away.

"But they aren't now," she said.

"Not exactly."

"There's a catch."

"You could call it that."

"Okay. A double crossing," she almost sang.

"You watch too many movies."

"Have you ever been caught?"

The elevator was brand new. It decelerated so gradually that it hardly felt like you were moving. Still, Charly felt something in his stomach. He was on an edge, about to fall.

"No. Close, a few times. But then, no."

"I'm intrigued, Charly. I'd like to hear more about this work of yours, if you have time."

"There's not much to say. It's as dull a job as any. And if it wasn't, I'd still have little to say."

"With me or in general?"

The rain was coming straight down outside.

They got lucky. There was a taxi at the curb, an old cabbie making notes in his book.

She gave a North Beach address. He gave the address of a record shop on Upper Haight. They went to North Beach first.

"Have a drink with me," she said.

There wouldn't be anything open at this hour. Which meant going to her place.

He weighed his options.

There was Tom Brown in the morning, in a few hours, in fact.

There was Yoshi...

He got out. She'd opened an enormous umbrella. It was like a tree over her.

He paid the cabbie and followed Mullen up a narrow flight of white steps. He admired her ankles, her black nylons, long thin calves for such a big woman.

A swimmer, he thought, that's what she is. Or was. It was something he'd overheard earlier. For Stanford. Olympic trials?

The apartment seemed vast. He couldn't tell. The woman didn't turn on any lights. She dropped her keys in a glass bowl, her raincoat on a chair, vanished down a hallway into a kitchen. There she turned on a light.

He heard her pouring drinks. He took off his coat, dropped it on top of hers.

"You take ice with scotch?"

"Depends. What do you have?"

"Black Grouse."

"Never heard of it. Ice it up."

She returned with two glasses.

They stood in the dark living room. There were paintings on the walls, big ones. A sea shore, a factory. He'd seen it before – the place, not the painting. Somewhere in LA.

The other was abstract, Pollock-like splatter and speckle.

Out the front window, the houses on the street, strung together, made one long dark sleeping creature. A couple Christmas trees flickered, fully lit.

Otherwise, silence. Christmas Eve.

"Merry Christmas, Charly," she said, holding out her glass.

"Is it that time already?"

"It's that time. Again."

Clink.

She leaned in close and pecked Charly on the cheek.

"Nothing special for the holiday, then?" Charly said.

"I'll work."

"Work?"

"I like what I do."

"Which is?"

"I'm a consultant," she said.

"I never know what that means when I hear it."

"Systems analysis."

"Well that explains things. What kind of systems?"

"All kinds."

He sipped his drink. He'd had just about enough. "And what do you *analyze* when you analyze a system?"

She shrugged, smiled, drank too quickly, licking her lip. "Data, Charly. I examine data and answer questions of application."

"Questions of application." He smiled. He hadn't said such a mouthful all day, perhaps all week.

"What to do," she said, "how and when."

"Not why?"

"We're not interested in why. That's given. The problem is there."

"The problem."

"The question."

Charly spun his drink, watched ice go round and round. "But how do you understand the problem without asking why it happens?"

"You're confusing how with why."

He drank his watery Black Grouse, poured down half the glass. Something was getting to him about this Mary Mullen. Not asking why things happen... Confusing how with why. Really!

"Confusing what with what? How?"

"*Why* something happens can be explained by how it happens. Beyond the how, where why is concerned, you get into philosophy. It's a mystery. We don't do philosophy."

Christmas morning, finally. And there he was, drinking with Mary Mullen, consultant, one time Olympic contender, practically a stranger – discussing the difference between how and why.

The sound of rain filled the air of the apartment. It was cold. It was not as big a place as it had seemed at first.

Mullen stepped forward. "Tell me about the catch."

"The what?"

"Things not working the way you expect them to."

"Oh, that."

Her wide breasts rose and fell. He imagined waking sore by a woman like this.

"Where to start."

"At the beginning."

"Robbery," Charly said, "is solitary work. Thieves..."

His glass was empty. The woman left, soft pad of her feet on the hallway floor. She returned with the bottle, filled his glass, set the bottle down on a dark coffee table.

"They often work together," Charly said, "enjoy the company of each other, yack it up at the bar, and are often great talkers, blabbers, they love to talk – at their own peril, of course. Marvelous liars. But behind all that, thieves are loners. That's the truth. They can't work together." He stared at his drink, the floor beginning to slowly rotate. "In the end... Anyone who says otherwise..."

Why was he telling her this? Where were the words coming from?

"So what you stole was stolen from you. Is that what you're saying?"

Eyes up, on her. "You're smart."

"But you managed to dupe the man who duped you. Before he duped you. Stole from him before he stole from you. And now he's back..."

Thin ice, Charly.

"Not bad, Mullen. Not bad."

"And now deceit is not his approach. He's being more direct. Coming to Yoshi's."

Yoshi.

"Deceit is always the approach. Some plans are just more direct than others. It all depends on –"

He thought to himself that the woman named Mary Mullen was not what she appeared to be. There was another woman inside of the woman before him now.

"You really were an Olympic contender?"

"Who said I was?"

"I don't know. I guess I overheard it. Yoshi."

"Yes."

"You were."

"I was."

"But you didn't go."

She was chewing ice. Her glass was empty. She set it aside and bent over, reached down.

"Like music, Charly?"

"Some."

"Like Beethoven?"

"He's okay."

The album started. *The Moonlight Sonata.* Of all things.

"I like Beethoven."

She stepped up to him. Eye to eye.

"You were saying," he said.

"... I came in second. In that race, second place was just second place. You go home."

The piano did something to the shadows in the hall. They were moving. Triangles of darkness lifted off the walls, shifted, searched for their proper places, their missing neighbors, the order that was shattered in the beginning.

She took his hand and pressed it against her breast.

Her mouth was big and soft. Her tongue was thick, her saliva hot and salty. She tasted good, Mary did.

He lifted, pulled at her dress.

The look in her eyes was feverish, starved, moving –

Like a dog. Don't flinch. Don't react to the threat.

She smells your fear.

She'll destroy you, Charly.

She was pulling him by his tie. Not undoing it. Pulling on it, downward, using it like a leash, turning him, her mouth locked on his face, around the room. His back to a leather chair, cornered –

Something was dripping loudly behind him, in the small entry of a dark fireplace.

She pushed him hard into the chair. He fell back.

She pulled her dress up over her hips and straddled him, shoving her stomach into his face.

He slid a hand, sucking on her tongue, up the inside of her thigh, between her legs, up her ass, top of her stockings, pulling hard, reaching, clawing, probing at the lips of her cunt –

Then he felt her knee press against the diamond in his pocket. Much more like that and it would cut him, slice through its paper wrapping, the lining of his pocket, his underwear, puncture a hole in his leg and bury itself under his skin.

"That's what you took," she said in his ear.

A string of saliva snapped back against his neck.

"What's what I took?"

"That." She squeezed, her massive thighs like the jaws of a whale. "In your pocket. The –"

She grabbed his crotch and pulled and he sat up straight.

I won't be able to stop her.

"I'm not stupid, Charly."

Her incisors, catching triangles of light from the kitchen, were enormous. Why hadn't he noticed them before?

"You know what I want – what I'd like, Charly?"

With that he pushed her away, pulled her aside, stood up.

"I gotta go. I have a meeting in a few hours."

It felt like a stupid thing to say. What with her dress pulled up over her hips, and those formidable legs. But he said it.

"On Christmas morning?"

"Yep. You're working. I'm working. We're all working."

"Fuck your meeting."

She stood up quickly. Mullen had a big body, strong, hard. It bounced once and settled. She came at him. He raised his hand.

"I can't. Not this one. Things are –"

"You're leaving. You're going out there..."

"Thanks for the drink, Mary."

"You know I'll make you regret this."

"I'm sure you will."

Her chest rose and fell. She was thinking, chewing something over in that square head of hers.

He put on his coat and stood in the darkness of the foyer.

"Night, Mary Mullen," he said to the darkness.

Mary stepped forward, glared at the man. She lifted her dress over her head and walked quickly down the hall in a black slip toward the kitchen, staggering and catching herself on the wall. "Fuck off. Pull the door closed."

He didn't look back. He didn't hear anything, for the rain, for his burning ears, pounding heart.

He felt her watching him, from the door or window.

She frightened him, he realized, the wet slap of his shoes on the sidewalk echoing over the street.

That's a woman who gets what she wants.

He thought of Yoshi, practicing her violin late into the night, into the early hours, alone, machine like, committed. He thought of her crooked finger pressing and releasing, regulating volume and tone.

But it didn't help.

He'd caught something. He could smell her in his hands.

He walked home in the rain, took a long hot shower and got into bed. He smoked. He read a few pages from *The Mysterious Rider*. He smelled his hands again. Still there, Mary Mullen.

Under his nails. Under his skin.

He could feel her tongue in his ear.

He put out the light. He heard a sound. He got out of bed and walked around. The mice? He looked out the front window, onto the street far below.

It was a black Mercedes, passing slowly, practically gone. Through the windshield, two hands on the wheel, bright white cuffs.

He was nearly asleep when he felt the cat climb onto the bed and settle down beside him.

It purred.

"Merry Christmas, cat."

~ 19 ~

What time was it? Raining, again. Still.

He called the travel agent. The ticket was ready. United 1395, San Francisco to Tokyo, Friday, 7:00 a.m. All he'd need was an ID at the ticket counter.

"That's a nineteen hundred dollar ticket. I got you a deal."

"At seven in the morning!"

"There was an eleven fifteen for almost twice as much."

"I'll stop by this afternoon. You'll be there?"

"Not today. Come tomorrow, after noon. If I'm not in, there's a dropbox."

"I'll leave it today."

"Suit yourself."

There was a mark on his neck that he hadn't noticed the night before. Below his ear. It looked like a hickey. But there was something else to it. He looked closely, straining his eyes down as he leaned into the mirror.

Maybe she'd bitten him. Mary Mullen, systems analyst, vampire.

He laughed at himself, remembering how carried away they'd been last night.

Another time, kiddo.

He put on a recording of Fauré nocturnes. He fed the cat. The creature ate like there was no tomorrow. He thought about it and then took the diamond from his pants and pressed it, wrapped in its yellow tissue, down into the bag of cat food.

He boiled two eggs and had these, soft, with bread and liverwurst. He had a cup of coffee and a cigarette.

The streets were dead. He drove over to Brown's.

A Mexican girl in a maid's uniform let him in. She led him to Brown's office, spread her hands at the chair Charly'd used before. "Signor Tom will be with you in a minute." She smiled brightly, lowered her gaze, made her exit walking backwards, pulling the door closed without a sound.

Christmas with the Browns.

The man walked in and sat down behind his desk. "You've got ten minutes."

"So it's settled?"

"That's what I said. We're even. Good work."

Charly said nothing. He looked at Brown, waiting for him to go on.

"You wanted to see me."

"Where's Frank Conway?"

Brown's face, a curious shade, latte brown, dash of yellow. Eggnoggy. December tans. If you looked too closely you might think Brown was ill. "I don't know." He sawed his jaw in and out. "That's between you and him."

Charly wanted to argue. He wanted, he realized, his employer to decry the injustice of Frank Conway's betrayal. That would never happen.

You get what you deserve.

"I won't waste your time. There's something I need to show you."

Now Brown sat waiting.

"There were diamonds in the crate."

"In what crate?"

"In *the* crate, Don Lincoln's crate."

"I don't know anything about any diamonds."

Brown stared at his guest. First the killing, now this. Drago Momcilovic. Nobody knew where he was. But he wasn't dead, that Brown intuited. Blood at the scene, he'd been told. But no body. Where was Drago Momcilovic? Why would Charly want me to believe the man was dead?

Simple: He thought he was.

"There was a bag of diamonds in the crate. I saw them, he saw them. We all saw them. Conway took them."

Brown thought this over. Quietly he said: "I'm listening. Go on."

"Go on? That's it. There was a bag of diamonds – "

"How many we talkin about?"

"I don't know."

"Five, six, *thirty?*"

"Five or six, I guess."

"Big, small?"

Charly smiled. He would like nothing better than to be on a mountain in Japan with Yoshi, all of this erased from memory. "Small."

"Five or six small diamonds. And?"

"And he took them."

"Yes, and?"

He was holding a card, Ace of Spades – tipping the balance – and Brown was forcing his hand. Brown wanted it out.

"What would you say five or six diamonds were worth?" Charly asked.

"How would I know?"

"Right. Did you know they were in the crate?"

"... Do you *think* I knew they were in the crate? Charly? There was supposed to be two million dollars cash in the crate. That's what we were told. We've been over this."

"So the diamonds were a surprise."

"I don't see what the problem is."

"The problem is... The problem is I'd like what is mine, what was *taken* from me."

"That's between you and him."

Charly lowered his chin, eyes on his hands in his lap. He had a small cut on his palm, meaty base of his thumb. He stroked it wondering how it had happened.

"Are you finished?" Brown said, getting impatient.

Charly sighed. "I took one of them."

"One of what!?"

"One of the diamonds."

"You took one."

"Yes. It's not like the others."

"You have it with you, show me."

Brown sat without moving. He was a neatly cut body wrapped in an arsenal of statements.

"I don't know what diamonds are worth either, but this one," Charly said, "this one I had appraised."

"And?"

Charly closed his eyes. He spoke with his eyes closed. "Eight million." He opened his eyes.

Brown took a deep breath. "Come again."

"There was a big diamond in that bag, with the others. I took it. It is worth about eight million."

"How do you know that?"

"I know it."

Kids squealed in delight somewhere in the house.

Brown looked fazed. He leaned forward, deep into his desk on his elbows. He blinked quickly several times, to Charly's amusement. "Wait, Charly," he said. "You're telling me... You're sitting there telling me there were diamonds in the crate, with the cash, okay, and that one of these diamonds was quite large, larger than the others, and worth, you say, eight million dollars. So –"

"That's right."

"So I say – how do you know this?"

Charly waited. He felt like he had something here, for the moment.

"And why," Brown went on, "should I believe you? ... Charly, you're set. We're set, we're settled. Take a vacation, friend. What are you doing? Coming here on Christmas morning, telling me Frank Conway stole diamonds from you, Momcilovic, from us?" Brown looked remotely exasperated. "What are you *doing*? What *is* this?"

"I'll sell it to Hamling. He names the price."

Brown swung back in his chair, opened his mouth and laughed. He smiled like a man warmed by the sight of a good friend doing something unexpected and wonderful.

"You'll *sell it* to Hamling! What are you...?!"

"I want him to have it."

Brown swung forward, extended his hand. "Show me."

"I don't have it here."

"But you can get it. Today... If what you say is true."

If what I say is true.

"I can bring it."

"So I'm going to tell Percy you're coming by later with a diamond for him, that you want him to *look at it* and consider purchasing it. It was appraised at eight million, I'll tell him. Appraised by whom?"

"A man who knows diamonds."

Brown stared at his guest, blinked, spark of recollection in his eye. "Daniel Ortiz," he said. And then: "I'll forget you said that."

"I didn't say anything. What I said was I want Hamling, or you as Hamling's proxy, to take the diamond."

Brown waited. "Why?"

"Because it's what Conway wanted all along. He didn't care about the money. A couple hundred grand in the shadow of this thing. No. He knew it was there and he knew he could get it. But something went wrong. Drago caught on, is what I think. So Frank turned to plan B. Only he didn't have a plan B. So he improvised. And in his hurry he didn't bother checking to see what was in the bag. He grabbed what he could and ran. And that's why –"

"He didn't check."

"No. Clearly. Or maybe he did. It doesn't matter –"

"He didn't check what was in the bag. You're sitting here telling me Frank Conway kills a man to get some diamonds and then doesn't bother looking in the bag to see if what he wants is there? Is that what you are saying?"

Charly thought over his words. Tom Brown was not a man to bullshit with. Although Charly was not lying, he was bending the truth. Brown impressed him as a man who didn't deal in bent truths. "I don't know if Frank checked or not. Maybe he did, maybe he didn't. Maybe he didn't wanna wait around. Didn't wanna go traipsing about the countryside looking for me. I don't know. What I do know, or suspect, is that –"

End of the game in sight, Brown said: "Conway paid up for you."

Charly nodded. "I thought so. A hundred grand, for eight million? Or more? Now he has me all to himself. He doesn't want the extra attention. No. He wants what he's wanted all along, which is a beautiful rock."

Brown said nothing. He sat in his chair without moving. "You're not finished."

"No. Get Conway off my back."

"You bring me the diamond and we'll move from there."

"Very good. I think my time is up."

"It is."

Both men stood.

"Thanks for coming by."

He drove around for thirty minutes, up and down the hills around Washington Square. Down Geary, speeding. He stopped at a Chinese donut shop. He had a glazed old-fashioned and a cup of coffee. It was good to sit and do nothing. Light rain falling.

A crowd stood gathered outside St. Mary's. Boys dressed up in suits, like men. Girls in white and red. He liked the organ there, liked the way the sound crept and crawled around overhead, through the strange space, the spaceship-like vaulted ceiling.

Celebrating the birth of our savior...

At his apartment he put two thousand dollars in a large envelope. He sealed it. He drove down to Bernal Heights, to the travel agency. He found the dropbox and left the money.

He'd need a map of Tokyo. And a Japanese phrase book.

Konnichiwa. Oishi kattadesu!

Don't get ahead of yourself, Charly.

At a payphone he called Yoshi. No answer.

He called Posner.

"Yes."

"It's done. Money's in."

"Good work. Listen, come by tomorrow. I need you for something."

"Need me?"

"What? You thought I'd give you a hundred grand for nothing? Don't sweat it. Easy work. But it's in LA."

"Great. Tomorrow. See you. But after this, I'm on vacation."

"Of course, Charly."

How much time did he have? Posner would find out that the money was for nothing, was still in its luggage in his apartment, waiting to go. And then what?

Wouldn't matter.

Back in the apartment he turned on all the lights, turned up the heat. He put on Vivaldi's *Juditha Triumphans.*

He felt like cleaning. Setting things in order.

He was watering his geranium when the street door opened and closed down below. The hand and shoulder of a big man. Blond hair, pulled back. Jaime. Slowly he came up.

Charly put on a pot of coffee. Made some toast.

There were two wooden chairs in the kitchen. Jaime took one of them and tipped it back. Charly waited for it to crumble beneath the big man.

"Cream and sugar?"

"No. Black. Thanks."

Jaime appeared to be listening to the oratorio, his eyes closed. He said: "There's an aria in this piece – it's Vivaldi, no? – that is absolutely ravishing. I heard it live once, in Venice. I cried."

Charly was taken aback. He leaned against the counter. "You're right about that. Ravishing."

The men drank their coffee. Charly had toast and butter.

The cat made an appearance, sat in the entry to the kitchen to study the visitor, and then left.

"I wouldn't have guessed that about you."

"Guessed what? That I've traveled, that I like baroque music?"

"None of it. You're a puzzling man, Jaime Dossantos. But enough. What's the low down, what brings you to my squalor this Christmas morning – "

"Can't it just be for a friendly visit, Charly?"

"That what you call it?"

"Expecting someone?" Jaime said. "Cleaning up. How's Sandra these days? You never talk about her. I saw her once –"

"Don't you have somewhere to be, people to –"

The telephone made a clatter in the hallway.

"I could say the same of you."

"One sec," Charly said, stepping into the hall. "Here comes your favorite part." He picked up. "Merry Christmas."

The man on the other end snorted and said, "You have something of mine."

"You don't say."

"Make things easy on yourself, Charly, and give it up. I'll pay you for it."

"With my money? That's ballsy, Frank."

"We can do it the other way."

"Which is –"

"I come and take it from you. And leave you with nothing."

"Like before."

"No. Not like before, Charly. This will be a whole new theme. I've reinvented myself."

"Into what? A good shot?"

"Heh, funny. I'm being patient with you, Charly. Giving you a chance. But look at your options. Use that clever head of yours."

"And?"

"I actually like you, Charly. Bet you didn't think that. But I do. And, really, I don't want to do this, but what choice do you leave me?"

"What choice!?"

"Enough palaver. I want the diamond. I'll call back in twelve hours and we're going to meet. You choose the place and time. This exchange is going to happen. Envision it and accept it. Otherwise – there is no otherwise, Charly."

Jaime was humming to himself in the kitchen. Smell of hot coffee, toast. He tried to picture the man on vacation in Venice. Big sunhat, sunglasses, a gondola.

Sunshine.

"I don't have it," he said.

"Don't lie to me. I know you have it, and I'm coming for it."

"Too late. Ring Tom Brown. But not today. He has kids and Christmas in the Brown residence is a *big deal.*"

"Fuck you, Charly. You're dead."

"Come on, Frank. Let's be nice. Where's your Christmas cheer?"

"Dead."

"I gotta go. Anything else?"

"Sure... You like fish?"

"What?"

"You like fish, Charly?"

"Do I like fish?"

"Sushi."

"..."

"She taste like fish, Charly?"

Click.

He returned to the kitchen, sat down. Lifting his mug his hand was shaking.

"You okay? You look like you just saw a ghost. Tom tells me, by the way – congrats – you're all done. I meant to tell you."

"Jaime –"

"Christ, Charly."

Jaime leaned across the table and grabbed Charly's shoulder.

"What happened? Who was that?"

"Frank Conway."

"Conway?"

Charly lit a cigarette. He stood and pulled down the bottle of Cutty Sark, poured himself a glassful. The glass didn't touch his lips. He poured himself another. "I'm going to show you something," he said. "But first –"

He went to the hallway and called Yoshi. No answer.

She's not at the conservatory today. Out with her brother? With Mary?

He dug out a phone book. Mullen, M.A. A North Beach address. Imagine that. He called. No answer.

He took out the cat food and put it on the kitchen table. He opened it and reached inside.

He set the yellow wad of paper on the table.

"Open it."

Jaime did. He whistled, turning the diamond between his index finger and thumb. "Now that's something."

"You couldn't guess its value."

"Couldn't I? Five mill."

"Close but no cigar. Anyways, I won't get what it's worth. And the longer it's here the – the more trouble I'm in. It's going to Hamling. Today."

"Okay." Jaime grinned as if in sympathy for a bad joke.

"Then I need Hamling to find Conway, get his dogs on Conway."

"Because?"

"Because! Because he wants this. It's all he's wanted. It's why he killed Drago, it's why –"

"The invisible man," Jaime said, staring into the rock, turning it, contemplating its countless facets, the refracted kitchen light a rainbow on his hand, the table.

"He's no longer negotiating," Charly said.

"But he was."

"I wouldn't say so. Anyways, now it's clear how he's going to do business. I need to –"

"What can I do?"

"Wanna do something? Get a Christmas bonus?"

"I can handle myself."

Charly thought about it. "Take the rock to Tom Brown. Right now."

"He's busy. You know that."

"Tonight then. Promise me, Jaime. It needs to be in his hands tonight. Do this for me."

"It's done."

"Call him."

Charly carried the phone into the kitchen, held it out. "I told you I'll take care of it."

"Call him."

Jaime looked put out. He made the call. Brown didn't answer. Jaime left a message, said he'd come by with something of Charly's at eight.

"Good," Charly said. "Let's you and me meet back here at nine. I'll fix you dinner. I'd like the company."

"Works for me. You know I don't eat meat."

"What's wrong with you?"

"The shit's bad for you. You have no idea what they do to animals."

"That's why I eat only organic."

"Bullshit you do. I've seen what you eat, Charly."

"You're right. I'm a sick man."

"You're a dead man is what you are."

"Funny you say that –"

Far away, behind the music, a commotion. Something out front. Charly went to the front room, turned the music down, looked out the window. A cold, gray, empty street. At the bus stop down the way someone waited, seated huddled in a black ball against the glass.

A stranger. Busses don't run on Christmas.

They finished the pot of coffee. Charly was feeling a little better when Jaime stood to leave.

The big man put the diamond in the inside pocket of his coat.

Charly walked him to the door. They shook hands.

Jaime looked down at him, as tall as he was, and pressed the tip of his finger into Charly's chest.

"Watch yourself. I'm looking forward to this dinner of yours. I've heard things. Anyways, it'd be nice to sit down and do something civil for once."

Charly opened the door.

The man called Chuchu was standing there. He smiled and the flash of his pointed teeth probably saved Charly, who innocently recoiled at the sight, pulling back just enough to have the tip of his chin nicked by the knife aimed at his throat.

An instant later Jaime shoved Charly aside and faced the killer, filling the door. Charly heard the man grunt, saw in the corner of his eye a splash of blood on the floor, heard what sounded like someone slapping a waterbed.

Jaime sighed and wrapped his arms around the little man in the door, hugging him like a bear against his chest, pushing him back, out of the entry, onto the landing.

Both men went over the railing.

Charly heard a second of silence and then a fantastic crash, of wood and bones snapping, crushed. The entire building shuddered.

They'd kicked over his geranium.

He looked down. The two men had fallen to the third floor landing. All he saw was Jaime's back. The man was motionless, face in profile. Eyes closed.

There was no sign of Chuchu.

No. There he was: a small foot poked out from the beneath the other man's leg. His shoe had fallen off. He had on white socks.

Charly went down. He rolled Jaime off the little man. Both of them were dead. Jaime's front, nice shirt, was all red. Stabbed again and again, full of holes. "Jaime." Cut up like a paper snow flake.

Chuchu had Jaime's blood on his shirt, hands and face. He looked peaceful, his head askew. The fall, with the weight of Jaime, had killed him fast enough.

The knife was still in his hand. A switchblade. If he'd connected, if Charly had been looking the other way when he opened the door, there'd be nothing to it. Sharp as a razor.

He took it, closed it, put it in his pocket.

He turned Jaime's corpse around, grabbed him beneath his arms and dragged him up the stairs.

So this is what they mean by deadweight!

Once back in the apartment he dragged the body through the kitchen to the backdoor. There was a small pantry there. He fixed the body seated upright against the wall.

He took the diamond from Jaime's coat. He took off Jaime's coat and draped it over the corpse's head. He went through the pant pockets. A wallet, car keys, small change, a stick of Wrigley's Spearmint gum. He took the wallet and keys. After a moment, he unwrapped the gum and put it in his mouth.

Charly never chewed gum. It was a good time for a piece of gum. Get the smell of blood and guts out of his mouth.

He went back to the stairs. Before looking, it crossed his mind that Chuchu might be gone, that he had been playing dead – he would have done such a thing. But no, there it was, dead as before.

You never know.

The killer's body was easier to move, weighing little more than a small woman.

He set it next to the other one, resting its head on the other's shoulder. Nice couple.

He went through its pockets. A fifty and some smaller bills. No wallet or ID. A bottle of pills. Adenosine. Another knife, this one smaller, thinner. Black Ray-Ban glasses, broken. Car keys. A Honda of some sort.

He called Yoshi. No answer.

He threw some clothes into a black duffel bag.

He was counting the minutes now. When's that flight again?

He washed his hands and face. He put a band-aid on the cut on his chin. It didn't do much. He was pressing a hand towel to the cut when he ran out the door.

Think Charly! Use that clever head of yours.

It was cold outside. The sky was low, scraping the rooftops. The rain had stopped. There was a sound, a strange buzzing, whining. It was a kid, the only form of life on the street, with a remote-control car zipping around.

He walked quickly up Lower Haight, looking for the Honda. Then down the other side. Nothing.

The buzz of the toy had stopped. The kid, antennae of his controller pointed at the ground, was looking at the figure in the corner of the bus stop.

Charly went closer.

"Go home kid."

It was Emmett. His head was down but he wasn't sleeping. His throat was cut, ear to ear, his front a black bib of blood, cord of blood pouring from the bench, his limp left hand, to the wet ground. There it ran into the gutter and washed away.

Around the corner he found the Honda. He drove it into the alley, up to the back of his building. He opened the trunk. He ran up the stairs, went inside.

Standing over the bodies, *déjà vu*. His hands were cold. From his bedroom he dragged out a Turkish rug. Pomegranates around the perimeter enclosed a walled garden, a fountain. He liked the rug very much. He'd bought it in Istanbul years before. He hated to use it like this, but what could he do?

What would you do, two bodies in your pantry and the police on the way? You have this great big rug and a car with an empty trunk parked downstairs...

He opened the rug in the kitchen and rolled Jaime onto an edge and then rolled him up like a burrito. He dragged this out the back door onto the landing, and then, step by step, down the stairs.

It's no small feat dragging a two hundred and fifty pound body down four flights of stairs in a rug. He didn't think he'd make it. But he did, and everything stayed inside.

Then there were the neighbors to think about.

He didn't think. He dragged the rug the remainder of the way, out to the Honda. Incrementally he raised and shoved the rug into the trunk, forcing it, bending it over. By some small miracle, it fit. He couldn't believe his eyes. He slammed the trunk closed.

The other body was no problem. It came down with Charly like a drunk friend. He sat it in the passenger seat, buckled it in, put on its broken Ray-Bans.

He drove down to a club off O'Farrell. They were always open. Old whores in pointed red hats stood by the entrance, arms crossed over their chests, smoking, shivering. Music thumped inside.

He parked at the curb, left the engine running.

"Hey mister!"

~ 20 ~

He walk-ran back to Lower Haight. He took the Volvo over to Yoshi's.

The tall new building looked like a mausoleum – white, sterile, hollow, its top in the clouds.

The door to her apartment was open a crack.

"Yoshi!"

At a glance, everything looked in place. He paused in the kitchen. In the bamboo dish rack, nothing but a knife, one of the Honyaki's, one of her father's, its oily steel full of rainbows.

Something on the air. Fish, no. Smoke, no. *Death!* And perfume. A woman. Mary!

But the place was empty.

Except, of course, for Yoshi, who was dead.

The body was in bed, naked under a white sheet. Its eyes were closed, face to the ceiling. Already stiff. Bruised around her throat. On his knees he pushed her chin one way, the other. There's blood on the sheet, by her hip, at her hand, but not a lot.

Her crooked finger was gone, cut cleanly off.

He pondered this for a moment, holding her stiff hand, looking deeply into the red and bloody stump.

Otherwise, the body was clean. Leaning in close, he smelled soap. Even the futon, except for the circle of blood left by the mutilated hand, was clean.

Had he washed her afterward? Done the laundry?

Something didn't add up. She hadn't showered and then been killed. No. She, the place, all of it was too clean for that. It was all so orderly, prepared.

It was a nicely prepared corpse, is what it was.

He went to the bathroom. It was, as he expected it to be, spotless. There was a little water in the base of the tub, near the drain. The tiniest of specks of mineral deposit in the water, glittering like silver.

He went to the kitchen. He looked in the fridge. Various things from the night before, in Tupperware and Saran Wrap.

He grabbed a beer.

He looked out the kitchen window. Soft rain falling, south of the city crawling off into the haze. He drank the beer. Something was turning in his stomach.

Why would he take her finger?

In the study, he immediately noticed that he'd taken the violin too. Where its case had been was now its dust-free shadow, a yellow rectangle of light.

He looked at the music on the stand, on the piano. The composer was Bach but nothing else made sense. "J.S.

Bach," he thought. As a young man, Bach once walked thirty miles to hear a guy play the organ.

I've never walked thirty miles at once in my life.

You might someday.

He sat at the piano and looked at the keys, the white ones, the black ones. He pressed a few of them. He finished the beer. He went back to the fridge, opened another, and returned to the piano, pressing keys. He stood and looked inside the instrument. It didn't look so simple from that angle.

When he finished the second beer he opened cupboards, looking for the Laphroaig that Haruki had brought over the night before. He'd never wanted a drink so badly. He'd finish the bottle.

He stood in the kitchen, all the cupboards open. No booze. Not a drop. There'd been some kind of purge. She must've taken it out in boxes.

"You are standing in the middle of a crime scene."

Clear head, Charly.

Something was coming. He felt it growing inside. Not just a cry, a scream, but a force, fury.

He took the diamond from his pocket, set it on the clean counter.

"Goddamn you! Look what you've done!"

That was nonsense, of course. And he knew it. But it had to be said. He also knew, remembering something Brown had said, that he needed to leave, right away. He needed to disappear.

Like Momcilovic. Get out of sight. Find the coign of vantage and work from there...

The phone rang.

It could be anyone.

No, not anyone. It's either her brother or Mary.

It could be for you, Charly.

Don't answer it.

It rang six times and then stopped.

He had to go, immediately.

"Yoshi. Poor Yoshi. What have I done?"

He kneeled down beside the body and kissed it on the lips. He kissed its mutilated hand.

"I'll get your finger back. It might kill me, but I'll get it back."

Outside the elevator, he heard the phone in the apartment begin to ring again.

Yoshi, naked, playing her violin, milky morning light high up in the room. Caught in the middle of a conflict you knew nothing about. If only you had closed your eyes and turned away, rejected it, rejected me, never even known me, you would still be here.

Charly, please!

Part Three

My Favorite Part

Black clouds, slag heaps of lead filled the sky. The fog had dissipated and the wind picked up. It began raining hard as he climbed into the Volvo.

He turned on the heat and the radio.

He took out Chuchu's knife and pressed the button. It snapped open. He pressed it closed. He opened it again.

He pressed its tip lightly into his jeans, his thigh.

The knife was very sharp.

He imagined cutting off Conway's fingers one by one.

How would he do that? He'd need to knock the man out, tie him to a chair.

He'd need tape, rope. He'd need equipment.

On the radio – he recognized it immediately – Hector Berlioz, *Harold in Italy*. The soaring viola made him feel young and careless. There was an army of demons back there, behind Harold, pursuing, but he didn't care. It didn't matter. The adventure mattered. Pressing forward mattered.

Don't look back.

He parked at the garage down the hill from his place. There was the BMW, just as he'd left it three days ago.

What day was it again?

Christmas. Celebration of the birth of our savior...

Police on the street. An ambulance. Various cars, flashing lights. They'd taken Emmett away.

"What happened?" he asked a cop at the corner, a young Mexican. The cop squinted in the rain and said something. He adjusted his hat. Charly pretended he hadn't heard. "A man *died*?"

"In the bus stop. Right over there."

"And on Christmas. That's..."

The cop turned and looked him in the eye. Then he looked away. "I tell you," he said, "the things I've seen. But I get time and a half for this."

Charly and the cop glared at the street, the bus stop down the way. Then Charly walked on. The cop sneezed loudly, blew his nose a moment later.

He went around back. He took his time, checking the ground. There wasn't anything. Everything was drenched black.

The steps were clean.

Inside he could still smell them, the big one, full of holes, the little one pressed flat.

He fried some bacon and eggs. He made a pot of coffee. He toasted and buttered some bread. He opened a jar of artichoke hearts and poured them into a bowl. He cut up cherry tomatoes, "Straight from Mexico," salted them, drenched them in oil. In no time he had a full spread.

He wanted a paper but didn't want to go back out.

It was getting dark. Finally, he thought, the holiday comes to an end.

The phone rang. He let it go, but it wouldn't stop. The anger coming back, rising up, pissing on the serenity of lunch, he kicked his chair over, ran into the hall, grabbed the phone, "What!"

"*Mother fucker!*"

Posner.

"*Vacation!*" the old man screamed. "All expenses paid!"

"I said I'd do the job. We're meeting, right? Lay the fuck off, Bernie. It's Christmas."

"I'll lay off when I see what's mine returned, *shit-for-brains!* I can't believe you did that! *When* did you know?"

"Know what?"

"Know what! Know that you didn't need the money. *My* money! Know what! *Fuck you, Charly!* You lied to me! Money's in! *Fuck you!* I don't see every fuckin bill of that money here tomorrow, I'm gonna *hide you* Charly. Know what that means?"

"Tell me."

"That's old fashioned for I'll whip you till there's nothin left. You'll wish Frank Conway found you first."

Charly didn't know what to say. It was all too much at once. He said: "You'll get it all back. I don't want to upset things. I only found out this morning, I meant to call you."

"*Meant* to call me! You don't get second chances, Charly. I'm all you've got in this world. I cut you loose and you're going down. Are we on the same page?"

"Yes," he said, imagining a page, columns of tiny illegible print. "Of course we are. I'll see you tomorrow."

The cat sat in the entrance to the kitchen, watching him. Its green eyes seemed otherworldly. It hardly moved, didn't even blink.

Charly went back to his lunch.

He poured some cat food into the dish. But the cat wasn't there – it had ran into the hall, toward the front room.

He finished his lunch. He thought about Yoshi's missing finger. He'd never find it, never get it back. It was one of those things – once gone, impossible to recover.

Gust of wind, crackle of rain against the window, a chilling breeze around his ankles, his small kitchen was suddenly very cold.

What's Felicia doing these days? Swimming naked by moonlight?

He wanted a shower. First he needed to clear the air. He'd put on Sibelius, the second symphony.

The front room was dark. Not even the flicker of a street light or ambulance or cop car in the window. As if someone had pulled the shades.

He flipped the switch.

Frank Conway was sitting on his couch, a white bandage wrapped around his head.

Charly swallowed, slowly raised a hand to his chest. "*Christ*, Frank! I'm having a heart attack."

"I would have said something."

"I thought we were meeting later. I name the place, re-member? How'd you get in?"

"Your front door was open."

The tall man looked comfortable on Charly's couch, his long legs crossed before him, his arm back. You might say, if it wasn't for the white bandage wrapped around his head and the gun under his belt, Frank Conway had just stopped by for a drink.

"Nice painting," he said. "You like art, Charly?"

"Get you a drink? Thanks, by the way, for your contri-bution to that other matter."

"Don't mention it."

Charly thought about the switchblade in his pocket. And beneath it, the little item everyone wanted so badly.

"Safe enough neighborhood," Frank said, "to leave your doors open?"

"I had company. Busy day."

"So I heard. Tough being you, I imagine."

The opening strains of the Sibelius, a walk down a path in the woods, warbling birds overhead. He wanted noth-ing more than to put it on and forget about Frank Conway, this dirty business. But he couldn't, not without, probably, a kick in the teeth.

"So where is it?"

"Where's what?"

"Where's what." Frank smiled and lowered his gaze. He had no patience for such games. He was a man already in significant pain and a hurry. "Mr. Chuchu came for it earlier. Don't suppose he has it. Haven't heard from him. He's very loyal, Chuchu is. Never lets me down."

"What happened to your head, Frank?"

Something flickered and went out in Frank Conway's blue eyes. He touched the tip of his tongue to his upper lip and took a deep breath. "Stinks in here," he said. "Smells like –"

"Where's my money?"

Charly was counting steps, counting seconds. The front door, over his shoulder, would be locked. The back door was open.

"I have the money," Frank said. He stuck a finger in his mouth, chewed on the nail with his front teeth. "It's not far. But first –"

"What's not far? You mean down in the car, out front, down where they just carted away a friend of mine? Is that what you mean by not far? Because – *not far*, Frank –"

"Shut up, Charly. Give me the diamond. You'll never see me again."

"Make me an offer. The other bidder, I'll just say –"

"How's this."

Frank pulled from under his jacket a gun, what looked to Charly like a forty-five, *big hole* on its business end.

Now he had something else to calculate.

Charly took one step back. That's what you do when someone points a big gun at you. You step back and reflect on things. Happier times.

In the corner of his eye he noticed the cat, again, at the other end of the hall. It had run back for its lunch. But then – and this time he turned his head and looked – the cat wasn't watching him. It was sitting, as before, but looking at something in the kitchen, the stove, the sink.

A mouse, perhaps.

"Great timing, fucker," Charly said under his breath.

"What's that? The diamond, you say?"

Charly held out his hands. Slowly he reached into his right pocket, slid his hand down the length of the knife, and took the diamond out.

Frank stood up, pistol at his hip.

To use the knife, Charly thought, he'd need – first – to take it out and open it – and then, second, get in close to Frank, which wasn't going to happen any time soon. Third – sweet misfortune – the hand that held the diamond was the hand he needed to get the knife!

Frank stepped forward and reached out. Charly dropped the diamond, its fine yellow wrapper, into the palm of the man's hand.

Frank smiled. He had such awful gappy teeth, teeth like raggedy hitchhikers, teeth like semaphores on a landing strip!

"Thanks, Charly. That wasn't so hard, was it?"

"Why'd you kill her, Frank?"

"Kill who?"

Kill who! –

"The girl! Yoshi!"

Now the hand was free...

Frank was stepping backward, toward the shaded window. He was his old self again. Unflappable to the core.

Kill who!

With the white bandage around his head, his tan slacks and leather shoes, he really did look like an RAF officer from some movie. Mary was right.

"I don't know what you are talking about," he said.

"Fuck you you don't! *Taste like sushi?* Fuck you, Frank! She had nothing to do with this. I want her finger back!"

"Her what?"

"Her crooked finger!"

"Her finger? Charly, you're losing it. Listen to yourself."

"*You took her finger!*"

He felt like he might cry. He had nothing left.

"I took her finger?" Frank glanced aside for an instant in thought. Then he raised the gun, pointed it at Charly, and said:

"I did no such thing. But it doesn't matter. Nothing matters anymore."

For a second, Charly was almost convinced – that nothing mattered, that he was dead, and that Frank had not killed Yoshi and taken her finger. He closed his eyes, accepted his fate, waited for the explosion that would send him to the other side.

It didn't come. He waited. He could hear seconds dripping in his head. He waited. There was something wrong; time wasn't working properly. He saw in his head that old light switch in the house up in the country: *Click, click, CLICK!* Nothing.

But then the dripping and the clicking fell into step and struck an odd rhythm, a march, an accelerating pitter-patter like a cat racing up the wall.

Or was it thunder? Or –

Someone was running down the hallway, behind him –

Flash, white gleam in the air, a shadow emerged from the hall moving fast, a black bolt and Charly felt his body cower, wince and duck, prepare for the blow, when the thing missed, passing him.

It was a man in a black jacket. It was screaming:

"KONO KUSOTTAREGA BUKKOROSHITEYARU!!!"

It had a meat cleaver raised over its head.

Haruki! Charly thought, one hand on the floor. *He came for me –*

As happens, the contest was over in an instant. The gun went off. A starburst of blood splashed across the ceiling.

Then the meat cleaver connected. Or maybe Frank lost his fingers first, it was hard to tell.

SHINK!

Haruki had aimed for the jugular, but Frank reached up, blocking the blow with his left hand, turning the gun upward with his right.

Off with his fingers! *Bump-bump, bump-bump!*

The first shot, through Haruki's gut, hardly stopped the man, he was airborne when the cleaver came down.

They tackled each other, face to face, their heels kicked out, triangulated, when Haruki put his hand under Frank's chin, pushing him back, nose to the ceiling.

The second blow, then, back-handed, was level with Frank's bandaged ear, aimed at the exposed throat. And there it landed, too far back, stopping only because of Frank's spinal column.

The second shot went through Haruki's heart. Charly flinched, blood in his eyes, chips of wall dropping on his shoulder.

Yoshi's brother fell straight to the floor, a lifeless heap.

Frank staggered, reaching out, backward with his bloody stump, his eyes rolling around trying to see what exactly had happened. The meat cleaver was lodged deep in the side of this throat, just under his bandaged ear.

Blood was pouring from his hand and spurting in pulses, like a lawn sprinkler, from around the edge of the cleaver.

He coughed, spitting blood. Blood seemed to be spraying from his eyes.

The man had a minute, two tops.

How was he still standing?

All the same, somewhere in his dying brain Frank Conway was still taking orders, following a plan. He swung the gun in Charly's general direction and

BAM! BAM! BAM!

fired three more rounds.

They all went wide, into the wall.

Frank groaned.

He reached out for the edge of the couch and collapsed, first to his knee, then onto his side.

Charly waited, crouched in the hallway. After a minute, he peeked into the room.

Frank had his forehead pressed to the floor. He was talking to himself. The wooden handle of the cleaver stuck out of his throat like the handle to an old-fashioned pump.

"Where's her finger?" Charly said from the hallway.

What came out of Frank's mouth wasn't clear. The words bubbled. "Her what?"

"Where's her finger, Frank?"

"I told you... I don't know... what you're talking about..."

Charly stood up and stepped into his living room, blood dripping from the walls, the ceiling. Frank groaned and coughed and –

BAM!

Another shot, way off its mark.

"You killed her and cut off her crooked finger."

"Charly!" Frank was having a hard time breathing. "You're wrong..."

Incredibly, the dying man laughed. Charly approached him, eye on the gun. Frank tried to raise his arm, the gun, but he could barely hold the weapon. He was shaking all over.

Charly took Frank's wrist. He took the gun and set it on the record player across the room. He looked at the other body, Haruki, on his back, eyes closed, his face calm, as if asleep. The blood running from his gut and chest was stinking up the room. Or maybe it was Frank's. Maybe it was something else altogether.

Frank collapsed to a shoulder, his bloody hand under his body.

"She was innocent," Charly said. "She had nothing to do with anything."

Charly looked into Frank's bloody eyes. There wasn't much there. They were swirling around, searching.

"Nobody's innocent," Frank said.

"She was."

Frank's eyes found Charly, worked at holding him in place. He then said quietly, clearly, "You were her purge, Charly. She used you..."

"Used me?"

"To get rid of... that cunt, Mullen... She only fucked you to..."

With a toe, Charly tapped the wooden handle of the meat cleaver. It was fixed hard, stuck in bone. Frank closed his eyes, a man lost in reverie. "You call that –" he whispered.

Some men take a long time to die. It's amazing what the body can do.

"You call that innocent? Charly? Say it."

"You didn't have to kill her."

"I didn't. Think..."

"What?"

"*Think*, will you..."

The color drained from Frank's face as a pool of blood expanded around him, covering the floor of the room.

"I..."

He was drifting off.

"Frank!"

The man winced, pain filling his face for an instant. And then nothing. His pupils dilated quickly. Great black holes.

Charly shivered, cold of death creeping over the floor, filling the room.

He took the gun from the record player. One side was smeared with Frank's blood. He wiped it off on his pants. It was heavier than it looked. In small print, etched in the steel side of the chamber: *Browning Practical. 9 mm. FN. Herstal, Belgium.* The clip slid out into his palm. He pushed out rounds with his thumb. Hollow points – seven.

"That will do."

From Frank's body he took the diamond and a wallet.

There was nothing on Haruki. That seemed curious, at first.

He didn't walk here.

But then it made sense. The other one – the tall one, Joe, the architect – was outside. Waiting.

We've been here before.

Get moving, Charly.

He washed the blood off his hands. He dressed in clean clothes. In two minutes he had everything he'd need. The black duffel bag and Posner's blue carry-on. The diamond. The Browning.

"So long apartment. So long stereo. So long woman in red dress."

He looked for the cat but it was nowhere to be found. He put the bag of cat food on the floor and tore down its top. He hesitated. He took out a large wooden salad bowl and filled it with the remainder of the cat food. But that too didn't look right...

Charly!

Front door or back?

Haruki'd come through the back door, by the alley. The man wouldn't park down there, waiting.

Back door then.

Good guess.

The black Mercedes was around the block, at the corner, facing the apartment.   What's he doing? Singing – is that – Gershwin?

The street was empty. Charly came up quickly in the car's blind spot.

Joe was singing along with Billie Holiday –

"Then you'll spread your wings – and take to the sky –"

If that back door's locked –

Another good guess.

He pressed the muzzle of the Browning against the back of the man's head.

"Drive."

Joe didn't hesitate. He turned the car on and drove slowly down Haight.

"Speak English, Joe?"

"No," the man said.

"But you can understand me."

The driver's eyes bounced between the mirror and the road. They approached Van Ness.

Charly tapped him on the left shoulder.

"Turn."

He directed him to the bridge.

He should kill the man. The logical thing to do would be to kill the man. He would know about the plan, the escape. He might be the only one who knows –

Charly's no killer.

They crossed the bridge. It was empty. Not a soul out.

He needed to get the man far away, and leave him there –

"Haruki is dead."

Stone face in the front seat. His eyes alone, machine-like, stitching the dark between the windshield and mirror, watching the man with the gun.

Charly lit a cigarette.

"I didn't kill him... The killer's name is Frank Conway. Heard of him? Maybe you have. It doesn't matter. He's dead too. Haruki got him... He's the one who..."

In Marin County, they passed a few other cars, revelers returning from parties. The occasional highway patrol.

Should Charly say anything, warn the man about how to proceed?

He's not stupid. And he's not here taking measurements for some kitchen back home.

Charly tapped him again when it was time to pull off.

"Slowly, here."

San Rafael was quiet, off to sleep. In a few minutes they were out in the country, the road threading its way through a darkness so vast that after a while it seemed the car and the small island of light that it occupied were going nowhere. The world had disappeared.

"Slowly," Charly said, tapping the back of Joe's head with the gun.

Ice gathered at the base of the windshield. Dusty rain whipped and curled in the high beams.

"So you like Gershwin."

"..."

"*Porgy and Bess.*"

"Billie Holiday," said Joe.

"I see."

Charly thought about seeing Yoshi's crooked finger for the first time. It was at the bar, after the concert, the Sibelius, when they first met. That's what it was, about her hand. Maybe it's what had brought them together. The crooked finger had summoned him.

The village was dark. They floated through without slowing down, as if in a dream. At the end of the road leading up to the house, Charly told Joe to stop.

"Get out."

Joe reached to turn the car off.

"No. Leave it."

They got out together, Charly a step ahead. He stood back. Joe was a big man, after all. Easily a head taller than Charly, with arms that...

He stood back. He made it clear what the Browning meant. He said: "Up this road there is a house. It is empty. There is food there. A bed. A telephone. The back door is..."

Joe didn't move. Didn't blink. His eyes were full of night. There was something in his lower jaw, a twitch.

"You have a pencil, paper?"

Charly made like he wanted to write. Joe reached into his coat and pulled out a pen and white card. He set these on the hood of the car. Then he took two steps backwards.

Charly thought about it. It wouldn't be easy. And he'd come too far to fuck up now.

"Get back," he said, putting the gun into the tall man's face. "Back!"

Joe winced, stepped back. He raised his hands, palms out.

"Up this road," Charly said, pointing, "there's a house! Go there."

The tall man looked up the road.

Rain blew in gusts around them.

"House!" Charly said. He drew the structure in the air with the gun. "Go!"

Joe started up the road. He hesitated, looked back. It was dark outside of the light of the car. Charly nodded, waved with the gun. Joe walked on, up the hill into the dark.

Charly got in the car. He watched the hunched back of the Japanese man climb the hill, finally disappear.

He didn't wait, didn't think. He turned the car around and left fast.

It was a few minutes to one. His flight was in a little more than a day. He'd go to the mountains. Rest up, clean himself, say goodbye to his friend.

On the radio, something from Bach's *Goldberg Variations*, and, from the soft murmur behind the keyboard, it sounded like Glenn Gould playing. That was fine, he thought, hearing the sound of the musician behind the recording. Being there, at the piano, with Mr. Gould.

~ 22 ~

The sun would be up soon.

It was freezing at the cabin. From the roof, like the teeth of giants, monstrous icicles descended, nearly touching the ground. Ice covered the windows.

He started a fire.

The cupboard was bare. In the fridge, a wedge of parmesan, half a dry sausage. He had a glass of Cutty Sark with his cheese and meat.

He sat in front of the fire and watched it burn.

He took a cold shower, scrubbing blood from his fingertips, from his hair, behind his ears, scrubbing until his skin was raw.

Then he fell into a deep sleep.

Burton woke him later, pounding on the door.

He was in camouflage. He had a rifle on his shoulder.

When Charly opened the door the big hairy man glanced quickly inside, over Charly's shoulder. "I'm going up the mountain. Put a jacket on."

Charly dressed in some things that stayed at the cabin. He took the 30-30 from the wall.

They walked up a fire road for an hour. Now and then Burton would stop and study something at his feet, in the dirt. He'd look up into the trees, up the mountainside. Everything was quiet and still.

Charly was sweating when they reached an opening on the ridge. They sat down on the ground. Burton took from his backpack a thermos and a couple sandwiches. He gave one of the sandwiches to Charly. He poured him some coffee in a paper cup.

"I was hoping to find this cat," Burton said, his eyes far away, at the edge of the world.

"A cat?" Charly said.

"There's a mountain lion. It killed some of my sheep."

"When?"

Charly finished his sandwich. He took out a cigarette. He was reaching up to light it when Burton turned, looked him right in the eye. "Please don't do that."

Charly looked at his friend, cigarette stuck to his bottom lip. Then he put the cigarette away.

"About a month ago was the first. A week ago was the second."

"And how do you know it's a mountain lion?"

"I know. It leaves clues... It happens sometimes."

The idea of a mountain lion excited Charly. He'd never seen one before. In pictures, sure, but not in real life.

He tried to imagine it walking along, sitting down, cleaning itself, devouring a sheep.

"What do they look like?"

"Big cats."

"Like lions?"

"No way. Just a cat. Only much bigger."

"They fast?"

Burton looked at Charly and smiled. "Fast? I don't know if they're fast or not. Haven't timed one. I guess so. They're shy. They can climb trees and see you coming from a long ways off."

"Maybe one's watching us right now."

Burton laughed. "I bet he is. The very one I want."

A minute later Burton asked, "Have a good Christmas?"

"No."

"No surprises?"

"Surprises plenty. But nothing I wanted."

"Sorry about that."

"I think I got what I deserved."

They sat for a little longer, watching the world. Then they descended the mountain the way they'd come. At the cabin Burton asked him if he'd be staying long. Charly told him his plans. Burton told him to keep the kitchen faucet dripping and to lock up when he left.

Three hours later that's what Charly did.

Before he left he drove up to a chalet made out of trees Burton himself had cut down. The man's wife, an enormous Swede, answered the door. Long golden locks fell in cascades down her shoulders onto her chest, around her magnificent breasts.

Her presence was stunning. Charly was speechless.

So this is where Vikings come from, he thought.

"Ethan around?"

"No," she said. "But come in, Charly. There's coffee. There's cake."

When she smiled Charly felt weak in the knees. He could feel the woman's grace.

"I can't," he said. "I have a plane to catch. I just wanted to –"

What he wanted to do was talk more with Burton. Maybe give all that he had to the man, maybe turn himself in. "Tell him thanks for me," he said. "Tell him I'll be away for a couple months. But I'll try and come up in the spring. We can all go fishing."

"I will," the woman said. "We'd like that, Charly. ... You take care. Safe travels."

Safe travels. It didn't sound right. It didn't quite make sense.

He gets to sleep with this goddess every night, wake up beside her every day. He tends his sheep, grows vegetables in his greenhouse, hikes to the top of mountains looking for lions.

What have I done?

He wanted to reach out and touch the woman, to feel her hands around his head, on his face. Instead, he turned and walked back to the Mercedes.

She waved to him from the porch as he pulled away.

My life, he thought, is a series of mistakes, one after another. And now I am falling so fast there is no way to stop,
no retreat, no hope.

If I get on that plane...

He parked up the street from Mullen's place.

North Beach was busy that afternoon. Despite the cold,
the wind, the drizzle blowing like cinder in the air, people
strolled about.

She wasn't home.

He started around the back of the building. The gate in
the alley was locked.

He returned to the front door. He smoked and watched
the street. Across the way he could see into someone's
bright and clean living room. There was a Christmas tree,
a white mantel and white fireplace, a gold framed mirror.
A young woman with a pony tail entered the room, a magazine open in her hands. She turned her head quickly, said
something to someone in the other room, tossed the magazine aside, shook her hips and disappeared.

He thought about Bernie Posner and what sort of job
he had for him in LA.

They get their hooks in you. One after the next.

He wouldn't do it. There had to be a way out. He was
getting on that plane.

He was thinking about Jaime Dossantos – "Just outen'about, getting exercise" - John Doe on a cold metal table – when Mary Mullen turned the corner, came up the hill with a woman under her arm. A short Asian.

They were coming up the steps when they first saw him.

They'd been drinking.

Mullen sneered, hardly paused as she came up to him. She took out her keys, said to the girl,

"Get lost Ping. I got work to do with this man."

Ping looked momentarily hurt. Then she shrugged, said in a sing-song voice, "Sure. That's cool. Call you later!" and she waved and skipped down the steps back to the sidewalk.

"Hungry Charly?" Mary said once they were inside. "Get you something?"

She didn't even stop, didn't even look his way. She was in the kitchen, rifling through the fridge, wasting time, waiting for him to make a move.

"Yoshi's dead," he said.

She poured two whiskies and pushed one along the counter toward him. She sucked on hers, "I know," and wiped the back of her wrist across her glossy lips.

Her eyes had that feel again, that glitter and meanness and distance.

Then she came right up to him, face to face, eye to eye. She put the whisky in his hand. "Drink," she said. And then: "I found her, Charly. I found her. On the floor. She was strangled."

"You?"

"Yes, me. Why *not* me?" Her voice was rising, building. "I was her friend, Charly! I was more than her friend. I loved Yoshi. I liked her – I liked her music, her ideas, the way she spoke, her body, her whole... That surprise you?" Her voice cracked. She was breathing fast. "You simple minded piece of shit thug!"

She slapped him hard across the face.

That stung. His ear rang from the blow. His eyes bobbled in his head, taking a second to realign themselves. His hand was wet with whisky. "Mary, I –"

"You have no idea how you've –"

There was no arguing with her. He had fucked things up. He knew that. But there was no going back, nothing to do – short of turning himself in, which was not an option.

He stepped back. He drank his whisky, set the glass down, shook his hand off. He watched her carefully. Fuming woman. He picked up his glass.

Why hadn't she called the cops?

"Why didn't you call the police?"

She glared at him, finished her drink, slowly poured herself another.

The idea came to him on a wave of nausea. The words were like shards of glass in his mouth.

"You took her finger," he said.

She drank, swallowed, sighed. "Correct, Charly. I took her finger."

"Her crooked finger!"

"*Yes*, Charly. Her crooked finger."

"Why, Mary? Why did you do that!?"

"Why?"

There were dirty dishes in the sink. There was a knife there, Charly saw. Not a great knife, like Yoshi's, or some of Charly's, but a knife all the same. A six-inch long chopper.

Mary picked up the knife, held it tightly over the sink, examined at its greasy blade.

"I like that finger," she said. "It's a good finger."

You'll have to kill her. You can't kill her. You'll have to —

Give her the diamond, Charly.

"You *cut off* her finger!"

Charly was flabbergasted. He didn't know what to think. So this is the person who cut off Yoshi's finger. Who does something like that? He sipped his whisky and thought about the question, looking Mary up and down, at her arms, her short cropped black hair, her dark blue eyes. He felt like the woman before him was not actually a woman but some creature, something alien, from another world or another time.

"What –" he began to say.

"I was the one who put her in bed. It seemed right. That she not be found the way I found her. ... She was a perfectionist, she wanted the purity of things... Almost... I cleaned her. I bathed her. It was something we did... She liked to wash after practicing. Did you know the strings of the violin stain the player's fingers? The steel or the lead, whatever – it turned her fingers... black... I bet you didn't know that... And then, after that, I took her body to the bed and..."

Mary sobbed. A look of absolute sadness, of Mary as a frightened child, quickly came over her.

"I couldn't leave her, Charly. But I had to! I knew that. So I thought I'd take something of hers. To never forget..."

Let her talk, Charly.

"And I thought – her crooked finger. It's her, it's everything about her, all... There was no question, Charly. I wanted it. I cut it off. Now I have it."

She finished her drink. She licked her lips and stared at him.

"I want it," he said.

"You can't fuckin have it. It's mine."

"I'll give you the diamond."

"You –"

From his pocket he took out the switchblade, which he set on the counter, and the diamond, which he set next to his drink.

It didn't look like much, this wad of yellow tissue paper. All of its recent action, hand to hand, was beginning to show.

It would need a proper container soon.

Mary opened the paper and looked at the diamond. She picked it up. She held it between index finger and thumb directly in front of her nose.

He could see the diamond reflected in tears in the corners of her eyes, on the side of her nose.

Charly'd left the gun in the car.

Mary squeezed the diamond tightly in a fist, looked down, looked into the sink at the knife. After a minute, carefully placing the diamond on the counter, she said, "Okay."

She left the room. She was gone for a long time. But then she came back with a small red leather case in her hand. It looked like something that should hold an expensive pen. Instead – she opened it – it contained a finger.

Charly took the finger out and held it up to the light.

Sure enough. It was Yoshi's crooked finger.

For a second, Charly felt relieved. He'd found it. He was breathing easier. He was warm inside. Like a kid on Christmas morning. He'd get his plane tomorrow, fly to Japan, and, who knows, maybe give Yoshi's finger a proper burial.

He put the finger in the red case and closed it. He put the case in the inside pocket of his coat.

"Thank you, Mary. You have no idea what –"

"Get out. I don't give a fuck what you think, Charly. Take the finger and go away... Good luck asshole."

He was at the door again, in her dark foyer. His hand was on the doorknob. He glanced into the living room, the chair, painting of the factory. He thought of Mary's beautiful thighs, her black stockings, her wide set breasts, her swimmer's back.

He was turning to say something when he realized what was about to happen.

One mistake after another –

Mary was coming for him. But not for that. Death, not desire, gleamed in her funny eye, no question. No. She was in the hallway, in the foyer, on top of him in an instant, the bottle of Black Grouse splashing in the air. She screamed as the bottle came down over his ear, exploding into a million pieces. Charly went straight to the ground, practically out cold, saved, perhaps, by all the cheap whisky in his eyes and nose. It burned. Hot blood pouring over his brow, into his eyes, into his mouth – "Mary!" – he squirmed on the floor, his hands slipping on the parquet as he tried to sit up, get back, stop the room from spinning.

"Mary, wait!"

She wouldn't, of course.

While Charly never thought of himself as a killer, Mary simply didn't think about it. Killer or not a killer, didn't matter. You ask her, anyone can be a killer. It's just a matter of motive and drive. Of necessity.

And Mary Mullen wanted that crooked finger. And she wanted that diamond. And she'd have both – and she'd kill Charly, this imbecile, if she had to.

"Mary!"

He put his hands up to block the next blow, and the jagged edge of the bottle sliced through the palm of his left hand, blood suddenly covering his wrist, running down his arm.

She *snarled*, spit in his face, in his eye, and fell on him, straddling him, knocking the wind out of him, reaching for his throat with one hand, raising the shattered bottle by its neck, knifewise over her head, with the other.

He managed to get a hand in between them, and pushed, and tore at her shirt, got a handful of tit and squeezed hard.

When he felt the end of the broken bottle puncture his back and rake his ribs, he finally realized what was what, what was going to happen.

She's going to kill you, Charly.

He took a deep breath and pushed the woman with both hands, with all his strength –

And though she had a positional advantage, she was also off balance, with one arm over his shoulder.

So, pushing, he rolled her onto her back and flattened himself over her. He grabbed her arm, the hand around the neck of the broken bottle, and slammed it hard against the floor. The glass went spinning away in a spray of blood.

He scrambled, covered her body with his, all his weight on her, his wrist under her chin, hard into her throat.

She started scratching. He watched stunned as strings of flesh came off his face, off the backs of his hands.

He slapped her twice across the face. That wasn't enough. She started snapping her teeth, spitting at him, screaming like an animal!

He hit her again.

She looked at him as if she wanted more.

He socked her hard across the chin. Crack of teeth, she was stunned, slackjawed. Her eyes rolled in her head.

Mary Mullen was in fact a very strong woman. But not strong enough. She'd underestimated Charly.

When her eyes found him again he hit her once more, splitting her bottom lip.

Her eyes closed. Something left her. He could feel it in her stomach.

"Wake up Mary!"   He slapped her, put his face down to hers and said in her ear, "Wake up!"

He bit her ear lobe. Her ear was full of sweat. Blood in her hair.

"WAKE UP!"

She coughed suddenly, catching her breath. He turned her over. She coughed up blood, spit out a tooth. She was panting, throbbing under him, between his legs.

"Damnit Mary! What... *Why!?* I'd *kill* you... If I could... But Mary... It's nothing. I can't. I won't... I wanted Yoshi. And you wrecked everything –"

"I didn't," she said.

"You did!"

"I..."

"The finger is mine, Mary. I *gave* you the diamond... Why'd you... You!... You have the diamond, what –"

"Fuck you Charly, you –"

She was coming back.

A fistful of hair, he smacked her head against the floor. She moaned. He watched her eyes turn white, rolling around in her head. "I'll let you go," he said. "But to make sure you – ... I'm going to call the people who want the diamond. They're expecting it. Tonight, Mary. And they are the kind of people – *are you listening!?* – ... They will do anything to get it. So... Now's your chance. Take whatever's precious to you and get out, get the hell away –"

"Fuck you Charly. You pussy. You worthless –"

Bam!

She was out. He wanted so badly to say more to her, to make her hear his side of things, but he couldn't. There was nothing to say. Not anymore.

He stood up and looked at what he'd done.

Blood ran into his eyes. He could feel small pieces of glass wiggling around the side of his head, in his hair, in his ear. He went to the bathroom and rinsed his face. He couldn't see clearly. He saw clear enough to see that he looked like hell.

There was blood running from somewhere. He felt it on his shoulder.

Left side of his head was round as a melon. Over his ear there was a wide open crack.

Is that bone?

You can't kill someone with a bottle of whisky.

Can you?

He pressed a wet towel against his head. He pressed hard, gasping, trying to push the melon back in.

The pain was significant. His cheek, eye to chin, four lines of blood where the skin was torn away, burned, and his eye was swelling closed. He could barely move his shoulder, or open his left hand.

With Chuchu's switchblade, he cut a bath towel into strips. These he tied around his chest and back, trying to stanch the blood running from a hole behind his shoulder. Maybe it worked. Maybe it didn't.

He tied a strip around his hand.

In the fridge he found some leftover spinach soufflé. He tried it. He zapped it in the microwave. He poured ketchup and mustard over it, sprinkled it with shredded parmesan. Much better.

He had a cigarette. He studied the ceiling. It was very white and clean. He studied the dishes piled in the sink.

How can people live like this?

Mullen moaned on the floor at the end of the hall.

Something has happened, he thought. We did something, she and I – and now we're connected.

Is it the finger?

It was coming this close to killing. It was a coolness of spirit he'd never known. A kind of automation of the body, a kind of transcendence in the act of fighting. It was a state of mind, like a carapace, from which he could kill. He knew it, he felt it.

He pressed a hand against his chest, feeling the red leather case in his pocket. He stepped over Mullen's body and began to open the front door. She was blocking his way. He crouched and pulled, sliding the body along the parquet.

"Take the diamond and get as far from here as you can."

He stepped outside and quietly closed the door. He lit a cigarette. Mary's little friend Ping was nowhere to be found. And the room in the house across the way was bright and quiet. No sign of life.

Off Van Ness he pulled into a Western Credit Union. He wired ten thousand dollars to a man in Guaymas, Mexico, along with this note:

"Tome Licia de vacaciones por duo meses. Estoy pospuesto. Te llamare cuando pueda. -CB"

He drove out to the beach. It was getting dark. Maybe there'd be a sunset. Under the heavy black clouds, on the horizon at the edge of the storm, a thin line of orange light. But in the end there was no sunset. It was day and then it was night.

23

Boom and shush of the ocean in the darkness. Down the beach tatters of surf froth appeared and disappeared, ghostly white, waving in the cold wind.

Just past midnight. He jumped the gate at Posner's place, took the stairs two at a time. It was raining hard. With the gale off the ocean, anyone inside probably didn't hear a thing. He took his time with the lock, snipping the chain. Light touch. Drive, cook, open a door without making a sound. "We all have our little talents."

As it turned out, noise wasn't an issue. Bernie and Marie-Laure in bed – what a racket! And at this time of night, at your age! He'd give himself a coronary.

He stood at the bedroom door and watched. On a bedside table, a reading lamp was on. Posner's glasses, *The New York Times*.

Over the bed, two large rectangular windows, clean sheets of darkness, rivulets of bubbling water running down. He noticed himself in there, his dim reflection. The intruder in the door.

Marie-Laure was on top, her big white back to him. Flopping around, all antics. But then she tucked her curly head, eyes on Bernie's bony feet, and, under her arm, she noticed him. But she didn't stop. She frowned, puzzled, pounding her man. She sat up and looked over her shoulder directly at him.

It took a moment. Then it dawned on Marie-Laure that something wasn't right – there's a man in the door watching her – and she quickly slid off Posner, swung around and pulled the sheet uselessly up to her neck.

"What?" Posner said. His face was bright red, greased with sweat. "What?" he repeated, reaching for her.

The man was oblivious. He got on his knees and began pushing Marie-Laure into position. She said something, whispering.

"What's that?"

Posner caught on.

He turned, looked.

"What the fuck!"

He jumped from the bed, his suddenly flaccid dick swinging in the air beneath his round pot belly. He was mumbling. He sat on the edge of the bed, his back to Charly, quick glances over his shoulder, as he pulled on some pants. Then he stood up, stepped on and over the bed, and roared, pointing, "What *the fuck* you think YOU ARE DOING!?"

He was coming quickly. Agile for a man his age.

Charly raised the Browning and fired twice.

Posner stepped back and dropped like a board on the bed, arms out. Two black holes in his chest, one above the other, twin fountains of blood bubbling up.

He was lucky he didn't hit Marie-Laure. The bullets passed straight through Posner, stopping in the books and magazines in the headboard beneath the window. He had no intention of killing the woman.

Then again, up to a few hours ago, he'd never thought he could kill anyone.

Marie-Laure had fallen from the bed. She was huddled up on the floor, shivering, whimpering.

Blood speckled the bed, the white sheet, the woman. He could see it in her curly blond hair.

She stood, grabbed the sheet, tugged sobbing against Posner's weight, let go and clutched a pillow to her torso. She stood trembling, the two windows at her left shoulder.

Charly remained in the doorframe. "Remember me?"

"What?"

"Remember me!?"

After a moment: "Yes."

Charly didn't know what to say.

"You seem like a nice girl. A smart girl."

"I am nice," she whispered. "And smart... Please!"

"I won't hurt you."

The boom of the surf filled the night, rain coming down hard on the roof, pouring, tearing at the roof, crushing the house.

He took a step forward. He stood over the body of Bernie Posner. Charly could see clearly out of only one eye, but it appeared the man he'd just shot was not getting up any time soon. "He forced my hand."

"What?"

"Forced my hand. He put me into a position, Marie-Laure. I didn't have a choice."

"You killed him! Charly, you killed him!"

"I didn't want to. I can't explain... Someday I'll pay for it."

He felt terribly clear headed. There was a simple solution to everything. The gun was warm, solid in his grip. It felt good there.

"But – Marie-Laure."

He wasn't six steps from her. She had sat down, wrapped her arms around the pillow, around her knees.

He thought about the windows. Who's out there, in the darkness?

"I'm leaving," he said. "You will never see me again. I will never see you again... You are going to forget about what's happened here. About what happened yesterday."

The woman whimpered. Eyes up, glimmer of hope in her glassy eyes –

Charly raised the gun. Half-way, to four o'clock.

The woman was shaking so hard he thought she might have a heart attack. He didn't want that.

He lowered the gun.

"You will say that a man in a mask came in, caught you in the middle of intercourse, said something to Posner, who then got up. As he was leaving the room, the intruder shot him. Then he left. Without a word. That's what happened."

"What?" Barely a gasp of air.

"Are you listening, Marie-Laure?"

"Yes, yes!"

"Good! Cuz if you fuck this up then it's curtains for you –"

"What?"

"Curtains! Curtains! How do you say curtains in French?"

"Curtains?"

"Curtains!"

"What? I don't know! Rideaux. But –"

"Then it's rideaux for you."

"But I don't understand."

He pointed the gun between her eyes. She pissed loudly all over the floor and cried, her small face balling up.

"Remember, Marie-Laure. Rideaux means dead. Tell them the killer said that. Rideaux means dead. Repeat after me. Rideaux means dead."

He had just opened the door when something occurred to him. He closed the door, turned and went back to the bedroom. Marie-Laure was still on the floor, sobbing.

"I lied," he said.

"Wha!"

"I'll sleep here tonight."

He took the body of Posner by the feet and dragged it into the living room. He covered it with a hand-knit blanket he pulled off the couch.

In the bedroom he flipped the mattress, sat down on the end of the bed, kicked off his shoes, climbed out of his pants, took off his shirt.

"Where's the shower?"

Marie-Laure stared at him, thumb in her mouth, eyes like golf balls.

"Marie-Laure! The shower!"

The woman sucked her thumb. He reached down and shook her gently.

He had the gun in his right hand. With his left he reached under her arm, pulled her up to her feet, pushed her from the room. They found the bathroom together. He sat her down between the toilet and tub. He took a shower.

It was an expensive tub and shower. Magnificent – all glass and brown stone and silver. He balanced the gun on a ledge cut into the wall and turned the faucet. Water sprayed at him from every direction. It was like standing under a waterfall. Streams of blood ran down his arms, his body, his bony legs, twirling down the drain.

He took a nice long shower.

He brushed his teeth with an electric toothbrush he found near the sink. The melon in the side of his head had grown, his eye swollen closed. It didn't seem to be bleeding any more. But the crack in his head, over his ear, wouldn't dry up. Yellow pus oozed out, filling the wound every time he wiped it away. The scratches down his cheek, four bright red lines, in comparison to everything else looked pretty good.

His hand throbbed, the gash in the palm drying into a thick scab.

"I'm turning into a monster."

Behind the mirror he found bottles of ibuprofen and Viagra. He tipped back his head and swallowed a dozen ibuprofen, washing them down with water from the tap.

He poked Marie-Laure with a toe. She bobbed gently back and forth like a buoy. He lifted her up, pushed her back into the bedroom and onto the bed, where she fell on her stomach.

"I won't hurt you," he said. "I won't even tie you up. I just wanna sleep. Just a few hours."

He put the gun beneath one pillow and lay down next to her, first on his back, and then on his side, facing her.

She wasn't moving. She began to shiver.

He stood up and looked around. Sheets on the floor, wet and bloody. He brought them to the bathroom and threw them in the tub.

He opened a closet, took down a heavy wool blanket. He threw it over the woman. He climbed back into bed.

He was exhausted but he couldn't sleep.

He was hungry, actually. His stomach started growling.

He thought of asking Marie-Laure to fix him something, but then decided not to. She'd been through a lot. He'd let her sleep.

He stood up. There was a digital clock on a shelf. He set the alarm for four. Hardly three hours away.

Posner's wrist watch was on a cabinet. He looked at it for a minute. He set its alarm for ten after four.

"You wear a watch, Marie-Laure?"

The woman didn't respond. She appeared to be sleeping.

"If I miss this plane..."

His reflection stared at him in the window. Its head was twisted out of shape, too big for its body.

He returned to the bed. He climbed under the blanket and pulled it up to his chin. He turned on his side, toward Marie-Laure. He looked at the back of her head, at her tight blond curls. He wanted to press his face into them, wanted to reach and touch her back.

He didn't. Who knows what she'd do.

The room smelled truly awful. Piss, blood, a strange sweetness, gun powder.

Be nice, Jaime said, *to do something civil for once.*

Do something civil.

He thought of Posner, rotting in the other room.

He thought of Mary Mullen. She was probably drunk, taking a bath, reminiscing about her days as a champion swimmer. Maybe she was in the hospital.

How does a guy like Bernie Posner get a girl like Marie-Laure?

Did Yoshi love Mary? Was Conway right – was she using me?

Think, Charly. If Conway didn't kill her, then who did?

What was his word? *You're her* purge, *Charly.*

My little purge. My...

Did Yoshi love Mary?

To answer this question, Charly got out of bed and took from inside his coat the red case. He brought this back to bed and opened it.

There it was: Yoshi's crooked finger.

He stroked it. He picked it up and smelled it, inhaling deeply its queer odor.

It did smell funny. There was more to it than just Yoshi.

What is that?

He put the tip of the finger in his mouth. It didn't taste like much. It certainly didn't taste like Yoshi. Maybe it had been on its own for too long, lost its Yoshi-ness.

I bet Mullen washed it. That's it. Or –

Charly's speculations were interrupted as Marie-Laure began to turn, to face him. Quickly he put away the finger, tucking the case beneath his pillow, near the gun.

"What was that?" she asked.

"You don't want to know. Go back to sleep."

He felt her staring at him. He reached over her head and turned out the light.

In the darkness he was sure that Marie-Laure was still staring at him. He could feel it, could hear it in her breathing.

No matter what, he decided, he could not let her see Yoshi's crooked finger. Above all else!

He pressed his swollen head deeper, harder into the pillow, until he could feel both the gun and the finger's little case in the back of his head.

And then it was like he was sinking into the bed, like the bed, the floor, the house, the earth far below, everything was coming up around him, folding over his broken body.

24

He woke quickly at the sound of the alarm. Marie-Laure was gone.

He looked in the bathroom, in the kitchen, in the closet. The woman was nowhere to be found.

The house was quiet. The wind was blowing hard but it sounded like the rain had stopped.

Terrified for an instant, he ran back to the bedroom and checked under the pillow. The gun and the finger were where he'd left them.

A few minutes later he was in the Mercedes, on his way to the airport. The highway was empty. At twenty to five he pulled into SFO long-term parking.

He left the Browning in the glove box. He locked the car and paid for two weeks.

Before leaving the garage he dropped Chuchu's switch-blade into a trashcan.

He didn't expect boarding the airplane to be that easy. More specifically, he didn't expect to get very far in the airport at all. There was every reason to believe that the consequences for everything he'd done in the last two days, for all of the crimes he'd just committed, would now become clear and present.

"My prints are everywhere!" he said, tempting fate.

The girl at the counter checked his ID four times, so smashed up was his face.

"May I ask what happened, Mr. Bingswanger?"

"It's been a long week."

"But your head?"

"I got bottled."

"Bottled?"

"Hit in the head with a bottle."

"Ooo. Ouch."

"Ouch is right. It was –"

"A bottle of what?"

The girl was busy typing, her hands racing like crabs over the keyboard, talking with her eyes on a screen Charly couldn't see.

"I was about to tell you."

"Oh."

Then she looked him in the eye. She was a petite dirty blond with pouting pink lips, clear blue eyes. He'd seen a million cheerleaders like her before. They're practically a crop in California.

"It was something called Black Grouse. It's scotch, I think."

"Oh I love Black Grouse!"

"Yes. It's nice, isn't it."

"And someone hit you?"

"That's what happened."

"Must have been some fight, Mr. Bingswanger."

"Some fight. Some woman."

"A *woman* did that to you?"

" ... "

"Maybe it's not a good idea to fly today, Mr. Bingswanger. I could check..."

He leaned over the counter, bringing his monstrous mug up to hers. She didn't move.

"Maybe it's not a good idea to be giving me advice just now," he said, peering with his one eye down at her name tag – "Kirsty."

Then it was all business.

"Right, Mr. Bingswanger. And will you be checking any bags?"

"No."

Does security stop you if you have a hundred grand in your luggage? Does security stop you if you have severed body parts on your person? Apparently not. Neither one, nor the other.

He was at the gate early. He had a scalding hot cup of Dunkin' Donuts coffee. He read the newspaper, looking for people he knew. He napped for half an hour.

From his luggage he pulled out *The Mysterious Rider*. He finished it. He set it down on the seat next to him and thought about it. The girl got the boy she loved in the end. And the villain, Buster Jack, got his comeuppance.

Nothing like that happens in the real world.

He went to the bathroom and brushed his teeth. He smiled at his reflection. A quarter of his head was puffed up like a melon. His left eye was swollen tightly shut. His right eye was bloodshot and watery. His gums were bleeding.

"You're the Elephant Man."

As he was boarding the plane, he noticed something in the corner of his good eye. A short figure in dark glasses. But when he turned to look, there was nobody there. He stepped out of line to look around.

The boarding area was practically empty. There was a janitor emptying trash. A kid playing his Nintendo, his mother asleep with her head thrown back, mouth agape. Across the way, passengers were boarding a plane for Santiago, Chile.

Then he got on the plane. He didn't expect to – he was still waiting for them to catch up, come on the plane and drag him away. "You're coming with us, Charly." But they didn't. Nothing happened. The airline representative checked his boarding pass, gave him a glance and a good morning, and down the ramp he went, behind two men in business suits.

His seat in first class was larger than he expected it to be. It was like a bed. He lowered it, raised it, played with the buttons. The next seat over was empty.

The stewardess was named Julie. He caught himself staring at her face, her ears. She smiled. He apologized, realizing how strange it must appear to her, this monster watching her so closely.

"Don't worry, Mr. Bingswanger. I'll handle things. You rest now."

She fixed his pillow behind his head. She smelled faintly of lilacs. She was so close to him, he felt heat radiating from her breasts.

Julie poured him a glass of champagne. When he finished that he had another. His eyes were heavy. Distantly he heard the plane rumble, felt his seat rock gently beneath him. The captain, who sounded southern, was introducing himself, commenting on currents, flight time, weather. Something crackled in his ears. Heavy eyes.

That's Julie. Those are her lips. Julie's smile. Julie's halo.

He fell into a deep sleep.

A warm ray of sunshine woke him. They were descending into Haneda Airport.

Now it will come, he thought. They'll meet me at the gate.

Charly followed a group of businessmen to customs, and he passed through along with them without a problem. A few minutes later he was outside, standing in a warm breeze, in Japan.

It was early in the morning. The sun was out!

He'd almost forgotten what it looked like, felt like. He thought he'd never see the sun again.

At the Tokyo Hilton, he checked into something called "The King Executive." It cost five hundred dollars a night. He said he would stay for five nights.

"Very good Mr. Bingswanger," said the young Japanese man behind the counter. He wore a suit and tie. He looked quite sharp in his suit, well groomed.

Charly admired that. That was another thing he thought he'd never see again – a man in a perfectly fitted suit.

The room was high up, with windows on two sides of the building. Tokyo was vast, a mindblowing jigsaw puzzle of glass and steel lines, curves, points like soldered nodes in countless overlapping circuits all the way to the horizon.

He couldn't hear anything. He touched the glass. It was very thick.

He examined the room. The bed was wide and the mattress firm. The closet was spacious. The shower was sort of like Posner's, only black – tile and glass and silver fixtures. The refrigerator was stocked with liquor, sake, wine, water, juice. In a cupboard he found a bottle of Johnnie Walker. He poured himself two fingers and sipped it slowly. He turned on the television. Almost every station was in Japanese. Then he found CNN, the BBC, baseball.

He took a long shower. After that he had another drink and a cigarette. He carefully lay down on the enormous bed. In a few minutes he fell asleep. When he woke, night had fallen.

He was going through his meager belongings, considering the potential of nearly a hundred thousand dollars, and considering ordering a steak, when there was a knock on the door.

A young Japanese woman stood in the hall. Her hair was straight, shoulder length, a shimmering black. Her face as expressionless. She wore a blue blouse with a high collar and a black skirt.

"Yes?"

"Will you be needing anything, Mr. Bingswanger?"

"No. Thank you."

"Are you sure, Mr. Bingswanger? Is there nothing we can service you with?"

"Service me with?"

The woman's English was accented but otherwise spoken clearly and with confidence. The syntax was off, puzzling to Charly.

But it didn't matter. He was thinking of various cars he'd worked on and driven. How many miles he'd done alone in a car in the American west.

"We can service you, Mr. Bingswanger, for any of your needs."

She bowed her head slightly at this, her eyes down at his navel. Her black hair was parted exactly in the middle of her head.

Then Charly caught on.

"Thank you, Miss –"

"Miss Kono."

A card materialized in her slender hand. He took it. There was her name and a phone number.

"Kono. Thank you. Good. For now all I want is some rest." He looked at the card, front and back. "I was in an accident, see."

"Indeed. Shall I send a nurse?"

"A nurse?"

"Yes, a nurse. Would you like a nurse?"

"... I'll call if I need a nurse."

"Certainly, Mr. Bingswanger."

She bowed. He closed the door.

He watched the lights of the city. He studied a building across the way, what looked like offices, and, higher up, apartments. Tiny people going about their daily lives, working, living.

It was like a machine, a living organism, the building across the way. Or was it something Kono had said?

"Service you..."

He sat down, put his feet up, watched TV, the news first, then baseball, then a fishing program, and then some action movie that was dubbed in Japanese. He recognized a few of the actors. He liked the car chases.

He fell asleep.

He woke several hours later. It must have been early in the morning. His head was sore. In the bathroom he saw that the swelling was going down. His good eye was clearing up.

Just a few more days, he thought. We'll be back to normal.

He ordered a steak, fries, salad, a bottle of Chianti. The food arrived fifteen minutes later. He took his dinner to the desk by the window and watched the sky in the east very gradually turn to steel, gathering light.

It was a Thursday afternoon when he went outside for the first time since arriving. A wind was blowing, and clouds had come over, but it wasn't raining, and it wasn't as cold as it was in California.

At a nearby Italian style cafe he sat in a wicker chair and had a cappuccino. Occasionally, young Japanese men and women would glance at him – his head was still noticeably in a bad way – but for the most part he felt anonymous.

The Japanese dressed very well. He liked that. He'd need to work on his wardrobe.

It was busy, there were so many people around. He'd forgotten what large groups of people moving around a city looked like. Everything was so hectic but still, in a removed and abstract way, orderly. Finally, he thought, feeling himself disintegrate into the sounds and sight of all these people, I might rest in peace.

He felt that he might disappear in Japan. He might check into a hotel, like the Hilton, hide away for two weeks, and come out only when he felt completely healed. Then he would change his name. Then he would rent an apartment in a small town up north and live a spartan life off the money he'd stolen.

He could find a job as a fisherman, on the docks. Let his mustache grow out.

All I need now, he thought, finishing his coffee, is some music. That would make my Tokyo holiday perfect.

Later that day, walking around Yurakucho, he saw something familiar. There was a poster, and in it a picture of a woman.

Imagine that, he thought.

There was Sandra Bizarro, standing before her piano, smiling ear to ear, her strong arms over her chest.

She was performing the Prokofiev second piano concerto with a local orchestra. The first show was Friday night at a nearby conservatory.

He examined the picture closely, not believing his eyes. No. It was the same woman, his Sandra Bizarro. He'd kissed those smiling lips, felt those same hands on his body.

Imagine that!

He immediately bought a ticket. Then he bought himself a suit, tie, and shoes.

That night, feeling rejuvenated and free and reckless, he had an expensive dinner of sushi moriawase take and beef sukiyaki and got tipsy on sake and, later, scotch. He flirted with some Japanese women at the bar. They were amused by Charly, perhaps by some of the ridiculous things he was saying. "And this," he said, pressing a finger against the long wound over his ear, "I got down on the docks last week, when this Malay pirate..."

In the end, though, he just frightened them.

It wasn't too late when he got back, so he immediately called Kono.

"Mr. Bingswanger. Thank you for calling."

"Call me Charly, Kono. Nobody calls me *mister*. Listen, I think you can help me. You wouldn't know anyone with –"

He was about to say "a crooked finger" when he changed his mind. There was only one crooked finger for him and that was Yoshi's. Still, he didn't feel like being with just any woman.

"Mr. Bingswanger? Charly?"

"With something different, Kono."

"Different?"

"With something wrong."

"Something wrong, Charly?"

"With something unusual about her body."

"Unusual?"

"Like ... A harelip."

"*Hair, lip*? What's that?"

"When the lip is like a hare's. Like a rabbit."

"Oh, of course, Charly. I know exactly what you mean. I think I can –"

"No, Kono. I don't want someone with a harelip."

"No harelip then?"

"No. With something else. Something more subtle, something hidden."

"We have someone with very big ears."

"Subtle, Kono. No. I don't like big ears."

"Enormous breasts, then."

"What do you take me for? *Subtle*. Discreet."

"Of course. A transvestite? She's *very* subtle."

"No."

"How about an amputee?"

"What kind?"

"How's one small breast?"

"No."

"One leg?"

"A pegleg!"

"Okay – how's one eye?"

"Hmm. She wear a patch?"

"Absolutely."

"Great."

The one-eyed girl arrived thirty minutes later. She had on a black patch. Her name was Ikumi. She was very quiet. Maybe she didn't speak English. While fucking her, he asked if he could take off the patch and see her bad eye. Ikumi shrugged and flung off the patch with a twist of her wrist.

The lids were tightly sealed, fused together years ago. She must have been a kid when something awful happened, an accident.

The socket was sunk in – ghastly, Charly thought. Skeletal, a spoon of gray flesh filling the hole.

He caressed her breast and licked the skin over her missing eye. Ikumi liked that.

He was deep inside her, Ikumi's heels high over her head, when something exploded outside. The room filled with colorful light. Fireworks, fireworks over the bay!

He realized then that it was a new year. And when he started to come, Ikumi climbed out from under him, grabbed his cock and pointed it at her face, at her missing eye. So Charly got to watch fireworks as he shot off in the hole of Ikumi's missing eye.

That was a first.

Nevertheless, for a different kind of woman, the hollow socket was fun only for a while. It was grotesque, actually. Charly decided he wanted something else.

The next day he called Ms. Kono.

"You didn't like Ikumi and her eye patch then?"

"Ikumi was sweet. Her bad eye was... Oh, clever, I guess. But I want something else. Something more subtle, more secret. Not so – violent."

"Okay. I'll see what I can do."

That evening a young woman named Sumi came to his door. She was much more friendly than Ikumi had been. She was excited to be with an American. Before undressing, she wanted to know all about Charly, about California and his job and his life. She never asked him about his injuries. He didn't say anything about them. Then she started on herself: where she grew up, what she studied in school, why she was a prostitute, and so on. Finally he interrupted her: "Take off your clothes."

She rubbed her hands together and smiled.

He stood at the window and watched Sumi undress. She had a soft, healthy body. It was impossible to tell how old she was. He'd guess twenty-eight, but she could have been pushing forty. It's hard to tell with some women.

Only in black panties, she climbed under the sheet.

Fucking her, Sumi was so cheerful!

There must be something wrong with her, he thought as she giggled in his ear. He'd never been with such a happy whore.

After ten minutes of fun and games he decided to be rough with her. Not to hurt her, but to maybe surprise her out of her cheerfulness. So he pushed her around, straightened her out, folded her up, really threw his weight into it. With each attack, however, Sumi managed, twisting and squirming, to turn around, bouncing right back up, all smiles. His play at aggression was ineffective.

It was like trying to grab hold of a greased pig.

Nearly an hour passed in this manner. Poor Charly was getting tired. And he was sore. He'd never got so much exercise fucking a whore.

"So what is it!?" he said, collapsing on his back, exasperated by Sumi's endurance.

"What is what?" the girl said, giggling, caressing his chest, pulling on his cock.

"What's wrong with you!?"

"Wrong?"

"There has to be something wrong, Sumi. Didn't Kono tell you I wanted someone with…"

"Kono told me."

He peeled the happy whore's hands off his body and got up.

Sumi was seated on the bed, her knees up, her legs folded beneath her. She's pretty enough, he thought. Soft and with a smooth round tummy. She'd hardly broken a sweat.

"So?"

"So what?" Sumi said.

"Sumi! You are…"

Charly was nearly moved to tears by the woman's evasiveness.

"You speak English, no!" he shouted. He spoke slowly, as if throwing each word at her. "We're speaking English here. Listen to me! I asked Kono for a woman with something wrong with her body. I like strange things about bodies. And from what I can tell, *Sumi*, there is nothing wrong with you except for the fact that you are so goddamn cheerful. And strong."

Sumi smiled and covered her mouth and blushed.

"Charly," she said. "You're wrong." Her tone changed. "I am not cheerful. The truth is, Charly, I am very sad inside. But I have learned…"

She looked directly at him, leaning forward, reaching out for him, her dark eyes drawing him in, hypnotic. This too was something none of the whores he'd been with had ever done. Talk so much, said things like "I am sad inside."

"You have learned?" he said. He got up and poured himself a drink. His erection was disappearing with all this talk. Still, there was a mystery here, a different kind of pursuit.

Maybe that was it – Sumi was impossible to dominate. She couldn't even act beaten.

"You've learned?"

"It's not important," she said. Her voice was different. It had lost its ring, its girlishness. Was that candor?

Charly drank his scotch and waited. He watched the girl closely.

"It's here," she said.

Is that defeat?

She pulled in her belly. She looked down at herself.

He couldn't see anything.

She pointed. She pressed her index finger against the top of her hip, just above a corner of her hairy cunt.

He blinked several times, not believing his eyes. But there it was.

He stepped forward, set down his drink, kneeled on the bed. Gently he pushed her down.

Sumi lay back and let him look.

It was skin, a button of reddish brown skin, an appendage protruding from the top of the inside of Sumi's thigh.

Amazing! Charly thought. Why didn't I see this?

You weren't looking.

He touched it. He wiggled it.

"Does it hurt?" he asked.

"Of course not," she said. "It's just a button of skin."

"What is it?"

"I don't know. I've always had it."

"What did the doctor say?"

"Leave it."

She touched it along with Charly, guiding his finger.

Charly kissed it, pulled it with his lips. It was like a nipple.

"It's like another nipple," he said.

She smiled at him, her face radiant in the dimness of the room.

"Sort of. Some men hate it. It really frightens them, Charly. If I can, I try to hide it."

"Why? It doesn't frighten me."

"It's my favorite part," she said.

Charly caught his breath.

It's my favorite part...

"Can I get you a drink, Sumi," he said. He stood up, suddenly excited. "I'd like to show you something."

My favorite part.

"I can't drink when I'm working. Maybe a little."

He poured her a scotch and held it out. It splashed over her hand. He opened the room safe and took out the red case. He lay down next to her.

"Now you can't tell anyone about this."

"What is it?" Sumi whispered, pulling herself up close to him, her hand on his chest.

He opened the red case. There was Yoshi's crooked finger.

Sumi transformed immediately, her smile replaced by a look of confusion, and then shock, and then horror.

She pulled away.

"Charly?"

"Sumi. It's okay –"

"That's someone's finger!"

"Yes, it is. But –"

"Charly, that's horrible!"

"But Sumi –"

The girl was quickly dressing, watching Charly carefully. He saw in her eyes that there was nothing he could do to stop her.

"Sumi, please."

"Don't ever ask for me again," she said. "Don't you dare –"

Dressed, Sumi ran to the door.

"It's not just a finger, Sumi."

She said something quickly in Japanese. Then, "I should –"

She was facing away from him, opening and closing the door, her shoes hooked on her fingers in her free hand. He didn't catch her last words.

She closed the door without a sound.

Charly was stunned. What had just happened?

He hadn't paid Sumi.

He opened the door and looked into the hall. Clean, bright, quiet, empty.

He closed the door. He put the finger away.

The concert was in ninety minutes. He'd be going alone, after all. He took a shower and put on his new suit.

25

But Sumi's sudden exit, her rejection of the finger, was only the beginning. The night did not improve.

Waiting for his taxi, it started to rain. In a minute water was bouncing off the street.

The taxi arrived. He saw the driver flap his hand at him in the darkness of the cab. He ran out to the car. His new shoes were soaked through.

There was traffic. The cabbie, a small old man with a thick white mustache, didn't speak a word of English. This didn't stop him from going on about the traffic, the weather, baseball and who knows what else, all in Japanese, the wet city gliding by.

Sumi's exit had left him feeling sick. He'd made a mistake in showing her the crooked finger.

He caught himself replaying the scene in his head, looking for details, an element to the event that he hadn't, at the time, noticed. Did she have earrings on? What kind of fragrance was she wearing? Were her armpits rough or smooth? What color was the purse she came in with?

He began to say something to the cabbie, to try and silence the man. Then he didn't care. Nothing he said would do anything. The man was unstoppable.

They made it to the conservatory at the top of the hour. The theater wasn't far from the entrance. It was hardly full. He took a seat on the right side, near the middle.

The first piece on the program was Claude Debussy's *La Mer*. Charly had only heard recordings before. The performance impressed him for the moment, but if you asked him afterward he wouldn't have had anything to say. Sumi filled his thoughts.

"I have learned..."

Sandra Bizarro was next. He waited. Clitter-clatter of the audience, a door opening and closing, click of heels, woman hurrying down the aisle to her seat. Silence came over the theater. He imagined Sandra waiting somewhere, listening for the silence to reach maximum depth. He closed his eyes and listened. *I have learned...* Still nothing. He'd stand and go. It couldn't be the same Sandra Bizarro, regardless of the photo in the poster he'd seen. There had to be a mistake. He'd misread the name, he was imagining things. He opened his eyes and studied the program, reading the name of the soloist letter by letter.

A panel swung back, left side of the stage, and Sandra Bizarro strode out in an armless red and black dress, neck to heels, her hair pulled back in a bun. She bowed once to the pitter-patter of welcoming applause. She looked good.

He leaned forward, resting his elbows on the empty seat before him, sitting up. He became aware, then, of how much taller he was than many in the audience.

Would she see him?

He didn't want to be seen.

In the moment before she turned and took her place at the piano, Bizarro looked over the hall, left to right, and he thought he recognized the smallest of turns in her lips, in the corner of her mouth, a smirk that said, "So that's all, that's it. That's what you came to tell me. I have work to do."

It pleased him to think that he was the only one in the theater who knew that about the woman on the stage. Then he began to think about other things he and only he knew of Sandra Bizarro, and he started to feel better.

Then it was Sergei Prokofiev's turn.

Sometime during the third movement, following a fierce growl in the horns, something shifted in Charly's vision, in the corner of his eye. It was his bad eye, but the swelling had reduced enough in the last day to allow for some use.

Someone was watching him.

Slowly he turned to his left. Sure enough – someone was watching him. It was a small, bald man in glasses. He was in Charly's row, but at a distance, near the left side of the room.

The lenses of the glasses were dark green, transparent enough, however, to reveal the stranger's eyes. The wall-eye, fish-eye, the wandering eye was impossible to miss.

Charly stared.

The man looked away.

He was seeing things, it could only be.

Sandra, in an intricate passage, her eyes closed, leaned forward, an overhead light gleaming off her sweaty forehead.

Charly looked back at the stranger. The man was whispering something to a woman seated next to him. They were clearly, now, just another Japanese couple.

Then both of them, the man and the woman, turned to look at Charly, the woman leaning forward. It was just a glance. The woman whispered something to the man. They both continued to watch Charly – even, he noticed, when he wasn't watching them.

For an encore, Sandra played the slow movement from a Schubert sonata, a piece Charly had heard her play many times before. He'd even sat with her at the piano while she practiced it.

Perhaps he was listening too intently. He felt himself starting to cry and he let the tears run from the corners of his eyes, covering his cheeks.

Then there was more applause, bows by the soloist and conductor. Shaking of hands. A girl in an enormous white dress brought a bouquet of yellow and red flowers up to the stage, reaching up, extending her arm from the shadows. Sandra Bizarro took the flowers and mouthed "Thank you" and bowed, and then turned and marched off stage.

There was an intermission. After that the orchestra played one of the Beethoven symphonies, Charly couldn't remember which. He wasn't listening. He was thinking about Sandra, about Yoshi, about Sumi, about the stranger who had been watching him.

He'd thought his injuries had more or less healed, thought the gash in his head was far less obvious than it had been when he first arrived in Tokyo.

In the bathroom he checked his head, his wound.

It looked good! It was healing. You'd need to hold him down to see that anything was wrong.

Then a young man standing beside him, washing his hands, said in English, "What happened?"

"What do you mean, what happened?"

"To your head. You were in a fight."

They were talking through the mirror.

"I was attacked. I'm feeling much better."

The young man smiled, dried his hands, left.

What had the stranger been looking at? Could he see me from that far away?

Sandra was in the lobby, in the heart of a crowd. She was taller than all of the other women. It sounded like she was speaking Japanese. He couldn't tell. He didn't get that close. He wanted to say something, to take her out, to get the watch she'd stolen from him back.

In the end he didn't do anything. He turned and left.

On the ride back to the hotel he concluded it was the right thing to do – to walk away, to not try and recover what was lost.

What is done is done.

Anyway, he probably would have frightened her. He didn't want to do that.

The phone in his room was ringing when he entered. It was Ms. Kono.

"Hello, Charly. Sumi told me that you have a finger in a box."

"She said what?"

"A finger in a box, is what she said. Do you know, Charly, that the transportation of body parts without the proper certification is *illegal* in Japan."

"I don't know what you're talking about."

"When you said *different*, Charly, *with something wrong*, I trusted you. You seemed like the kind of man I could trust. And I meet all sorts. *I* am a good judge of character. But now I'm thinking otherwise. Now I'm thinking you must be sick. A very sick man."

"Listen, Kono. Sumi's exaggerating. She misunderstood."

"So you don't have a finger in a box? Is that what you are saying?"

"Exactly. I don't know what you – what Sumi said – what any of this is about."

"She was very excited, Charly."

"We had an argument."

"An argument?"

"Yes, it was –"

"Do you often argue with prostitutes, Charly?"

What's with all the questions?

"Yes," Charly said. "In fact, I like arguing with prostitutes, Miss Kono. I like fucking them and then debating –"

"I won't listen to any more of this! Explain it to the police, Charly. Argue with them."

"The police."

"They will be there any minute now. I called them. Sumi was not exaggerating. You have someone's finger. You should be questioned. The victim must be identified. There will be an investigation. You *will*..."

Billions of lights filled the cold glass, Tokyo glimmering in the rain all the way to the horizon. The woman in the phone went on and on. He'd thought only American women could talk like that. So angry and with so much to say. Talk and talk and talk and talk. In the end, do words matter that much?

Charly thought he heard the ocean, far away. He thought of the California coast, of the night he spent there in his car. How long ago was that?

He set the phone down on the bed and packed his things. He didn't have much to carry. His duffel bag, Posner's blue carry-on, the crooked finger's little red case. He went out wearing the suit he'd come in in. The man at the front desk, typing at his console, hardly noticed him.

Outside, he lowered his head and walked quickly through the rain. In eight minutes he was at Seibushinjuku station. He bought a ticket and boarded the next train. A little more than an hour later he got off at a desolate stop called Kuki. At a news stand there he asked the vendor, a woman fortified behind stacks of magazines and papers, for directions to the nearest hotel. She shook her head irritably and pointed at a queue of taxis. Charly walked away.

He didn't want a taxi. He didn't, after a moment's reflection, even want a room. He needed to get away, far out of the city, quickly.

He left the station, walking along a row of brightly lit colorful shops. It was late, nearing midnight, and cold and wet out, but the area was busy. People were out eating, shopping, strolling.

He decided to stop for a few minutes, to watch the goings on, to reflect on the situation.

In a cafe he ordered a coffee and a handful of tiny cookies. They were salty. When he looked closely he saw that the cookies were made out of fish. This both disgusted and intrigued him. He ate the last few slowly, scientifically, nibbling with his front teeth.

He finished the coffee and decided he would need to steal a car. He went looking for the nearest underground parking lot.

Under a black overhang a large man sat on a folding chair playing a bass clarinet, the *Concierto de Aranjuez*. At his back, the blinding, flickering fluorescence of some shop; before and around him, a glass box, sheets of rain.

Charly left him some money.

Then, outside of an arcade and video shop, a vehicle came to a sudden stop at the curb. The driver, a teenage boy, leapt out and ran inside. He left the motor running.

Charly didn't think twice. Almost in one motion – walking around the car, glance into the shop, opening the door – he climbed behind the wheel and pulled quietly away.

Nobody seemed to react. With one eye on the mirror, he carefully watched the entrance of the arcade. Nothing. The driver was still inside. That was good. Buy him a couple minutes. What was he doing – playing games? Leave his car running on the curb to go play a video game?

It's almost the right thing to do, Charly thought at a stoplight, stealing the kid's car.

Three-quarters of a tank. Everything where it's supposed to be. Easy as pie.

He turned up the heat, flipped through the radio. He didn't care what came on. He needed the sound to cover everything else – the women, the diamond, the money, the finger.

Drive, Charly.

After a few aimless minutes, doing his best to avoid the street he'd come from, he found himself on a highway, going north.

Three hours later, when jerks of sleep became unbearable, he pulled off, followed a dark road into the countryside. He pulled into what might have been a park or barn yard, he couldn't tell.

There were tall trees all around. Not much else.

He got out. The rain had stopped. It was very cold, like in the mountains in California.

The air smelled good. Clean, fresh.

He pissed in the gutter.

He listened to the sounds of the night, the woods.

Drops of rain pitter pattering in the canopy, all around him.

He had a cigarette. He got back in the car. He put the seat back and fell asleep.

~ **26** ~

Before sunrise he awoke to a tapping sound. Something dripping. It took him a moment but then he saw in the footwell of the passenger seat a puddle, water dripping from under the glove box.

The car was parked at a tilt, on the shoulder of the road. That shouldn't matter.

It was freezing in the car. His hands were stiff. His back hurt.

He followed the road into a small town. There he purchased gas, paid in cash. Then he returned to the highway and continued north. Along clean, well-maintained highways he went north all day. He stopped around sunset in the mountains, outside Semboku, at a motel in the woods. There was snow on the ground. There were pools of sulfurous steaming water out back.

The room had a futon on the floor, a low bedside table and lamp. That was it. Wearing only shorts, he tip-toed out into the dark, slipped down into the spring. The water was blazing hot. After a minute, immersed to his chin, he exhaled, relaxed.

That night he paid for a massage. After gently inspecting the stab wound in his back, the woman left the room and came back with someone else. A nurse of some sort, Charly guessed. This woman applied an ointment to the wound. She also worked on the palm of his hand, which wasn't healing as quickly as it should. The gash there was yellow and black, gaping like a bloody mouth if he opened his hand fully. She also looked at his head.

His back and shoulder tingled, his hand burned.

The next day, after a small breakfast of rice cakes, oranges, and tea, he went back to the spring. Alone he lay naked in the water, so deep that only his eyes and nostrils emerged.

Dark trees rose beyond the steam at the edge of the pool. Like a prehistoric animal, his eyes climbed incrementally up the towering forms to a gray opening far overhead, the low dark sky.

Spread your wings and –

He heard nothing. He heard the water of the spring bubbling in the murky void beneath him, groaning, something under the ancient rock churning.

In the afternoon, the nurse came to his room to check his injuries. She seemed pleased with her work, which pleased him.

She had an extraordinary touch. He'd never felt fingers like hers on his body before, such delicate work. He thought to himself that she, in touching him, didn't see a body in her hands – it was something else. A plant, maybe. A spiderweb.

He did this for a few days. Soaking in the steaming spring, resting. He ate almost nothing. He slept ten hours a night. He spoke hardly a word. Except for the nurse, he met no one.

Once, wanting company, he brought the crooked finger into the pool with him. He washed and scrubbed it. He carried it around the surface of the pool in the palm of his hand. When he let it go, it sank, swinging back and forth. He followed it down to the gray muddy bottom. It was hot down there. Silent. He watched a tiny cloud of particles slowly rise up and fall around the finger. He pictured it landing on the moon.

The next day he discovered near the lobby a tiny library, an alcove where books in many different languages were shelved. He looked through these quickly and pulled out a paperback. On the cover was a black and white photo of a young woman glancing over her shoulder, fear in her eyes. She wore a shawl. She was in something like a castle. It was an old story, a romance from the nineteenth century. He didn't normally care for such things. He preferred adventure stories.

"But what the hell."

He dropped some change into a little wooden box.

He sat in the common room and had a cup of tea. He turned to page one.

Later, returning to his room, he stopped in the lobby to flip through a stack of brochures. One caught his attention. In it were pictures of a sandy beach, palm trees, smiling men with fishing poles and fish in their hands, smiling girls in bikinis waving.

It was snowing outside.

There was a simple map in the brochure. The place was in the south. That would be his destination. He could do it in one day, with fair weather and no trouble. He wanted to sit on that beach, to feel that sun on his face, to hold that fish in his hands.

Two days later he woke at dawn, wrote the nurse a thank-you note, folded it, placed it on a stack of money, and left.

~ 27 ~

Hotels in Shirahama were aligned like dominoes on the beach. Concrete slabs, garish and decadent, in comparison to the cabin he'd stayed in in Nyuto. Reminded him of Mazatlan.

He kept driving. He found a small road-side place outside of town. The sign on the road was in Japanese, but beneath the characters was the word "motel" and beneath this, in buzzing red neon, a sea horse.

The place had a sandy yard out front. It was empty. There were twelve rooms in a row. A wooden plank walkway under a rotting overhang lay before them. At the end of the lot, through a tall stand of bamboo, a narrow path led down to a secluded beach. The beach was small in width, but, for the shallow shore, long and flat.

It rained the entire first day of his visit. He stayed inside, reading. The story was getting to him. There was a ghost, maybe. Or was it just in the imagination of the lovers? They'd murdered a man, the husband of the young woman.

The conscience is a mysterious thing.

That evening he lowered the window shade and took out Yoshi's finger. He brought it bed with him, where he read to it. He fell asleep with the light on.

He woke suddenly in the middle of the night, disturbed by a strange sound outside. Quickly he hid the finger in the refrigerator, behind the beer.

The next day the sun came out. It was warm. He opened his window. There was a breeze and he could smell the sea, hear seagulls cackling, bamboo rustling in the wind.

At a five-and-dime he bought shorts, sandals, a sun hat, a thermos, a folding canvas chair, and a transistor radio the size of a credit card that took a watch battery. He went down to the beach. He read throughout the day, dozing on and off. He drank a thermos of tea. He tried to find something on the radio but couldn't get a signal. He didn't see a single person. A mangy dog came down the path and sniffed around, but that was it.

Far out at sea he saw small fishing boats, rising and falling on gentle waves. Further out, gray and unmoving, like fossils, larger vessels.

The next day was warmer. The water was calm.

"California is right over there," he said to the empty beach.

He walked down to the water. He went in. The water was cold, but after a few minutes it began to feel good. He swam far out, toward the open ocean.

He lay on his back and watched seagulls chase each other around the sky.

Is it possible? Did I get away?

Was it just last week when –

The next day, dozing on the beach, he woke at the passage of a shadow over him. A figure stood in the sun above him.

He shaded his eyes with his hand. It was a young woman. She was in a tank top and shorts. She was tan, her sandy blond hair pulled back into a coarse braid.

"Didn't mean to wake you," she said.

"You didn't."

"I saw you down here. You don't see –"

Looking down at him as she was, her chin puffed up, making her look very young. She couldn't be twenty. Not a Brit, but –

"Where you from?"

"Cairns. Queensland."

"That's Australia?"

"Right. ... You?"

"New Mexico."

"Mind if I sit?"

"No."

She dropped down into the sand next to him. Her shoulders were round, tan and freckled.

She watched the ocean. In his beach chair, he watched her, curious. Then he watched the ocean, the low soft waves going up and down the shore. He adjusted his chair, picked up his book and kept reading.

"What's your name?"

"My friends call me Charly."

She looked at him, curled up her tiny nose as if smelling something unidentifiable. "I'm Audrey."

"Nice to know you Audrey. Why you here?"

"Here here, or in Japan here?"

"Japan."

"Surfing."

"Surfing?"

"Why not? When I have time I travel and surf."

She did look like a surfer, now that he thought about it.

"Surfing's good around here?"

"In some places. Not here exactly. As you can see."

He nodded.

Audrey kept her eyes on the water. They were brown.

"Not bothering you, am I, sitting here?"

"Nope. Sit all you want. I like the company. Even if I don't have anything to say."

"Good book?"

"Not bad."

"What's it about?"

"Love and murder. A threesome."

"Hmm."

Audrey jumped to her feet and took off her shirt. She had on a black top, her breasts pulled tight up to her chest. She had, he also noticed, some kind of jewel in her navel. "I'm going swimming." She dropped her shorts and walked quickly down the beach into the water. She swam away, chopping her arms in the low waves, kicking hard with her big legs.

He was dozing when she returned. She was rosy cheeked, breathing hard, smiling ear to ear. She threw herself down in the sand.

He was confused. It seemed strange, this young woman appearing as she had, undressing, swimming, collapsing like this at his feet. They were strangers.

"How'd you find me?" he said.

"I'm in the same place as you, a couple doors down. I saw you leave yesterday and this morning. I've been at a different beach, down the way, with some friends. Today I thought I'd see what you were up to."

"So no surfing today."

"I went earlier. Crappy waves." She was on her belly, her face on her crossed hands, her red eyes up toward him. "Tomorrow we'll try again."

Audrey closed her eyes.

Charly watched her back rise and fall as she slept. He watched beads of water evaporate in the small of her back, watched a fine line of white skin where the fabric of her black swimsuit pulled down on her hip.

She had a tattoo on the inside of her ankle. A black straight razor, opened in a V.

He was walking back to his room, his chair tucked under his arm, his book in the other hand. The sun was going down. It was winter, still, he had to remind himself.

She came running up behind him.

"You didn't wake me."

"You were sleeping."

"You would've left me? Alone in the dark, in the cold?"

"I did leave you. But you woke up. So –"

"What do you do, Charly, in New Mexico. I bet you're an actor. You remind me of a theater friend I had –"

"I have a gallery."

"You're an artist!"

"No. I have a gallery. I sell art."

"What kind?"

"You don't want to know what kind. No more questions, Audrey, I'm on vacation."

"Swell. Listen, I have some beers in my room. Come and join me?"

Swell. Listen, I have some beers in my room, come and join me?

"Sure. Why not."

They sat in front of her room in two plastic chairs. Evening lights were coming on up and down the street.

The stars came out and the air turned cold. They went inside. The place was a disaster. Duffel bags, clothing, wet suits, swimsuits, bottles of different soaps and ointments, an empty bottle of Jack Daniels on its side on the floor, crushed plastic cups, an overflowing ashtray, magazines, books, two surf boards, shoes and sandals and... How it was possible for one person to carry so much shit, let alone live in such conditions, was beyond him.

He shoved a pile of clothing from the bed and sat back, kicked his shoes off and put his feet up.

She turned on the TV, flipping through channels. She stopped on a baseball game. The Buffalos versus the Swallows. That's all Charly could make out.

She climbed on top of her things and sat next to him. He could smell her. Something acrid and fishy. They finished their beers. She brought out two more and popped them open.

"Where're your friends?"

"Out. I don't know. They're stoners."

Charly had a cigarette. Audrey asked for one. His eyes on the TV, he put another between his lips, lit it and handed it to the girl.

When she finished the beer she climbed from the bed and went to the bathroom. She was throwing off clothing. "I'm taking a shower. Then let's go get something to eat, I'm starving!"

It was the top of the eighth. The Swallows were down by two and at bat. The last hit was a double, putting men on second and third. There were no outs. Next up was real bull, a slugger. The pitcher, practically a kid, slender, too small for his hat, looked sick, pale, drenched in sweat. He was doing everything he could to hold his wobbling knees still.

Charly listened to the shower. He imagined Audrey scrubbing salt and sand off her body, from between her toes. He thought again, "Is it possible? Am I getting away?"

With a crack, the slugger connected, peeling the skin off the ball, fouling.

There wasn't a purse in the room, as far as he could tell. He opened an old canvas wallet. ID. Sure enough: Audrey Bessing from Cairns, Queensland.

In the photo, Audrey seemed to be laughing, not exactly smiling, her mouth open and tongue curling up. Her eyes directly at the photographer.

She had a large, lovely Welsh chin.

He flipped through. There was a university ID, a library card, a credit card, cash crumbled and crammed into its slot.

He poked a finger into various piles of clothing. Faded Levis, underwear, socks.

When the shower turned off he put the wallet back where he found it and returned to his place on the bed. He lit a cigarette.

The bathroom door opened suddenly and Audrey rushed from a cloud of steam with a towel wrapped around her body, armpits to knees. She stood on the other side of the bed, tossing through clothing, her hair down around her cheeks and shoulders, dripping on everything. She found what she wanted and returned to the bathroom. She left the door ajar.

"How long you here for?" she said.

"Couple weeks. You?"

"It's open ended. I'll go back when I go back."

Charly thought about that and couldn't make sense of it.

"You in school or something?"

"Not any more. I might go back. Or might surf my way around the world. I know a guy who did that."

Charly pictured a guy surfing around the world. Seemed like a silly thing to do.

Suddenly, a commotion in the TV. The crowd booed, hissed, the commentators went to town. The kid hit the batter. In the replay, there it goes – the slugger twisting away, chin up like St. Teresa in ecstasy, taking it in the side, beneath the elbow. What a gentleman. His eyes on the ground, the bull tossed the bat aside and jogged to first.

"You go through my things yet?" she said behind the bathroom door.

"What'd you say?"

"Find anything you like?"

"Why on earth would I go through your things, Audrey? What do you think I am?"

"You're a man, Charly. It's okay. I have nothing to hide. Nothing you can steal. Except for the board. But I'd catch you. I have ways."

"I'm sure you would, you do. But no. I did not go through your things."

Then she stood before him, next to the TV, smiling, her hands on her hips. She'd put something on her lips.

"Well I gave you a chance. Now let's go!"

"How old are you, Audrey?"

"How old do you think? I'm older than that."

At a restaurant down the street, Audrey took the menu and told him what to have. She spoke enough Japanese to order. They had goya chanpuru, umi budo, katsuo no tataki, and beer.

Later, two tall blond men came in and sat at the bar. After a minute one of them said something in English across the little place. Audrey waved, got up and went over to them. They turned in their seats in unison, one on each side, to face her.

So those are her friends. In a day, Charly thought, watching the three chatting, hearing nothing, none of this will matter. We'll all be gone our separate ways.

Audrey came back to the table and immediately continued eating. She raised her eyebrows and said, her mouth full, "My friends!"

"I see that."

Back at the motel, they stood outside of her room, listening to the night, the surf, to moths buzzing around a yellow bulb overhead.

What were they waiting for?

Then he smiled at the girl, said goodnight, and went down the planked walkway to his room.

He turned on the TV. Nothing on. He lit a cigarette and read his book. There was beer in the fridge. He didn't feel like beer.

He went out, down the street to a small grocery. He bought a bottle of Cutty Sark.

At his room he took the only glass he could find and filled it with scotch. He sipped a little and then poured himself some more, filling the glass to its brim.

There was a table in the room, near the window. There were two chairs. He took the one in the corner.

Now and then a car passed down the road. They didn't drive too quickly here. Or maybe it was the hour. Then a bird of some kind made a fuss – a strange distant cry out in the dark.

The birds that come out at night here may not be like those you find in California. Different types of owls, probably.

He thought of Audrey. Was she alone in her room? What was she doing? Reading a surf magazine? Waxing her board? Writing a letter to a friend back home in Cairns? Taking a shower?

He lowered the window shade. He turned on the radio. A piano – pianos. After a moment he recognized a movement from Ravel's *Ma mère l'oye*. He lit a cigarette and listened.

When he turned out the lamp the room was completely dark. It was a strange sensation, the soft tinny music, the darkness, the red glow of his cigarette.

They make very good window shades in Japan. Maybe it has to do with the fact that it's a crowded place. Even for a roadside motel, what superb window shades. And this transistor radio, the size of a credit card. Imagine that!

He put the light back on. He took a quick shower. He turned up the heat. He poured himself another drink and climbed into bed naked.

I could stay here for a long time. They'd never find me. How?

He read for another thirty minutes. Then he put out the light.

He was just closing his eyes when there was a knock on the door.

It was late, well into the small hours of the morning.

He wondered who could be there, behind his door. He flipped through characters, faces and names in his head. There were only a few possibilities. Unless it was a stranger, which was a remote possibility.

But at this hour?

A stranger could only mean one thing.

No. A stranger could mean many things, Charly, mean just about anything.

Mary Mullen came to mind for a moment, that strange conversation about confusing how and why.

There's the knock again, a little louder this time.

He was thinking about the glass ashtray, beside him on the bedside table, in reach. He knew exactly where it was, could feel it in his mind, in the dark.

If that door opens, will the ashtray fly like a frisbee?

And then what?

Then, whispered: "Charly?"

Audrey.

There's always a simple explanation. Posner said that.

Look at Posner now.

He turned on the lamp. He went to the door and opened it a crack.

"What do you want?"

"Nothing. I can't sleep. What are you doing?"

"Reading. Don't you – you're up in a few hours, aren't you?"

"Yep," she said. "Pour me a drink?"

He closed the door. He pulled on some pants. He opened the door. "Come in."

He filled a plastic cup with Cutty Sark and handed it to her.

"Isn't that hard – getting up at dawn?"

"Nah. Now it's routine. It's like... The body does everything. Awake, asleep, doesn't matter. Thirty minutes before sunrise my eyes open and I get out of bed, grab the board and go to the shore."

"Sleep walking?"

"Kind of. My legs know what to do. It's muscle memory."

"Is that right?"

He returned to bed, picked up his book, flipped pages. He tried to read but he couldn't take his eyes off the girl by the door. She was in red shorts, white t-shirt, big brown tired eyes.

She watched him, drink in hand, thinking.

After a minute she said, "I tell you what's hard."

"What's that?"

Her brown eyes had something to them. Something fluttering in the darkness – that yellow beetle, desire.

She finished her drink in a toss. She came toward him, climbed onto the bed, hands and knees.

"Not getting any when you want it," she said.

"When you want it?"

"Sometimes it hurts."

"Hurts?"

"When I need it more than anything."

"You have friends for that, Audrey. For your needs."

Her face was up to his, her lips at the corner of his eye. That powerful chin nudging his cheek. She took the book from his hands and tossed it on the floor.

"They're friends, Charly. We don't fuck."

"I thought that's what –"

"What is it with you?" she whispered, angry. "Still learning English? You brain damaged?"

She was on her knees beside him, over him. She pressed her breast against his face. He put a hand on her bare leg.

"You say no," she said, "and I'll kill you."

"I believe you might."

Without a word she stripped and climbed on top of him. Her body was hot and damp, feverish, as if she'd just stepped away from a fire.

He grabbed her above her hips, squeezing her tightly. He felt himself expanding, breaking apart.

She was not heavy, but there was a lot to Audrey Bessing. There was muscle, legs that seemed to go on forever. Her skin was tough. Her breasts heavy, meaty. She grunted as he turned her over, threw her on the bed, fell on her. He buried his face in her breasts. He pushed her hard up into the headboard and dug his tongue into her wet cunt. He heard her hiss, sigh, snap her teeth together above him. Then she gasped and threw out a hand, knocking the lamp, the only light in the room, from the bedside table.

When the lamp hit the floor the bulb exploded in a flash of white light. The room was pitch dark – forcing the two to press themselves even closer, tighter, eye to eye, eye to skin, to insides. When he tried to say something, her hand came up out of the dark and grabbed his face, his cheeks, his lower jaw, and she growled in her throat, digging her fingers into his mouth. Speechless, the man and woman clung to each other in what was not exactly sex, but rather grappling in the darkness, in blindness, full of slaps and kicks and grunts and coughs – like two desperate animals facing off, clawing at each other in a burrow far underground.

At one point – her leg hooked firmly around his jaw, his head turned in just the right way, his chin pressing hard against her clitoris, his arm twisted and pinched beneath her back – he felt himself losing his balance, sliding off the edge of the bed, and he thought: "That's it. Now she's going to break my neck and take my money."

But that didn't happen. What happened was a few minutes later they finished and he, on his back, fell quickly, briefly, asleep. When he opened his eyes and reached out he found the girl was gone.

He brushed his teeth, the bottle of Cutty Sark on the toilet. "Enough's enough." He collapsed on the bed and fell instantly asleep.

He woke up many hours later, terrified that something had gone wrong. He opened the window shade. There was the street, the dusty front of the motel, the red sea horse flickering in the late morning light.

He checked his things. What remained of his money was still there, where he'd left it. And the red case with the crooked finger, in the fridge behind the beer, was also where he'd left it.

Late in the afternoon a few days later, Audrey discovered everything.

They were developing a routine, a need for each other. She'd come back late in the morning, and he'd strip off her wet suit and lick the salt from her body. They'd shower together. Then he'd do whatever he wanted with her. Sometimes she resisted, but not very hard, and not for very long.

Soon he couldn't get Audrey Bessing out of his head. He could taste her all day long. He could smell her cunt on his hands, on his clothing. He knew she was going to leave soon, or he'd leave, but that didn't matter. All that mattered was getting more of her – later in the day, that night, the next morning.

He thought of taking her with him.

Would it be easy? Simple?

Nothing's simple, Charly, *especially* this –

He'd left her alone in his room. He said he had an errand to run, he'd be back in the evening. She was half awake, naked on her belly on the bed. Flushed cheeks, her eye half open, shimmering under the heavy lid. Sleeping like a cat.

He drove down the highway to the next town, to a port. A large ferry was docked there. He bought a ticket. He waited till the last minute and then joined a line of cars. A powerful horn sounded, echoing around the port. His was one of the last cars to board the vessel.

He stayed in the car. He pushed the seat back, smoked, dozed, daydreamed of Audrey's anus.

An hour later the ferry stopped at a small resort island. They disembarked. Two minutes later he parked at a Holiday Inn.

The island boasted rain forests, lagoons, spas and the like. Charly'd had enough of spas.

At a western-style diner he had a hamburger and fries, milk shake, cup of coffee.

Across the street was a small movie theater. It reminded him of the place he liked on Haight, back home. They were showing a Godzilla picture. *Gojira tai Megaro.* Megaro was a giant bug. He was tempted to go in.

Megaro or Audrey?

He returned to the ferry. He walked on and it left a minute later. He stood on the stern and watched the island grow smaller, sink into the horizon.

He took a taxi back to the motel. The sun was going down. Audrey was in his room, watching TV.

He was pissing when he heard her say, "I found the money, Charly."

He came out, zipping up.

"What's that?"

"The money. The bag. Where'd it come from?"

He stared at the girl, scenarios playing out in his head. He hadn't expected this.

"So you went through my things?"

"Course I did. You stick fingers in my ass. I can go through your things."

There was no argument.

"It's from a job I did for someone," he said.

"A job," she said, a smile bent up the side of her face. "You a hit man or something? Yakuza?"

"No. And if I was, sweetie, I wouldn't tell you. Or I'd have to kill you."

"Would you?"

" ... Would I? Tell you or kill you? Neither."

"Good. I didn't think so. So guess what else I found?"

Laughter in the TV.

"You didn't."

"I wanted a beer and I didn't have any. There it was. ... There it was... Where'd you get it? What's it for?"

" ... "

There were times when Charly had nothing to say, times when he had plenty to say but reasons not to, and times when maybe he said too much. But now, here, taking this from Audrey, he was finished, facing a wall. It was like she had cut his tongue out.

"What's it for, Charly? You cut if off someone? ... You can't be yakuza because you're American. Only Japanese men can be yakuza. Did you know that?"

She tipped her head toward her shoulder, like a secretary holding a phone without hands. Her tone was easy, casual, almost like that of a precocious child. Her body was saying something else. He saw it in the way she was tightening up, sitting up straight, holding her breath.

He said: "Is there anything to drink? Scotch?"

"Nope."

"Beer?"

"Nah."

He walked around the bed, pulled a cigarette from a soft pack on the table and lit it.

Her feet were bare. Tiny bristles of blond hair glimmered in the evening light on her legs. Her tattoo, the black straight razor on her ankle, open.

V is for what, Charly?

"You shouldn't have seen that, Audrey. I wish you hadn't found it... No. To answer your question. I didn't cut it off. It belonged to... I'm not a gangster or anything like that. I didn't hurt the woman who..."

He sat down on the edge of the bed, facing the TV. A cooking program was on. They were making cake. Sandra used to make cake, baking all night long, filling the place with the smell of butter and sugar, getting flour in her hair, on her hips.

Suddenly he hated the idea of cooking, of ever cooking again. He'd buy everything he ate from now on. The idea of even touching something fresh or raw disgusted him.

"And the money?" she said.

"It's stolen. The man who stole it before me – he's dead."

"You killed him."

"I did."

"And so you're hiding."

"You could call it that."

"And the finger?"

"The *crooked* finger, Audrey... It belonged to a woman I knew. She was murdered."

"And you cut it off?"

Questions, questions, questions! Can't a man have any peace?

Charly felt anger stirring in his gut. It had been awhile. But there it was. The old meanness coming back.

"I didn't cut it off!"

"But if you didn't, then who –"

He put a hand on her ankle and squeezed.

They were separating egg yolks and whites in the TV. He reached out and turned it off.

After a minute, Audrey said, "You wanna put on some music?"

He found the transistor radio and turned it on. It hissed and buzzed. Then there was something – a Mozart opera

– but it seemed to be a local station run by kids who kept interrupting with comments and laughter.

Then they stopped playing the opera altogether and put on something experimental, what sounded like synthesizers and banging trash cans. He turned it off.

"There's nothing on."

"What did you do, Charly?"

"I got myself tangled up…"

"So you don't run a gallery in New Mexico, do you? You're not even from New Mexico, are you? You're a criminal. You're some kind of criminal. You're on the run."

"That's about right. That's what I am. That's what I'm doing."

"But you won't tell me what happened, where the crooked finger came from – except for this murdered woman –"

"It's a long story. I couldn't even begin. It started with…"

Charly turned on the bed and faced the girl. He stood up. He climbed onto the bed, straddling her long legs. She didn't move. He climbed up her body. Her hands were at her sides, inside his knees.

He couldn't hurt her. And yet –

Audrey was strangely relaxed, this criminal of some kind on top of her, pressing her down.

"Audrey," he said, his face up to hers, "some things can't be said. Some things – we won't, we don't talk about. This is one of those things."

She'd kept her eyes on his. Then she looked down, away. Something twitched in her mouth, in her lips.

"Okay," she said.

"Okay."

Charly went to the door. He stepped outside. Night was falling but the air was still warm.

Swallows whipped around in the darkness overhead, chirping, barking, leaping from the blue night air for an instant and then returning.

How can it be so warm? It's January.

"I'm going for groceries. I hope you're here when I get back. I'd like to tie you up."

Audrey had turned the TV back on. She was mindlessly clicking through channels. She stopped on a sumo wrestling program. "We'll see about that."

He walked down to the market and bought a six-pack of beer, a bottle of Cutty Sark, a pack of Marlboros, cellophane wrapped sushi, a bag of seaweed chips and a bag of fish cookies, and twenty-five meters of nylon rope.

Back at his room – Audrey was still there – he tossed the girl a beer and the bag of chips.

"Have something to eat," he said.

"I'm not hungry."

"You need your strength."

"I'm strong enough."

He swallowed a beer and opened another.

"You think so."

He lowered the window shade.

"Take off your shirt. Turn over."

He pulled off her shorts. He tied her elbows to her knees and her wrists to the headboard. He made a lasso and dropped it around her neck.

"I want you to do something for me."

"Anything!"

He put his feet up, drank a beer, looked at what he'd done.

"What would you have me do, Charly!?"

Her face, bright red.

I'll never see her again.

"Take it out with you. To the ocean."

"Take out the crooked finger you mean."

"Take it far out and leave it, drop it. It will sink. I don't want to ever see it again."

" ... And then?"

"And then nothing. I'll forget it, I'll forget I ever saw it. I'll forget I ever saw you, forget I asked you to do this."

"Whatever. Just –"

"You'll do it for me?"

He walked around the bed. She tried to turn and find him.

"It's done!"

"Far out, Audrey, take it far out there. I don't want it coming back. Washing up in the night."

"Like in that movie!"

Then Audrey laughed, her whole body shaking, the whole bed shaking beneath her twisted form.

"I don't know what you are talking about," he said.

Charly untied the girl. She collapsed on the bed. She panted like a dog, her tongue out, red lines crisscrossed over her back, breasts, neck, stomach, thighs.

They finished the beer, ate the sushi and seaweed chips, smoked and watched TV late into the night.

~ 29 ~

When Charly woke the next morning Audrey was gone. The crooked finger was gone too.

"That's that."

Now just to get rid of this cash.

A clean slate – a new man!

After a cup of tea, he went down to his regular spot on the beach. It was a warm breezy morning. The sand was cold on his feet.

He went into the water for a swim.

Will you let me go, he thought, gazing at the sky.

Charly – if you have to ask...

He sat on the beach and read his book.

It was getting close to the time when he usually returned to the motel, for the first turn of the day with Audrey.

A man in a sun hat stood behind him, over him. Charly didn't hear the stranger approach. Charly didn't hear the stranger approach because the man took a long time coming down the beach, walking as if the sand were deep and slick. Unsteady on his feet, the man limped, his shoe filling with sand.

The stranger hated beaches. He hated sand and bright sunlight, hated sun bathers and their hotdogging boyfriends. He'd rather have a root canal than look at another picture of a beach.

When Charly turned, he saw a man in a sun hat, in a light blue windbreaker, in dark glasses. A smear of sunscreen ran down his nose, bubbled on the tip of his chin.

"You look comfortable," the stranger said.

Charly held a hand to his brow, for the sun. It took him a second to recognize the figure, the voice. "So it's true," he said. "I was beginning to think I was going nuts. That none of this was what it appeared to be."

"Always too much..." The words out thick, a mouth full of marbles. "Always too much of a head on you, too much for your own good."

"Posner's people send you?"

"Posner? Never heard of him."

"Then Hamling."

"Him neither. Why'd he bother? ... I sent myself."

"How'd you find me?"

"Like I found Conway. And Felicia. I know how to find people, Charly."

"Like Conway... So you caught up with him?"

"It's not so complicated. The answer's right before your eyes. It's been there all along."

Charly wasn't looking. All his eyes could see was ocean. Flat waves running up the beach and receding, hissing and sparkling in the sunlight.

"You caught up with him and…"

"And he started talking," Momcilovic said. "He told me the whole thing. What a story. So simple. An exemplar of simplicity. But sometimes… What do they say? … I let him go. Because I knew –"

"He'd come after me. We'd sort things out. You'd pick up the remains."

"… I'd get what I wanted. You see – I had Conway's number. From the get-go. I had the man by the balls."

"Until the plan went crooked. And Conway died."

"Until then. Yes."

About this time, Charly thought, the crooked finger is on the bottom of the ocean, cold silence, darkness, covered in a fine layer of white sand. An object of curiosity for the fish.

"So I've had to play catch up, again," Momcilovic said.

"I don't have it. I got rid of it. I gave it to …"

"But I'm good at this game."

Momcilovic took a straight razor from the pocket of his windbreaker and unfolded it.

"So what," Charly said, "now you shoot me with the gun I left you? That old thing?"

"No. Nothing like that. I'm not that clever, Charly. … You know what your problem is?… It's hard getting guns on planes. Did you know that?"

"I never thought about it."

"It's true."

"So."

"So what, Charly?"

"So you bought something here."

"No. That's another thing. Getting a gun in Japan is not easy. ... I hate this country. Things are too small. Too close together. I can't breathe here, Charly, it's... It's..."

Momcilovic cleared his throat and spit in the sand.

"You're too late," Charly said.

"Am I?"

"It's on the bottom of –"

"Be that as it may –"

"Can I ask you why?" Charly said.

"You can ask."

"Then why are you doing this?"

When Charly turned to look, taking a second, again, to shade his eyes from the sun above them, finding the man, finding his bad eye in the murk of that thick lens, seeing nothing, it was too late.

"What're you reading Charly?"

Momcilovic closed in with the razor.

"It's by –"

It was like swatting a fly. Quick, effortless. With one hand on the top of Charly's head, the other brought around the razor. It was a very sharp instrument. Jugular and larynx, sliced open like ripe fruit. Blood sprayed upward and out, on the killer, on the sand, on the book.

For a moment it looked like Charly had something to say. Then he tipped over, fell from his chair onto his side.

Momcilovic watched him die. He picked up the book. On the cover was a black and white photo of a young woman glancing over her shoulder, fear in her eyes. She wore a shawl.

"Theresa Raquin."

He put the book, opened to its middle, over the body's face. He took from the body a key dangling from a red plastic sea horse.

Was Charly hearing anything then, in the instant of his death? Did music play in his head?

I don't think so. Dead is dead. And Momcilovic knew how to do it.

But who can really say?

What the living man heard was the wind, the waves, the cackling laughter of gulls.

A crab popped up from the sand and climbed nimbly up the corpse's shoulder, looked around.

Momcilovic shuddered. It was too much for him. The beach, the crab, the book. Nature.

He took out a handkerchief and wiped the razor clean. He closed it and returned it to his pocket.

He turned and marched up the beach toward the bamboo stand, back to the path. He was met by a brown mangy dog. Quietly it sat there, watching the man approach. Serene creature, its body gone to hell. It had one eye. Its hair had fallen out. Its body was covered in red and white scabs. Enormous black flies sucked at its sores.

~ 30 ~

Not much later that morning, Audrey returned and went directly to the beach instead of her room. She wanted to tell Charly that she hadn't let the finger go, that she'd kept it. She'd brought it out with her, far out, as she promised to, but in the end she couldn't let it go.

She thought he was sleeping at first.

Then she saw the blood on the chair, black in the sand, the flies and crabs feasting on the corpse.

She took the book from its face. It was stiff, sticky with blood.

She'd never been much of a reader.

"They found you."

It was fascinating, how its neck opened up like that, like another mouth.

Then she remembered the bag of money.

She ran back to the motel.

When she entered his room, she didn't see the man at the table, sitting in the corner. She wasn't looking there. She went to the other side of the bed, knelt, and reached underneath, pulling out the blue carry-on. There it was. A lot of cash – about a hundred thousand dollars, he'd said.

"You must be Audrey."

She looked over the bed at the man in the corner. He was deformed, his head smashed flat on the side, almost concave, one eye clearly useless, staring off at the wall.

"What do you want?" she said, kneeling behind the bed.

"Where is it?"

"Where's what? The money!? ... It's here, right here."

She lifted the bag onto the bed.

"Not that," the man said, standing.

Her heart was racing. She struggled to keep calm, to breathe. The door stood open.

Audrey counted to three in her head and then jumped, running for the door.

But the man moved fast, he was moving before she'd even left the floor, practically leaping over the table. His palm in her face, he knocked her head back, grabbed a handful of hair and kicked her feet out from under her. He caught her in the stomach with his knee, slammed the door closed with his heel.

He had the razor out in an instant, its square corner pressed into her neck, under her jaw.

Gasping for air, sobbing, her eyes racing around above her head, over the floor, Audrey held very still.

"You take it?"

"Take what?"

"The diamond! Give it to me!"

Audrey slapped her hip, her pocket.

Momcilovic sneered and, keeping his eyes are hers, pulled a slim red case from her shorts.

He took a step back, put the razor down. He opened the case.

"What in hell?"

Momcilovic took the crooked finger out and dropped the case. He held it up, studying it closely. He smelled it, flexed it, the crackling bone.

Just as the man appeared to be figuring things out, Audrey kicked him hard in the knee. The joint buckled backwards, turned inside out.

The man cried out and crumbled to the floor.

The finger went flying across the room, bounced off a mirror and fell behind the TV.

Momcilovic was growling, shouting, cursing as he held his leg and tried to get back on his feet, one hand going for the razor. But Audrey Bessing, younger, faster, and desperate, had slid back, pulled herself away on her elbows and was now climbing on the bed, kicking out and screaming.

She grabbed the bag of money and swung, and though it caught Momcilovic in the side of the head, he saw it coming – he'd turned away.

She was off balance with that.

Still, she came at him, the half-man teetering on one leg, the bag of money in her hand, her other hand opened like a claw.

They caught each other, arm in arm, their hands scraping and scratching, the blue bag sliding down her arm to her elbow as the razor rose as if to cut open the ceiling.

One of the last things Audrey considered was how she seemed to be pushing a finger into the man's head, straight into his skull. But that couldn't be. It was the light. It was blood on her hand. It was a hallucination of adrenaline, of panic.

On a string around the man's neck – "Is that?" – a big ear.

She was as tall as the man but not nearly as strong. And once Momcilovic got a grip on her wrist, he didn't let go. He pulled down hard and it was all over after that.

Outside, the ocean air was milky, warm and breezy. The twitter of birds filled the air.

It was an idyllic January morning in Southern Japan. It could have been a day in early spring.

They say the planet's warming up.

Momcilovic groaned, reached down to hold his leg steady. He felt feeble, like an old man. He was hurting inside. He looked himself over. Didn't seem to be spilling anything, losing anything.

Except...

He stood in the doorway. He looked toward the beach, at the bamboo at that end of the motel. There was his car, a bright red Toyota Corolla.

He looked the other way. Two Japanese men were standing there. One was very tall and thin, dour faced, with huge lips, the other, in a beige trench coat, was stockier and full of smiles.

Trench coat said, "Meester Bingswanger!?" He smiled. He had beautiful, white teeth.

Momcilovic caught his breath, stood up straight. He wondered if there was blood on his face, if his hands were clean. "No," he said. "You just missed him." When Smiles didn't appear to understand, Momcilovic went on, raising his voice: "He's down at the beach."

"The beach!" said the man in the trench coat, smiling, his lower jaw dropping.

"Down that way." Momcilovic flapped his hand in the air. "I'm a friend of his. I was getting more beer," he said, holding up the room key.

"Beer!"

"Yes. But there is no more."

"On the beach."

"Right, right! He's on the beach. Not here. There!"

"The beach?" said Smiles, pointing and nodding.

"Yes, yes. That way."

He was hurting all over, head to toe. It took everything he had to raise his arm, to point.

His flight back was in a couple days. Maybe he could get an earlier flight, on stand-by?

"Oh," said Smiles. "Thank you." He lowered his head ever so slightly.

His tall partner, stone faced, did the same.

The two men left. They followed the wooden walkway to the edge of the motel, to the bamboo stand at the end. There they stopped. The man in the trench coat looked back. "This way?"

"Follow the path," Momcilovic said.

"The path?"

"There's a path!"

"Oh, yes. I see. Thank you!"

The two men disappeared around the corner.

You have four minutes.

He let himself into Audrey's room. It was simply stunning, how much clothing the girl was traveling with. He almost didn't bother. But then he made a cursory check of the room, looking in the obvious places.

Nothing.

Just a goddamn finger and a bag of cash.

He wondered if there were any good fishing holes nearby. He'd go but for the sun, which was making him nauseous. Maybe further up north, where it was cold still. Or maybe he'd stay inside the whole time, go back to Tokyo, order out, take hot baths, watch fishing shows on TV, get a pretty whore for a day and a night.

Limping, Momcilovic went back to his car, got in, and drove away.

Note to the reader:

I first self-published *The Crooked Finger* in 2014 as Max Ruen. Some years later I revised the book, cutting out the dirty bits, and published it as *Smorgasbord* (2022), which is more or less what you have just finished reading.